**'Who are *you*?'**



Narrowed eyes rake
until Shanna felt her

'The war has not yet deprived me of my manners, I assure you, but good food and half a bottle of Abraham's best has somewhat dulled my senses. Allow me to introduce myself. I am Rafe Amberville. I expect you have been told about me?'

'No, Mr Amberville, I have not.'

**Dear Reader**

This month, as well as two historicals from Mills & Boon, we also launch two historicals from our American sister company. Their approach is very different from ours, but we hope you find the extra scope intriguing.

In Elizabeth Bailey's HIDDEN FLAME, we have a wonderfully gothic Regency, and you may recognise Linda Shaw from Silhouette. Her hero, Odessa, is quite a character! Enjoy. . .

*The Editor*

**Valentina Luellen** began writing at school—mainly because she loathed maths! It took her twelve years before she had a book accepted, but has since been published regularly. Historical romances are her favourites, because she loves researching into so many different countries.

She and her husband moved to Portugal when he became seriously ill, and there his health improved. Her hobbies are restoring antique furniture, decorating, cooking and dressmaking.

**Recent titles by the same author:**

TO PLEASE A LADY
THE WEB OF LOVE

# ONE LOVE

Valentina Luellen

MILLS & BOON

MILLS & BOON LIMITED
ETON HOUSE, 18–24 PARADISE ROAD
RICHMOND, SURREY, TW9 1SR

*First published in Great Britain 1993*
*by Mills & Boon Limited*


*This edition 1993*

ISBN 0 263 78238 7

*Set in 10 on 11½ pt Linotron Times*
*04-9310-78679*

*Typeset in Great Britain by Centracet, Cambridge*
*Made and printed in Great Britain*

# CHAPTER ONE

THERE would be a storm within the hour, Shanna thought as she gazed out of the window and in the distance glimpsed a vivid flash in the black sky. She hated these early summer storms. . .the rolling thunder which reverberated throughout the house, shaking the crystal chandeliers and rattling the windows . . .the lightning which invaded every nook and cranny as if determined to seek her out and make her jump every time it penetrated the rooms. It had been humid all day and the sultry heat drifting in from the rice fields and beyond them, from the swampland where she had not yet dared set foot, had drained her of all energy.

Not that she possessed much these days. Recovery since the collapse which had followed close on the heels of the news of the death of her beloved father had been slow and the weakness that had plagued her limbs was only now—after weeks of rest—beginning to disappear. Had Alexander Amberville, a close family friend, not brought her to the peace and quiet of his home, she wondered what would have become of her.

She had known what it was like to be alone and defenceless against the intrusion of enemy soldiers into her house, looting, destroying, brutalising any woman unfortunate enough to come in contact with them, and she never wanted to experience such a nightmare again. Here in South Carolina, the horrors of war seemed so unreal. The countryside was peaceful for Confederate forces still controlled here in strength. Here, she knew, in time she would grow well and strong again. But when the war was over. . .? She did not want to dwell on that thought. She no longer had a home to go back to, no family. Apart from Tante Lea, who had been part of her life since childhood, she had no one. . .possessed nothing, except a deep, burning hatred of the blue-coated soldiers who had taken everything and everyone she loved from her.

She pulled the curtains across the windows, ensuring they were tightly closed, and turned to look at herself in the long wall mirror beside the dressing-table. She grimaced at the reflection which stared back at her and one thin hand rose slowly to examine the long hair cascading over her robe and reaching almost to her waist. Once the raven tresses had hung down her back like a cloud, but now they were lustreless, lacking both texture and shine. And her skin had become quite sallow during her illness. She looked terrible. Like a ghost!

The wide grey eyes she had inherited from her beautiful mother darkened with despair as they contemplated the change in her.

She rarely ventured out of her room, although as it had grown warmer she had taken to sitting out on the balcony and Tante Lea would bring her a tray of food—which, on most days, she barely touched. There were times when the warmth of the sun on her face revived her and she promised herself she would go riding the next day. She was an excellent horsewoman and Alexander Amberville had offered her the choice of his fine stable, which contained mostly animals of Arab stock.

But at other times, as she closed her eyes, the book on her lap unopened, her thoughts wandered back to the old plantation house at Baton Rouge, and the memories that came flooding back brought more tears—more anger at the senseless, bloody war which was dividing families, pitting brother against brother—more loneliness.

She was by no means poor. In fact upon the death of her beloved father she knew she had inherited all the family wealth, a considerable fortune, she suspected, but, as yet, she had no heart to make the journey into Savannah to discover just how rich she was. What did it matter, anyway? What good was money to her? It could rebuild her home, if the Yankees had left anything standing, but for what? To live there alone with Tante Lea? Alone with nothing but memories. She would not contemplate such an existence.

She would never marry. She had no love left to give. The young man she had been betrothed to and sent off to war with a brave smile and a hug had been part of her life since childhood. The marriage had been arranged, as most marriages were by the best families in New Orleans, when she was only twelve. All those years of preparing herself to be a wife and mother destroyed within two short months. Her grief had barely begun to recede when, the following year, her brother also gave his life for the South.

Death had come to claim all the members of the de Lancel family! The frightening thought would not leave her and haunted her day after day, night after sleepless night. Now it had taken her father too. When would it be her turn?

'It is over, child. Do you think Tante Lea is going to let anything happen to you? Didn't I take care of you at Baton Rouge? New Orleans?'

A faint smile touched Shanna's ashen cheeks as she turned to look at the woman who had come silently into the room. How long had she been standing there watching? she wondered. She rarely knew what was going on behind those jet-black eyes that could see into her very soul.

'I am not alone, am I, Tante? I shall never be alone while you are with me,' she said, and her lips quivered as she considered all that they had been through since they took flight from New Orleans. Tante Lea had saved her from the Yankee soldiers then and again at the plantation outside Baton Rouge when they had come riding their horses over the lawns and gardens and forced their way into the house, which to their delight—and amusement—they found defended by only two women and a handful of coloured servants. Half of those had turned and run when they saw the blue uniforms. Tante Lea had killed for her. Had she not, Shanna knew she would not have survived that dreadful day.

The Creole woman moved forward and gently drew Shanna into her arms. She had been brought into the de Lancel family home when she was twenty, and the quivering girl in her arms ten years old. Upon the death of her mother two years later, she had become Shanna's constant companion, adviser, confidante.

She had not aged in ten years, Shanna thought as she looked up into Tante Lea's face. The honey-coloured skin betrayed not one line or blemish. She wore a bright red blouse and skirt that clung to the curving contours of her figure and open-toed sandals on bare feet. Shining mahogany hair was concealed beneath a white scarf knotted on the top of her head. Perhaps it was true what the other servants had only dared to whisper about her—that she was the daughter of a Voodoo priestess and had been taught the secret of eternal youth. She knew so much about the art of healing and she was so wise that Shanna had always believed it to be the truth.

'The darkness is fading.' Long, slender fingers touched Shanna's cheek and as always she found the touch reassuring. 'It is time you made a new life for yourself. There is nothing you can do about what has happened. You must live now—for yourself.'

'Yes.' Shanna accepted at last the wisdom of the words which had been spoken to her every day for the past week. 'I have been a poor guest for the Ambervilles. Whatever must they think of me?'

'Tomorrow will be different, *ma petite*. I shall fetch you a spiced tisane and you will sleep. In the morning life will begin again, *n'est-ce pas*?'

'Yes, Tante. Tomorrow,' Shanna promised.

* * *

She was awakened from a deep sleep by the booming of thunder overhead and, despite the closed curtains, the lightning, as the storm intensified, had become so brilliant that she could still see it outside the windows. She shivered and drew herself up on to the pillows, hugging her arms about her knees. She would not sleep again until it had passed. She tried to relax, but it was impossible. Somewhere below a shutter was banging noisily and the old half-timbered house groaned and creaked beneath the mighty force of the wind, and the rain which lashed the window-panes. Despite the fury raging outside, the bedroom was stifling. She threw off the heavy covers, wondering if a glass of warm milk would help her. Perhaps Hannah or Abraham, the pair of coloureds who were in charge of the household, were still up, but as she slipped her feet into the slippers beside the bed she realised that had they been one of them would have paid some attention to the noisy shutter.

As she reached for the robe at the bottom of the bed, she heard another noise, closer at hand, that was not obliterated by the thunder. The distinct sound of something being knocked over in the next room. Tante Lea, of course! Knowing Shanna's dislike of storms, she had remained near at hand. She would not have to go down to the kitchen after all.

Turning up the lamp which had been burning continuously for the few brief hours she had managed to snatch some rest, Shanna crossed the thickly carpeted floor and opened the door which led to a large and very comfortably furnished sitting-room.

When she had first arrived at Wildwood and been given these rooms, the latter had contained a heavy mahogany desk, the top covered in deep red leather, two leather armchairs, and bookshelves which covered two whole walls. . .but there had been no comforts such as a woman required, no pretty curtains at the windows, chairs brightly covered and carpets on the polished wood floor. A man's room, Shanna had thought the moment she saw it.

Alexander Amberville had solved the problem for her in one day, installing a long, velvet-covered sofa in burgundy brocade, two matching chairs—removing the others to the attic upstairs; new drapes had been hung at the windows and the floor covered with a beige and pink carpet into which her feet sank at every step. She was only now beginning to realise—as the pain of her loss dulled and she accepted she must continue to live—how welcome she had been made in the house by her father's friend and his son. Both visited her daily, had tried on countless occasions to persuade her to venture downstairs—to take a carriage ride and put some colour into her cheeks—and had never tried to force her otherwise when she stubbornly declined.

Tomorrow she would show them how grateful she was not only for offering her a home, but for the concern they had both shown. She had neglected not only herself, but her obligation to the people who had befriended her—and that was not how she had been brought up.

The lamp cast an eerie glow across the floor, illuminating first the small table where the embroidery she had started a week ago lay folded upon the work basket, unfinished, and then slanting further as she advanced into the room, accustoming her eyes to the gloom and seeking whatever it was that had fallen to the floor.

'Tante Lea? Are you here? I heard a noise. . .'

Her voice froze abruptly as, from behind and slightly to the left where the sofa was, she heard the distinct, ominous cocking of a pistol. Terror seized her! Yankees! No, that was impossible, they were hundreds of miles away! A deserter. . .

'Turn around and hold the lamp higher so that I can see your face,' a voice demanded and, her heart in her mouth, she slowly turned, obeying the order. The pale light framed her ashen features, the long hair as black as a raven's wing in the lamplight, her trembling lips and the fear in her wide eyes.

The man who rose from the sofa was tall, over six feet, and well built, yet he moved with the litheness of a mountain cat as he moved around it and confronted her. Narrowed eyes—she could not determine their colour in the poor light—raked her from head to toe until she felt her cheeks begin to burn. No man had ever stared at her so boldly; she would never have allowed it! He wore the uniform of a Confederate officer—a very dirty uniform, and in places in need of repair. The jacket was open and the well worn shirt beneath revealed a chest matted with blond hair to match the unruly thatch above the cold, suntanned features. On the floor beside the sofa had been tossed a pair of boots, caked with dust. Beside them a battered hat, equally grimy.

'Who are you?' Shanna's voice was less steady than she would have liked.

'Who the devil are *you*?' the stranger ejaculated. For a moment more he stared at her until his piercing gaze forced her to lower her eyes; only then did he return the pistol in his hand to its holster. 'And what the hell are you doing in my rooms? The last thing I expected was a welcoming committee. . .'

'I am Shanna de Lancel, Mr Amberville's guest.' She felt quite faint with relief that he had put away the weapon. Since Baton Rouge she had grown afraid of every stranger—every shadow—every strange sound. . .

'I didn't know he was after another wife. I do suppose you mean Alexander Amberville and not Wayne. . . No, my brother likes to keep his women out of sight of my father,' came the humourless comment.

'Your brother. . . Father. . .' Shanna stammered. Someone had told her Alexander Amberville had two sons, she could not remember who, but as she had never seen the other son, and neither of the two men who came to visit her ever mentioned him, she had thought no more about it.

Had she not been subjected to such a fright, Shanna knew she would have found it amusing to see the man step back and sketch a flourishing bow—still clutching in one hand the remains of a half-eaten chicken leg. And then the aroma of whiskey hit her full in the face. Not only had he taken the leftovers from dinner that evening, but he had helped himself to Abraham's corn whiskey!

'The war has not yet deprived me of my manners, I assure you, but good food and half a bottle of Abraham's best has somewhat dulled my senses. Allow me to introduce myself. I am Rafe Amberville. I expect you have been told about me?'

'No, Mr Amberville, I have not.' Shanna stepped back from him as he made his way somewhat unsteadily back to the sofa and collapsed down on to it, stretching his long legs over one of the arms.

'Out of sight, out of mind. My dear father and brother obviously have missed me.'

What was it she heard in his voice? A hint of laughter, yet there was no smile upon the brown face. Sadness? And an underlying bitterness she could not understand. Rafe Amberville, home from the war, and she was installed in his rooms! How could his father have been so thoughtless?

'I will go and wake Hannah and have her make up a bed for you in another room. Tomorrow you will have your own rooms back, I assure you. I had no idea. . .'

There was no answer from the direction of the sofa. She stood quite still for a moment, wondering why he was so silent, and then, hesitantly stepping forward, found his eyes closed. He was asleep! How silly of her not to have realised he was exhausted! She started towards the door then realised that she had not been downstairs yet and did not know where the housekeeper slept. But she did know there was a huge linen closet on the same landing as her room. Tante Lea had inspected it quite recently and told her it was full of bedlinen, curtains and other items, all neatly folded and stacked and obviously not in use.

There had to be something there. . .but she could not move him! He would have to stay where he was until morning. The thought did not appeal to her, but what else could she do? Carefully making her way along the shadowy corridor, she opened three doors before finding what she wanted. Behind each door had been an empty, unused room. Wildwood was far larger than she had imagined, she realised as she grabbed up a heavy comforter and returned to the sitting-room.

Rafe Amberville's long torso was spread across the sofa in a most awkward manner, she discovered when she tried to wrap it around him. But in the end she did succeed with her task and then paused, considering the unshaven face with compassion. What little she had seen of the war had horrified her. What terrible thoughts were in his mind now, a man fresh from battles, daily conflict, death? He was older than Wayne by several years, she thought, although not as old as the growth of beard made him appear. Without that he would be quite handsome.

He muttered in his sleep, disturbed by something so violent that as she watched his closed fists pushed away the comforter. The war had left no one untouched, she thought bitterly as she carefully replaced it. Her dreams were no longer peaceful ones, of loved ones and her home. They were full of blue uniforms, men with laughing faces, the noise of rifle and cannon fire. How much worse it must be for him.

Lean brown fingers with the strength of tempered steel in them closed suddenly around one wrist as she began to move back from him, holding her fast.

'Stay. . .' The single word fell from his lips. He uttered no others.

'Please, let me go. It is impossible. . .' Shanna began before realising he did not hear her.

Who was it he clung to like a small child awakening from a nightmare in the night and seeking something—or someone—to give him reassurance, an untroubled sleep? She eased herself back from him, waiting a few moments before she tried to prise away the fingers around her wrist. But the moment she touched them they tightened and only when she relaxed again did they also lighten their tight hold.

'I will stay,' she whispered to the gaunt, unshaven features. 'Sleep. I promise nothing will disturb you again.'

She made herself as comfortable as possible on the little space left alongside him, resting one arm along the back of the sofa. During the weeks she had spent nursing wounded soldiers in New Orleans before it fell to the Yankees, she had become accustomed to spending night after night with some of the more critical patients, forcing herself to withstand more hours than there were in the day—to shut her ears to the groans of the wounded all about her, the pitiful pleas for morphine when no more was available, the screams of agony from a man undergoing amputation.

Each time she left the overcrowded hospital, she would return to an empty house, save for Tante Lea and three servants. She had allowed those who wanted to leave to do so. They would have run off anyway, she had reasoned, to seek the golden future they had been promised. She had had no heart to stop them, although it saddened her to see them go, knowing that they believed they would find a better life than beneath her roof. Most of them she had known since childhood.

Tante Lea would prepare a hot bath the moment she walked through the door and immediately whisk away the bloodstained apron or gown she had worn so that no signs of the nightmare day remained. But for Shanna it was not so easy to forget—to wash the stains from her clothes was a simple matter, but however long and hard she scrubbed her hands and arms she could still feel the stickiness, the warmth of life blood on them. It was a feeling which would never leave her.

It had been on one of those long, drawn-out days when she had returned exhausted that she found the news of her brother's death awaiting her. A plain envelope containing an impersonal but polite letter to inform her of the loss of Captain James de Lancel upon the field of battle. He had distinguished himself with a show of great gallantry and died a valiant soldier.

Valiant—but dead! She wanted a live brother, not a dead hero. Not memories! Two men gone from her life in one short year.

Valiant and buried in places with strange-sounding names. . . Bull Run which had claimed the man she should have married; Shiloh, her brother. And now, almost a month ago, her father at a place called Resaca, as the Confederate general Joseph Johnston and his army retreated before the advancing Federal forces towards Atlanta.

She had been nursing the wounded the day they brought her that news too, but this time there had been no tears. As she read the letter, all emotion had drained from her. She felt cold, as if the hand of death had touched her too. She would never love anyone again, she'd told herself that day, it was too painful. Never, never, never!

Her eyes closed tiredly now and she dozed without realising it. When she awoke the storm had passed and it had grown light outside the windows. The man on the couch still slept soundly and while she slept he had released the hold on her wrist. Carefully she drew away from him and reached for the comforter to tuck back around him, only to find herself enfolded in two very strong arms and drawn down against his chest. Before she could gather her startled wits he had crushed her mouth to his, exploring it with a hungry expertise which made her begin to struggle frantically to free herself. Then, just as abruptly, she was pushed away from him. Had he awakened from a dream believing her to be someone else, or was he still the worse for Abraham's corn whiskey? He looked at her so strangely, with blue piercing eyes that seemed to see down into her very soul.

'You are wrong, sir,' she said in a low, fierce whisper, wishing her voice did not tremble so. It was more from fear than indignation. Unknowingly he had revived the memory of the last time she had been subjected to such brutish treatment—and she hated him for it. 'The war *has* made you forget your manners!'

Aware of his eyes lingering on her flimsy night attire, she fled into the bedroom and not only locked the door, but propped a chair beneath the glass knob. Rafe Amberville was nothing like his quiet, friendly brother. Perhaps there was good reason why his name was never mentioned in the house!

Shanna turned from the window at the sound of someone trying the door. Several hours had passed since she had locked herself in. She had dressed and sat on the long window-seat with the curtains open, watching the sunrise. Although there had been some movement from the other room not long ago, no attempt had been made to invade her privacy. Hopefully he was suitably ashamed of his outrageous conduct, she thought. From the other side of the door came Tante Lea's voice and she quickly removed the chair and unlocked the door, weak with relief.

Over her shoulder Shanna saw that the sofa was empty and the curtains drawn back, flooding the room with early morning sunshine. There were no boots or hat on the floor and no sign of the man who had appeared in her life in the midst of the stormy night. Had it not been for the comforter folded over one arm she might have thought she had imagined it all. That—and her bruised lips. It had not been a gentle kiss.

Tante Lea said nothing, but turned to stare pointedly at the sofa, her head to one side slightly as, from behind her back, she produced a half-chewed leg of chicken.

'Are you in the habit of raiding Hannah's pantry, child? Ten minutes ago poor Benjamin was on the receiving end of her tongue for stealing the leftovers and Abraham found one of his corn-whiskey jugs almost empty. I didn't know you had a liking for strong liquor either.'

'Don't be ridiculous, Tante.' Shanna grabbed her by the arm and pulled her back into the bedroom. 'Have you not seen him? Has no one seen him but me? Mr Amberville's other son, Rafe. He was here last night. . .these were his rooms and he certainly did not expect to find me in them.'

'Rafe Amberville is back?' One black brow arched in surprise. 'Now that will stir some embers from all I have heard. He and his father can hardly bear to be civil to each other and he has no more time for his brother.'

'That would explain why neither of them mentioned him,' Shanna said with a frown. 'But it is as if the moment he went off to fight they forgot about him.'

'Out of sight, out of mind,' had been the bitter comment. But why? What on earth had he done to deserve such treatment?

'What have you heard about him, Tante?' Shanna asked curiously.

'Nothing that would interest you, child. Now, are

you going to let me do something with this hair this morning? You did promise.'

'Only if you tell me about Rafe Amberville.'

'Very well.' With a sigh Tante Lea fetched the silver-backed brush from the dressing-table and began to brush Shanna's long hair.

'There is very little to tell. One thing I do know, Rafe Amberville has more than his fair share of the devil in him. He goes his own way. Is his own master. No one will ever rule that one. Nor steal his heart. It belongs to this plantation—to Wildwood.'

'I see nothing wrong in that; it is a lovely place.'

'And neglected since he went off to war. When he was here he was in complete control—now that overseer Jack Hanson is in charge because the younger son has other things on his mind and is too busy to attend to business. He is a bad man. A cruel man, too ready to use his whip on those who cannot defend themselves.'

Tante Lea had been the result of a union between a Creole woman and the son of a prominent plantation owner in New Orleans. The disapproval of his family had not prevented the young man from setting up the woman he loved in a comfortable little house, with servants and money to provide for her every need. Lea had wanted for nothing as a child, but after his death there had been no more money. The house and contents had been sold to support them as their lifestyle deteriorated. Had Thérèse de Lancel not taken her into her household, the future would have been very bleak. As it was she had lived in comfort and her new mistress had settled enough money upon her mother to keep her for the remainder of her life. She had never known what it was to be beaten, to have the skin ripped from her back the way some of the poor devils at Wildwood had. They were worked until they dropped and then beaten for being too weak to get up from the ground.

'Tante, are you dreaming?' Shanna had been trying to get her attention back for a full minute. 'Surely Mr Amberville knows what is going on? If it is as bad as you say why does he do nothing about it? He seems such a kind man.'

'A blind one, if you ask me. He sends one son off to war because he cannot stand the sight of him and ignores the faults of the second because he has spoiled him since the day he was born. Wayne Amberville can do no wrong. He drinks too much, but that is put down to high spirits. He gambles with money belonging to his father—where he gets it from is anyone's guess. . .and he doesn't give a fig about this place. When his brother sees how the place has run down during his absence there will be trouble.'

'Poor man, not to be made welcome in his own home,' Shanna said with a frown, and became aware of Tante Lea watching her closely.

'And just how did you happen to encounter him upon his return?' the woman asked.

'I thought it was you—in the sitting-room. I heard a noise and I was going to ask you to fetch me some warm milk. Instead. . .' She shivered slightly, disturbed by the remembrance of the pistol being cocked behind her. 'Instead. . .he was there. . .very tired, and rather drunk. He did not touch me,' she added quickly as she saw the way Tante Lea's eyes narrowed. What she would do to Rafe Amberville if she discovered he had dared to lay a hand on her was beyond her imagination. She never wanted to see the woman angered again! 'He fell asleep on the sofa and I fetched a comforter. I did not know what else to do. He must have awakened very early.'

And have a head like a rock, she thought to herself, after the amount of corn whiskey he had consumed.

'It looks a beautiful day out, Tante. I shall go downstairs for breakfast this morning. Is there somewhere outside that I could sit?'

'The south veranda catches the first warm sun. I'll show you where it is and then I'll have Hannah fix you something to whet your appetite. It's time we put some flesh back on those bones. Time you began to look like a woman again, not some scrawny girl of seventeen.'

'I shall be twenty-one next week,' Shanna protested. Tante Lea was the only person she would ever have allowed to speak to her in such a fashion and she was right. Even though her hair now looked quite presentable and the pale blue dress she wore hugged her figure in all the right places, she was too thin and did indeed look years younger than she really was.

Twenty-one. A grown woman—and yet not a woman, for there was no one to relieve the emptiness inside her, nothing to bring a sparkle to her grey eyes, a flush of colour to her wan cheeks.

She had been too grief-stricken and bone-weary from the long journey from Atlanta to take notice of the house when she arrived. She vaguely remembered a long approach to the house itself past shade trees festooned with Spanish moss, a colonnade of tall white pillars gleaming in the strong sunlight, wide verandas and wrought-iron balconies on the upper storeys where honeysuckle and bright purple and pink bougainvillaea entwined in profusion.

Of the inside of the house she recalled little—a wide staircase which had led to her rooms, nothing more. It had been the peace which remained in her memory. After the noise of the trains, it was a blessed relief. She had been squeezed between Alexander Amberville and an enormous woman who had insisted on talking incessantly about the war and her troubles as if there was not another person about her who did not have enough of their own. Shanna's nerves had been stretched to breaking point. There was no other topic of conversation for anyone but the war, and with General Sherman driving back the Confederate forces towards Atlanta every carriage had been full to capacity with refugees seeking sanctuary elsewhere. Some had disembarked at Macon, but more had taken their places, hoping that Savannah, Charleston or Augusta would be far enough away from the enemy soldiers to keep them safe.

Had Alexander Amberville not shown her the last letter her father had ever written, asking that he take her under his roof and care for her, she would never have left Atlanta. She cared little what happened to her. But the sight of it had reduced her to tears, dashed away the last vestige of courage left in her, and she had given in to his persuasions. Now she was glad she had done so. As she sat down on the veranda and Tante Lea disappeared back into the house, with the sun on her face, the sound of doves cooing somewhere on the roofs above her, the smell of freshly cut grass wafting under her nose and sweet-smelling magnolia blossoms planted a few feet away, it felt good to be alive. She savoured the moment because it reminded her of home and for the first time she realised she could dwell on the ruined plantation house where she had been born, without pain.

'Why, Miss Shanna. Now aren't you a sight for these old eyes?' Abraham appeared at her elbow with a tray which he set down on the long pine table. A glass of freshly squeezed orange juice was placed before her and a large plate of ham and eggs. 'Hannah told me to tell you she don't want no little bits left at all and there's plenty more where that came from. I'll bring the toast and coffee in a while.'

Shanna knew she would never manage all the food with her meagre appetite, but she did not want to hurt the servant's feelings. Tante Lea had taken an instant liking to him and his wife Hannah, both well into their fifties, and that was good enough for her. She smiled up into the wrinkled face, wondering if it had been he who had told Tante about Rafe Amberville's relationship with his family.

'I shall do my best. It smells delicious. Thank you, Abraham.'

There was a look of surprise in the old man's eyes as he turned and left her, as if he was not accustomed to such civility. Shanna had been raised in a house where the coloured servants were treated more as part of the family than slaves; her mother had insisted on it. She knew her father had not altogether agreed with the treatment, but he had bowed to his wife's wishes and she had controlled the household firmly, but without whip, or angry words. For all her quiet ways, there had been a strength about her mother that had sustained her through everything, Shanna thought wistfully, even a prolonged illness that had confined her to her bed for the last year of her life. Yet never had she complained, never had the servants taken advantage of her disability, and when she had died, and Shanna assumed her duties, they were as respectful, as considerate towards her as they had been to their old mistress.

The drumming of horse's hoofs drew her attention towards the paddocks off to the right of her, in time to see a huge black stallion soar over the high surrounding fence and thunder past the house without faltering in his long stride. She glimpsed a hard brown face momentarily turned in her direction and then horse and rider were swallowed up in the trees. It was several minutes before she realised the features had been familiar, but the last time she had seen them they had been covered in a growth of beard.

The breakfast proved too much for her, as she'd known it would. She stared regretfully at the two pieces of ham and the plate of buttered toast which she had not touched and pushed the plates to one side. Perhaps in a while she would take a walk to the stables and inspect the animals there. If Rafe Amberville's horse was anything to go by, there would be an excellent selection to choose from. And tomorrow she would go riding, she told herself resolutely. Little by little she would get her strength back and then she would take Tante Lea with her and go to Savannah to call on the lawyer whom Alexander Amberville had appointed to deal with all legal matters pertaining to her dead father's affairs. She had been left a great deal of money and jewellery upon her mother's death; now there would be more—and the house in New Orleans, at this moment occupied by Union troops, and the plantation at Baton Rouge, left unattended and at the mercy of the elements.

'If you send that plate back to the kitchen Hannah will have your hide,' a voice remarked so close by that she jumped in alarm. Six feet of bone and muscle lowered itself into the chair opposite, piercing blue eyes slightly amused as they considered her. 'I did not mean to startle you. If you aren't hungry, I'll help you out.'

And with that Rafe Amberville piled the ham into two pieces of toast and bit into it with relish. Shanna hardly recognised him as the unkempt soldier she had met only a few hours ago. Although he was now clean-shaven, she still found it difficult to assess his age. It could have been twenty-eight or thirty. The blond hair had been bleached by the sun. It was thick and curled slightly at the nape of the neck. He wore a fresh white shirt, open at the neck, the sleeves rolled back over berry-brown arms and dark trousers. The boots looked new and were highly polished. He looked every inch a gentleman, yet she sensed something about him that disturbed her—an inner turbulence, which, although controlled, lurked very close to the surface.

How she wished she possessed his powers of recuperation: to look so fit and well after the way she had seen him. . .

'I hope I have been forgiven for intruding on you last night.' He helped himself to more toast, stretching long legs out in front of him.

'You were not to know I had been given your rooms. No apology is needed,' Shanna returned politely. 'I shall have Hannah move my things within the hour.'

'You will do no such thing. There are plenty of rooms for me to choose from. Besides, I shall not be here long. A few days, perhaps, and then I shall be receiving fresh orders. You will be here much longer, will you not, Miss de Lancel?'

'I am surprised you can remember my name.' The words slipped out before she could contain them and brought a tight smile tugging at the lean mouth.

'The whiskey dulled the pain of my thoughts, not my wits. That is not the only thing I remember. . .' he added, and watched bright pink colour stain her cheeks. 'It has been a long time since I have seen a woman blush so delightfully. And an even longer span of time since I held anything—or anyone—so soft in my arms. A pleasant memory when I am alone some night. Don't worry,' he said quickly as he saw the alarm which sprang to Shanna's eyes. 'It is our secret. Your reputation would not be enhanced by a rumour that you had spent the night holding my hand. I doubt if anyone would believe anything that innocent could take place if I was a party to it.'

Abraham came out on to the veranda and set down a plate in front of him. It contained two of everything, Shanna saw. Eggs, ham, tomatoes and thick wedges of bread, baked not long ago by the smell of it.

'Hannah said you went out at the crack of dawn, Massa Rafe. I guess you had to go and see for yourself. The way you rode Balthazar back I knew where you'd been.'

'It's lucky I didn't meet my brother on the way or I would have broken his neck,' came the grim retort, and a fork was jabbed viciously into a slice of ham. 'What the devil has happened to the place while I've been gone? The roof on the cotton barn is falling apart. The slave quarters haven't seen a lick of paint in two years and someone has put the fear of God into people who once looked upon this place as their home. And the whip has been used, Abraham. I will not tolerate that. It was not needed before.'

The blue eyes glittered with sudden anger and once again Shanna was aware of an underlying conflict in him which he was having difficulty in fighting.

'But you are not here, Massa Rafe, and Massa Wayne has hired an overseer—a man by the name of Jack Hanson. . .' Abraham supplied the name with reluctance.

'Hanson! That trash! Isn't my brother capable of running this place with my father? From what I've seen neither has done very much since I left—except allow the place to run down.'

'It's the war, it's bad. So little money for repairs. Our cotton is still stored in the sheds at Savannah. With the blockade it is impossible to get it out.'

'Two grown men incapable of a full day's work. It won't be the war which destroys this place, but my own family. Over my dead body, Abraham. When I know where I shall be, I'll write to you. I want to know what is going on here, do you understand me?'

'You'll even know when a leaf drops from the trees,' the old man promised. 'I'll bring your coffee, just the way you like it, hot, black and strong enough to stand the spoon up in it.'

Shanna had listened in silence to the conversation, knowing it was not her place to say a word. She was a guest, not part of the family. As she did so she found herself in full agreement with what she had been told by Tante Lea. Rafe Amberville did go his own way and his heart belonged without a doubt to Wildwood. And the disquiet in him she now knew to be the violence of a temper she suspected he at times found it hard—if not impossible—to control. She believed had he encountered his brother after his inspection of the plantation, he would have taken out his anger and frustration on the younger man—with words or fists or both!

Rafe Amberville finished the last piece of bread

and sat back in his chair to enjoy the large mug of coffee Abraham had brought him. Shanna had seen the old man smile to himself as he removed the empty plates.

'That was the best meal I've eaten in the past six months,' he said. 'My men and I have seen no meat in that time and very little of anything else. We have just withdrawn from the Shenandoah Valley,' he explained and Shanna nodded, understanding at once how hard life had been for the men fighting there, defending the approach to Richmond.

'I hear the Yankees are being their usual pleasant selves towards defenceless farmers,' she said, her quiet voice tinged with bitterness. 'Is it really true that General Sheridan has given orders to burn their barns and confiscate all the livestock? How will those poor people live? And our soldiers—how can they fight when they do not have a decent meal inside them? Oh, how I hate this beastly war!'

'Sheridan is out to destroy the heart of the South. If he succeeds, Richmond will be isolated. It will take a miracle to beat them back now, especially with Sherman almost at the gates of Atlanta. If that falls, God only knows where he will make for next. He and Sheridan are two of a kind. Live off the land and to hell with the poor devils who have to try and survive after they have gone.' The hardness faded slightly from the man's face as he looked at Shanna. 'You have had more than your share of pain and grief. Abraham told me about your father—and your other losses. You are safe here. . .for the moment.'

He could have bitten off his tongue for such

thoughtless words as Shanna gave a soft gasp and one ringed hand fluttered nervously to her heart. He wondered what the man had been like she was to have married. She looked so young and frail, yet from all he had been told he knew there was great courage and resilience within that slender frame. A wan smile lit up her pale features and he thought how different it made her look. With colour in her cheeks she would be quite pretty. He wondered if his brother had tried to charm her into his bed yet. She was just innocent enough to whet his appetite and, he suspected, in need of a friendly shoulder to lean on. Wayne's speciality. Without knowing why the thought of her being touched by his brother angered him.

'Do you ride, Miss de Lancel?' Now why was he bothering himself with her? He had more than enough to do on the plantation before he was recalled to duty. His first task would be to get rid of Jack Hanson, although where he would find a replacement in these troubled times he did not know. The only men left were old or crippled, incapable of running a place as large as Wildwood, but he would not have what he had built up over the years destroyed by a stubborn father, a lazy, womanising brother and an overseer who could not get a good day's work out of the hands without his whip.

'Please call me Shanna. Yes, I do. I was wondering about making the effort tomorrow. The stallion you were riding is a beautiful animal. Are all your father's horses as magnificent?'

'My horses. The stables are mine. If you feel up to

it, then, I will pick you out a reliable animal. Balthazar will allow no one but me to ride him. I will show you over the plantation, or would you find that disturbing?'

Because of what had happened at Baton Rouge, or because of the overseer's heavy-handedness? she wondered.

'I would like that very much. Thank you, Mr Amberville.'

'The name is Rafe.' The words were accompanied by a broad smile which caused her heart to flutter unexpectedly as she became aware of his attractiveness as a man for the first time. There was a touch of mockery in the smile which deepened the corners of his mouth. He had learned all about her from the fountain of information in the house—Abraham. Was he wondering what she had been told about him?

'I hope you are not planning anything too strenuous for your first day,' a voice remarked from the doorway, and Rafe slowly rose to his feet as Alexander Amberville appeared on the veranda. For a long moment father and son stared at each other, but made no move to shake hands or embrace each other. They were like strangers. 'I was told you came back last night. You will be here long?'

No warmth in the voice, no sign of being pleased to see him safe and well. Shanna was shocked. With her Alexander had always been kind and considerate. She, a guest, was treated better than his own flesh and blood.

'I am waiting for new orders. Don't worry, Father,

I will not inconvenience you for too long. A few days, perhaps.'

'I want no trouble between you and your brother while you are here,' came the harsh warning.

'He may be a little bruised when I leave, but he will be intact,' Rafe replied with a shrug of broad shoulders. 'Which is more than I can say for Jack Hanson.'

'Hanson was hired by me,' his father thundered, his features reddening. 'And should I see fit to fire him, I will. But I do not. He gets the work done and Wayne trusts him.'

'And you trust Wayne.' The hardness had returned to Rafe's eyes. Shanna could feel his frustration mounting. 'You haven't changed. Still a blind fool!'

She rose to her feet so quickly that her chair toppled backwards on to the floor. She was unaccustomed to family quarrels and wanted to hear no more.

'I think I shall go for a walk and enjoy this fresh air, Mr Amberville. Please. . .' she paused, looking from one to the other in a silent appeal '. . .do not waste precious time in remembering old grievances. I only wish it had been possible to spend more time with *my* father. . .'

Her voice broke. Picking up her skirts, she hurried down the steps and began to cross the lawn towards the stables. Barely a moment had passed before Tante Lea appeared from the back of the house and hurried after her. Rafe watched the two of them wander out of sight with narrowed gaze. At least she had someone to watch over her, although he doubted if the companion would be able to keep Wayne from her mistress's door if he became insistent.

'A very intelligent young woman—for one so young,' he remarked as he returned to his chair and searched through his pockets until he found a cheroot. His father frowned as he lighted it. He did not smoke and drank in moderation. There had been times when Rafe had done both to excess. He had been penalised for it whereas his younger brother's exploits had been attributed to the high spirits of youth—or to 'finding his feet'. But then Rafe was the unloved son, the troublemaker, the nuisance. He had not known love since the day his mother died, her heart broken through the indifference of the husband who despised her, and since that day he had never known his father to utter a kind word towards him or to speak well of him to anyone.

'She is not for you,' Alexander said coldly. 'You will have nothing to do with her while you are here.'

'I rather think that is up to her. She has a mind of her own and she would not have survived this long if she had not learned how to use it.' He blew a cloud of grey smoke into the air, his head tilting to one side as he added, 'Or do you have plans for her?'

'She is alone in the world. I intend to offer her a home here and I shall do everything possible to find her a suitable husband. She is a wealthy woman in her own right now. She must be protected.'

'By you—or Wayne! My God, you cannot mean to marry that innocent off to him!'

'They are ideally suited.' Alexander's lips tightened in anger at the remark and it grew as his son threw back his head and roared with laughter.

'Wayne and her money are well suited, don't you mean?' Blue eyes, so intense in their scrutiny that they made him feel uncomfortable, searched Alexander's face. He had aged considerably in the past three years, Rafe thought. The lines at the corners of those indifferent eyes had deepened and his hair was almost white now. Not with worry over him. Wayne perhaps? Was he at last realising the potential he had overlooked in his elder son—the love he had turned his back on? He doubted it. If he was considering his younger brother as husband material for Shanna de Lancel then Wayne was still the golden boy at Wildwood. 'Is this place in such a bad way that you sink so low to get money?'

The words were hurled at his father with a quiet fury behind them and as Rafe saw him flinch he knew he had touched a raw nerve. What was happening to his beloved home? He had been shocked when Abraham and Hannah had told him of the attempted runaways whom Jack Hanson brought back in chains, beaten and cowed. No one ever ran away from Wildwood! And the only time he could remember a slave being whipped was when his stepmother had claimed that one of the young coloureds, Samuel, one of Abraham's sons, had made an improper suggestion to her.

Alexander Amberville had taken down the long deadly bullwhip from his study wall and had the offender tied to a tree outside the stables. And there, with everyone gathered to witness what happened, including Rafe, had proceeded to beat him senseless. As soon as he had recovered sufficiently to travel, he had been sold. The incident was still as clear in Rafe's mind as if it had happened yesterday. He had grown up amid the negroes and at times been happier in their company than that of his own father. At the age of ten, the bloody spectacle had stirred the first unrest within him and made him question the depth of his loyalty to a man who ignored him. One short month later, Julianna Amberville, Alexander's second wife, was killed in a riding accident as she showed off the new mare her husband had bought her before her Savannah friends who came frequently to the house. To Rafe it seemed like a judgement.

He was convinced she had lied. She had been years younger than his father; he had long suspected her of lying in order to keep his attention upon her alone. But because of those lies an innocent man had been flogged and sent away from the only place he had ever known as home, from his family and the boy who had looked upon him as a friend. That day, as he had watched the blood flow, Wildwood had become no better than any other slave-run plantation. Rafe had vowed it would not happen again.

'I will do whatever is necessary to keep this place for my family,' Alexander replied coldly.

'For Wayne, don't you mean?' Rafe rose to his feet, crushing the half-smoked cheroot beneath the heel of one boot with a fierce expletive. 'I'm not going to get my head blown off just to please you, Father. When this mess has been resolved, I shall be back for good. This place is mine as it was my mother's. She gave it to you as proof of her love, not knowing you are incapable of understanding what the word means. Wildwood will never belong to anyone else but me. Remember that, and if my precious brother wants to keep his precious head on his shoulders you had better make sure he understands it too.'

From the doorway behind his father, Wayne Amberville watched his elder brother stride across the lawn in the direction Shanna had taken, before stepping out on to the veranda. Five years younger than Rafe, he bore little resemblance to either father or brother, but favoured the mother who had captured the heart of the widowed Alexander with her flashing eyes and inviting smiles and caused many a tongue to wag in the county by allowing him to rush her off to the altar only six months after the death of his first wife.

He was tall, but slender as a woman. Light brown hair reached almost to the shoulders of his impeccable blue coat. The eyes which followed Rafe's progress were of a deeper brown. Eyes that were never still and missed nothing and did not hide the hatred inside him for the man who had returned to upset his carefully laid plans. His skin was pale for he avoided the sun like the plague—it always made him turn as red as a beetroot—and the hands which cupped a cool glass of mint tea showed no signs of manual labour.

'Damn him!' At the venomous comment Alexander turned, shaken from deep thought, and a frown creased his craggy brows. 'Why did he have to come back? All the men who have died and he rides back as healthy as you please.'

'That is no way to talk about your brother.' There were times when even Alexander began to wonder at the hatred Wayne held for his own kin. His younger son was vain and selfish as his mother had been, but he had been idolised by his father since birth and, after Julianna's tragic accident, what affection remained in Alexander had been lavished solely on this one son.

Rafe was strong. Rafe possessed his mother's strength and there had been times when Alexander had been proud of him, but he had never told him so. They had grown so far apart over the years that even the simplest of conversations had become impossible. And the war had hardened still more his embittered heart. There was nothing between them now—but Wildwood. The one thing that could link them together—or drive them apart forever!

'Please, Father, you don't have to pretend with me.' The sarcasm in Wayne's manner stung him, but he refrained from commenting. He was still seething from Rafe's scathing rhetoric. 'You are no more pleased to see him than I am. He will undo everything I have tried to do if we let him. I——' Wayne hastily corrected himself, knowing it was not wise to antagonise his father with Rafe present to take advantage of any disagreement '—we agreed Hanson would have full control and come to us only in an emergency and so far it has worked well. We shall have a full crop of cotton again this year. How many other plantations can match our output? Cotton is what has always brought us money and will continue to do so.'

'Meanwhile we pay exorbitant prices in Savannah for items we could grow ourselves. I agree the cotton is our first concern, but it is time we accepted the possibility this plantation could see blue uniforms—and in the not too distant future.'

'Rafe told you that?' Wayne looked startled. It was something he had never taken seriously. Most of the Union army was too concerned in the attempt to capture Richmond to bother with the deep South.

'No, I am remembering the panic in the faces of those people I saw fleeing Atlanta. The train was full of men and women who had believed our man Johnson could hold back Sherman's forces. But he failed and I'm afraid Atlanta will fall to the Yankees unless a miracle occurs—and, with the limited resources the South has at this moment, the only miracles we can expect will come from the Almighty himself.'

'Very well, I will have a word with Hanson this afternoon. And I'll see Abraham about setting down some more smoked hams and bacon.'

'I was wondering about letting Shanna take over those kind of chores,' Alexander said, and Wayne's eyes glinted expectantly at the news.

'She has agreed to stay, then? When did you ask her? Did you tell her about the birthday party?' Shanna de Lancel and her vast fortune were the best thing to come his way in many years and the prospect of her remaining at Wildwood dispelled some of the unpleasantness caused by Rafe's return.

'I have said nothing to her yet, but I will—soon.' Before she became too friendly with Rafe. 'I intend to ask her to take over the running of the house. It needs a woman's touch and it will keep her mind occupied. We must do all we can to stop her dwelling on her father's death. I am sure you will find ways to amuse her. Take her riding, for carriage rides to our neighbours. Make her feel accepted among our friends. Make her feel one of the family.'

'There are times when you amaze me, Father,' Wayne chuckled. 'Am I right in assuming you hope for a match between the girl and me?' A fortune at his fingertips! What did it matter if he did not care for her? He had charmed women before when it suited him and without such a tempting reward at the end of his labours.

'I am an old man, Wayne. I want a grandchild before I die. Give me one and you shall have more than just your wife's inheritance—you will have Wildwood.'

'And Rafe? He will never agree to that.'

'Wildwood is mine to do with as I please. When you marry and settle down and provide me with an heir, the place will become yours. I give you my word on it.'

'You shall have your grandchild, Father.' And he would be master of Wildwood, his brother disinherited. The knowledge was headier than any aged wine. The plantation and a rich wife to indulge him in the kind of life to which he had become accustomed, but could not afford to keep up without forging further cheques in his father's name to give him that extra money. 'You have my word on that.'

# CHAPTER TWO

SHANNA allowed her gaze to wander slowly down the line of horses for a third time, her eyes full of admiration for the beautiful animals Rafe Amberville had so proudly called his own.

'That one—the chestnut mare with three white stockings,' she said, at last making up her mind, and the tall negro beside her nodded approval.

'One of Massa Rafe's finest. She's as docile as a kitten. Not like old Balthazar over there. He's part devil, that one. Maybe that's why Massa Rafe likes him. Won't let anyone else but me care for him.'

'Hey, boy! Didn't I tell you to saddle my horse?' an angry voice declared behind them. 'See to it before I take my whip to your lazy hide.'

Shanna took an instant dislike to the man who stood in the doorway, feet astride, a coiled whip in one hand. She neither liked his tone of voice, the look of him, nor the way his eyes raked her from head to toe in a manner that made her instantly bristle. It was not the way Rafe Amberville had looked at her. This was a cold, calculating stare as if in his mind he was mentally undressing her.

'The overseer Jack Hanson,' Tante Lea whispered contemptuously. 'Without that whip he would be nothing.'

'Watch your tongue, girl, or you'll feel its sting on your back,' the man growled, moving towards them.

'You will not lay a hand on her.' Shanna's grey eyes darkened like gathering storm clouds. 'Tante Lea is not a slave.'

'She's black and she's on this plantation. To me that means she gets treated like all the rest.' Jack Hanson's eyes lingered on the firm swell of Shanna's breasts beneath the blue silk gown until the colour began to rise in her cheeks. 'And you ain't no Amberville, so I take no orders from you. I've heard all about you. This ain't New Orleans, so keep your fancy notions about black liberation to yourself. That kind of talk ain't welcome in these parts.' He wheeled on the negro, lifting the whip menacingly. 'My horse—now!'

'Yes, Leon, saddle his horse and then escort him off Amberville property,' Rafe declared. No one had seen him enter. Shanna wondered if he had heard the insults tossed at her and then saw by the tight line of his mouth, the glittering eyes, that he had. 'If you set foot here again, Hanson, I'll use your own whip on you so that you will remember the pain you have caused others.'

'You can't fire me! Only Mr Amberville can do that,' the overseer retorted. The fingers clutching the ugly whip tightened until the knuckles grew white. He was afraid, Shanna realised. Blustering, defiant—but afraid of the blond-haired man who stepped towards him. She caught her breath as he lifted his hand warningly. 'Stay back. I'll lay you out cold and your brother will thank me for it.'

'I am sure he would,' Rafe drawled, undeterred by the threat. 'You have one minute to get on your horse and get out of here before I give you a taste of your own medicine.'

The ultimatum was delivered so calmly and quietly that he could have been discussing the weather, but Jack Hanson knew from past encounters with Rafe Amberville never to trust the outward show of restraint. He had felt the power which lay in his fists, the hardness of his body, toughened by years of hard work. But his greed was far greater than his fear. He and Wayne Amberville were the true power at Wildwood, not this man, nor their father who had become content to allow all matters pertaining to it to pass into their hands. Wayne made a show of consulting him, but it was only a gesture so as not to arouse his suspicions. For every runaway slave Hanson brought back, another was sold to plantation owners who asked no questions. Between them, they were making a nice little profit. Wildwood would never suffer for a few lost negroes, not if he wielded his whip a little harder.

At the same time as he raised the whip, his other hand snaked down to the knife at his belt. Before he could use either, Rafe's clenched fist thudded into the man's jaw. It was a savage blow with all the anger he had refrained from unleashing upon his father behind it. Hanson's eyes glazed and he dropped like a stone to the ground.

Leon, the negro stableman, chuckled and he bent and lifted the unconscious man and flung him across the saddle of his horse as if he were a sack of potatoes.

'A man of few words still, I see, but you sure get things done,' he said, and a wide grin split his features from ear to ear. 'Massa Wayne is going to be mighty put out over this. They always has their heads together as if they was plotting something.'

'My brother only has one thing on his mind ever,' Rafe returned, rubbing bruised knuckles. 'Money—how to get it as easy as possible and the quickest way to spend it. Take Hanson to the main gates and make sure he doesn't sneak back tonight. You have my permission to stop him if he does, any way you can—short of killing him, that is.'

'Are you not being a little unfair to your brother?' Shanna ventured to ask as Leon and his unconscious companion rode out of sight. 'After all, he has been looking after the plantation since you went away. It cannot be easy these days with money so scarce.'

'Not so scarce he has had to let the place deteriorate as it has.' Rafe led Balthazar out of his stall and inspected him critically. As always when he had been ridden, Leon had rubbed him down the moment he arrived back in the stables. Not even the war or the abolitionists' wild talk of freedom had managed to break the ties of friendship between them. He knew neither his father nor brother would have considered giving a negro a position of power, but in his estimation Leon could manage the job of overseer very well. He would not use brutal methods with his own people, but he was capable of keeping them at work, of convincing them that the road to the North was not paved with gold and that when they arrived there they would not be treated any better by the people who preached freedom and equality than they were at Wildwood.

The stallion shied nervously as he sensed strangers and Shanna stepped backwards, awed by the size of him.

'Touch him,' Rafe said quietly. 'He will not hurt you. He's as gentle as a kitten with people he likes.'

'Even kittens have sharp claws,' Tante Lea muttered, staying well back as Shanna hesitantly lifted her hand and stroked the animal's nose. 'That is no kitten and he has big teeth. Take care, child.'

Balthazar nuzzled Shanna's fingers and instantly her apprehension vanished. She was aware of Rafe's eyes on her face and as she looked up at him was again conscious of the intimacy which leapt unbidden between them. Tante Lea felt it too, as strong as a sudden gust of wind, and a small frown puckered her brows. A man of violence and an innocent child! Such a match could never be.

'Do you feel up to going riding with me?' The question was so unexpected that it took her breath away. 'Now my temper has cooled, I had better try to undo some of the harm Hanson and my brother have done around here. And when you see over the place you will realise I have not been talking out of the top of my head.'

'It is so long since I have ridden. . .' Shanna sensed Tante Lea's disapproval of the idea, but as her gaze rested on the chestnut mare she silently brushed it aside. What harm was there in accepting the invitation? It would be good to talk to someone who would understand her abhorrence of the war and to be for a while in the company of someone she liked—other than Tante Lea, who had borne her morose silences and long spells of depression without one word of reproach. 'Yes, I will come with you.'

She did like Rafe Amberville. She was more than a little wary of the disturbing feelings he was arousing in her, but, she told herself, he was at Wildwood for only a short time. When he went back to the fighting he would forget her. She was a moment of relief from what he had left behind—as he was for her. They both wanted to relax and forget.

'Give me a few moments to go and change into something more suitable.'

Why was she so excited? She knew why when she saw the pleasure that registered in his eyes at her acceptance.

'That one is as bad as his brother,' Tante Lea said as she hurried after Shanna towards the house. 'Back for a few short hours and already he thinks he has made a conquest. This is not wise, child. Believe me.'

Because Rafe Amberville had looked at her and made her aware of the fact that she was a woman? Even the pink-cheeked young man she was to have married had never made her feel like that. They had been too close, having grown up together and accepting, without question, that both families wanted them to marry one day. Accepted it and believed friendship to be love. Shanna had never known the deep fires which true love could ignite!

'Well, what do you think of Wildwood now?' Rafe reined in Balthazar on the edge of the cotton fields and looked expectantly into Shanna's face.

The sun had brought a flush of colour to cheeks that had possessed none at breakfast. She looked barely eighteen instead of almost twenty-one—although he could not deny that the tight-fitting riding habit she had changed into did not cover the figure of a young girl. It had been many years since he had felt himself stirred by a woman. There had never been anyone special in his life and he had strongly, and so far successfully, resisted all attempts to persuade him to step up to the altar.

He had indulged in several short-lived affairs over the years, satisfactory at the time, but never binding. Nothing had managed to occupy his time as Wildwood did. It had taken a war to drag him away from the only important thing in his life.

For a brief instant he remembered the woman with whom he had spent his last night before leaving home. Young, beautiful, experienced—and married. The thought of leaving Wildwood had so disheartened him, he had broken his own golden rule and bedded a married woman. In comparison, Shanna de Lancel was an innocent. . .an angel! And, if his father had his way, the next mistress of Wildwood.

'I think you are very lucky still to have your home,' Shanna said, wondering why his eyes had suddenly grown so cold. They were looking straight at her, but she surmised he did not see her. He was lost in thoughts she dared not ask him to explain; they were too private. And painful. There was not only anger in him, but a deep festering wound which would not heal. Whoever had hurt him had made sure he would not recover. 'I miss my home very much—the plantation we owned outside Baton Rouge. Tante Lea and I fled there when the Yankee general issued his hateful decree. It was impossible to live in New Orleans after that. No woman was safe!'

Even Rafe had been shocked at the callous order that went out to the Union troops occupying New Orleans, from their commanding officer, Major-General Benjamin F. Butler, who had been the military governor.

The general order number twenty-eight, issued on the fifteenth of May 1862, had stated that if any female by word, gesture or movement, insulted or showed contempt to any officer or soldier of the United States, she would be regarded as a woman of the town plying her avocation and treated as such.

The women of New Orleans had reacted no differently to any enemy in their midst than any other women in the world—they had rebuffed him, scorned him, avoided him like the plague—and they paid dearly for it.

'The Yankees found us there too,' Shanna continued at length. She sensed he was waiting for her to unburden herself at her own speed. He hooked one booted foot over the pommel of his saddle, produced a cheroot and enquired if she would mind. She shook her head. Her father had smoked a pipe. As the smoke drifted beneath her nose, she realised she would never again sit at his feet and fill it for him as had been her practice.

'But you managed to escape,' Rafe said quietly, loath to interrupt her. How he wished he had someone to unburden himself to, but no one could solve his problems and they could not be forgotten. Only at the height of a battle, with gunfire all around him, men falling right and left, screaming, groaning, the sound of his own voice yelling at them to press on obliterating all else, did Wildwood vanish from his thoughts. But at night, however exhausted he was, it returned to haunt him before sleep claimed him, closed his mind to the horrors of the day and gave him a brief respite.

'They came at night, like thieves.' Shanna closed her eyes as the nightmare returned, then she forced them open again, knowing it was over and that she was safe. Nothing would harm her here. 'Most of the servants had gone. There were only six, but when they saw the four soldiers they ran and hid. They came out again when it was all over, but they did not stay—there was nothing left to stay for. They burned the house after they had ransacked it—the barns, the stables, everything. They were like animals. . . ravaging under cover of darkness. . .

'Tante Lea saved my life when they came after me. She killed for me that night. Since I was ten years old she has looked after me, and until that night I thought I knew her. I grew up overnight. The little girl accepted reality. It was frightening. Without her I would never have survived. Somehow we reached Atlanta. I took rooms in a lodging house to be near my father. . .after all that had happened I never wanted to be parted from him again. . .'

Bright tears appeared in her eyes. She tried to suppress them, but the floodgates of her memory had been thrown wide open. She had not cried when she had learned of his death; now she could not stop.

She was not aware of Rafe dismounting, but his arms were suddenly reaching up for her, lifting her from her horse and carrying her to the shade of some trees a few yards away beside the riverbank. She felt the strength in them as he cradled her against his chest. Her tears soaked the front of his shirt. He did not speak, but set her down on the slope and sat beside her, holding her close until the tumult began to pass.

When it did, Shanna lay spent and limp against him, her cheek against the smoothness of his shirt, her eyes tightly closed. How long she remained that way she did not know, then, as if suddenly realising how possessively the arms held her, she pulled free, cheeks flaming, and dashed the last tears from her eyes.

'Whatever must you think of me? I have not cried like that since my brother was killed.'

'It is not good to bottle up your emotions,' Rafe said gently, watching as she pushed an unruly strand of hair back behind her ears.

'That is easy for you to say. If I were a man I could lash out at people I dislike, as you did Jack Hanson earlier, but for a woman it is different. She is expected always to be in control. My mother once told me that, although men treat us like china dolls, we are the strong ones.'

'Your mother was a very wise woman. *My* mother

was a fighter. All her life she fought to keep a man who was barely aware of her existence—as he is of mine. She fought to keep peace here when his rough methods alienated our neighbours. She fought to keep the two families together—hers and my father's—and in the end it killed her. She died unloved, unwanted in the room next to mine. My stepmother wanted that room, but I threatened to burn it rather than allow her to set one foot inside. I think that day my father and I accepted we would always hate each other. She would always be between us——' Rafe broke off, a smile masking the pain in his eyes that the memories had aroused. 'I thought I was consoling you. You have a way about you, Shanna de Lancel—a peaceful way that makes a man feel good to be with you. I haven't been this relaxed for a long time.'

'Tante Lea said I was born under a lucky sign,' Shanna said, embarrassed by the compliment. Once she would have fluttered her fan and accepted it without a second thought afterwards. She had never been without an escort in New Orleans. She was beautiful, the daughter of a prominent man and a society mother and heiress to a small fortune. She was accepted into all the houses that her parents considered suitable and looked upon by all the men she met as prospective marriage material. She had learned very quickly that a stolen caress, or a kiss out of sight of the watchful Tante Lea, did not mean the man was in love with her—only that he wanted her. Sometimes she despaired of ever finding a deep relationship such as she shared with her father and brother. Most of her friends had married by the time they were eighteen; her fiancé had wanted them to marry before he went to war, but she had refused, convincing him it would soon be over and they would be able to start their married life together without a threatening cloud looming over them both.

How she had reproached herself when he was killed. But as time passed she accepted the true reason why she had made that decision. She had not loved him. Not as her parents had loved each other. Not as she loved her brother James. She sought a love that would endure despite the worst hardships that life could produce. One love—forever. Was it such an impossible dream?

She suspected Rafe Amberville did not make idle comments to women. He was good-looking and sure of himself. And man enough to take what he wanted from life. There was no indecision about him. His life was here at Wildwood. It *was* his life. An all-consuming passion that left little room for anything—or anyone else. The woman who loved him would have to accept that, or risk losing him forever.

'You like my domain, then?' Rafe said, allowing his gaze to wander slowly over the surrounding scenery. Along the riverbank were the rice fields; beyond that acre after acre of cotton beginning to flourish in the June sunshine. It would be a good harvest and invaluable to them after the war—if the plantation survived.

'Your domain,' Shanna echoed softly, 'where you are king—and reign supreme?'

'As my mother once did before she lost her mind and married my father.' His eyes followed the clear flowing water back the way they had come, past the paddocks and stables, the slave quarters and cotton barns. On the way back they would ride past the smoke house and the grain barns, past the horses grazing on lush green grass, the pig pens where Hannah was fattening the swine for special occasions. Back to the house where memories and hatred awaited him.

'Why *did* she marry him, then?' Shanna wondered if she should pry into his obviously painful past, but he did not appear to mind the question. She sensed almost relief that he was able to speak of those earlier years—the same kind of relief that she had felt in his arms moments ago.

'Let me say—having no wish to offend those delicate ears——' he gave her a grin that was positively wicked '—that my mother and father were something more than friends before they were married. She was two months pregnant when he was "persuaded" to marry her—*her* father was a very wealthy man. But the marriage was never a success. Day by day the situation worsened. Separate rooms, separate lives. I was her whole world and she was mine. And I have unburdened my soul sufficiently for one day. I brought you out to forget your own troubles.'

'And you have. You have made me realise there are other people in the world who have suffered the loss of someone they love. I am not alone,' she replied. She felt the breath catch in her throat as he turned and looked at her with the same piercing gaze that had set her heart racing before. This was foolishness, she told herself reprovingly, they were little more than strangers; how could he have this effect on her? No other man ever had. She was allowing the sentimental moment they had shared to cloud her judgement. Rafe Amberville was a soldier, soon to return to the fighting. She wanted no more heartache.

She knew she should have pulled away when he reached out and took one of her hands in his, examining the long, slender fingers one by one. His touch was impersonal, but not so the blue eyes intent on her face. The sudden glitter in them should have warned her of his changing mood; instead, as if mesmerised, she could not move. Not even when he drew her back against his chest and bent the dark face close to hers.

'You were very kind to a tired soldier last night, little Shanna, and I have shown you little thanks for it,' he murmured.

'I—I would have done the same for anyone in such a position,' Shanna stammered.

'But you did it for me and I think it only proper that I show my appreciation for your ministering. I was in no mood to do so last night and for that you must forgive me.'

'I thought we had settled that. There is nothing to forgive. You were tired—and the welcome, such as it was, could not have been what you were expecting,' Shanna protested before words failed her.

'Welcome!' Rafe ejaculated. 'There is no welcome for me here from father or brother. From Abraham and Hannah, perhaps. Yes, most certainly. And

Leon and his younger brother—we have all shared much together. But no one else.'

He made it sound as if he was alone in the world, yet he possessed a family. She did not! No matter how bad the situation was between them, they were of the same blood and it was unbelievable that he could turn his back on them, dismiss them as if they did not exist. Yet had they not done that to him? If he lost one of them surely he would feel pain? Or if he was taken by a Yankee bullet. . .would his father not mourn? God forbid that it should happen.

What was wrong with her? Her reason was going to think such a thing. He meant nothing to her! His face came closer. She could feel his warm breath on her cheek as light as a breath of wind. One hand reached for the combs securing her hair into place and, before she could stop him, he had removed them. The carefully arranged mass of hair that Tante Lea had wound into a thick coil at the base of her neck cascaded in wild profusion down over her shoulders. He wound a lock of it around his fingers and gently tugged at it so that her lips came still closer to his.

He was going to kiss her, Shanna thought in panic. She must not allow it to happen!

'We should be going back to the house,' she protested, trying to pull back, but discovered she was held fast.

'Before I have shown my gratitude?' Rafe teased.

Shanna had been kissed before, but she was totally unprepared for the fire which leapt through her body as his mouth took hers. Not in the dominating manner of the night before, but with gentleness, cherishing it and imparting into each and every long, drawn-out kiss an expertise that made her senses clamour for more. She knew it could not be possible but it felt as if the ground was moving beneath her.

For a moment only did she try to resist him and then Rafe felt her sink against him in silent surrender. He pressed her down upon the ground, losing himself in the magic—or was it madness—of the moment? The sweet fragrance of the loose hair, so soft against his cheek, the light perfume she wore which reminded him of orange blossom, the fierce beating of her heart beneath the thin fabric of her blouse, the firm breasts pressed against his chest reminded him how long it had been since he had made love to a woman.

It was that thought that sobered him, made him draw back. Shanna was not like the other women he had associated with over the years. The childish eagerness of her lips had revealed that. She was indeed an innocent and did not deserve to be a victim of his hunger—or his desire to thwart his father's plans. She was not for him!

The tide of emotion which had swept over Shanna, washing away all natural caution, slowly began to recede, leaving her drained, puzzled by his change of attitude.

'I—I do not understand. . .' she faltered, as he took her hand and lifted her to her feet. What had she done wrong? Her words brought a momentary glitter to Rafe's blue eyes, then, smiling, he shook his head.

'No, Shanna, you do not, and that is exactly why I am taking you back to the house right now.' He brushed some dirt from the folds of her skirt and ran a critical eye over her appearance. The flushed cheeks could be attributed to the warmth of the sun. Tante Lea would not think anything of that. Rafe suspected she would be somewhere close, watching for their return—as would his father.

As he helped her to remount, his hand lingered on hers, all mockery vanishing from his voice and his features. 'I would like us to be friends, Shanna.'

'We are,' Shanna replied, quickly gathering up the reins he held out to her. Friends—but nothing more, his tone implied. How could there be anything or anyone more in his life when Wildwood occupied it so completely?

They were almost to the stables when Rafe reined in Balthazar behind a group of negroes diligently weeding the floral borders which lined the pathways. She followed suit, watching curiously as he bent low and slapped the upturned bottom of an old woman. The face which was slowly turned in his direction lighted up with an expression of pure joy as he was recognised.

'Massa Rafe, you is home again! Now everything will be all right.'

'I wish I could stay, but in a few days. . .' Rafe lifted his shoulders in a shrug of resignation. How calmly he accepted that he must return to the fighting, Shanna thought, when he did not know what lay ahead—only that he could be wounded, captured and sent to one of the Federal prisons, which by reputation were more to be feared than any battle—or killed! 'You look well, Mamma. How are Jacob and Lisette?'

At the question tears sprang to the old woman's eyes. Several of the other workers had stopped to watch and listen even though they knew that if they were seen by the hated overseer Hanson they would feel the bite of his whip across their backs. There were no exceptions for man, woman or child. And the younger women unfortunate enough to catch his eye had even more to fear from him.

'Jacob died last fall, Massa Rafe. The fever took him. Mr Hanson, he said it was nothing and my man should go back to work. He did and it killed him. Every night since I have prayed for God to strike that man dead.'

'Hanson will not bother anyone at Wildwood again,' Rafe said through tight lips. How many more needless deaths had there been because the faces had been black and the people considered unimportant? 'I had Leon escort him off the property earlier. He won't be back.'

'Bless you, Massa Rafe, we knew it would be all right when you came back.' Her words were echoed by the men and women close by. Shanna could feel their relief at the news, see the tension ebbing out of their faces.

'And Lisette?' Rafe repeated, recalling a bright-eyed girl who had been fifteen when he left and had already aroused the interest of his brother. His warning of what would happen if he touched her had been delivered to Wayne with a colourful rhetoric that had turned him ashen.

'She ain't here any more. Massa Wayne sold her when he found she was with child. No one knows where she is.'

'Perhaps I can find out before I leave. It can't last much longer, Mamma, and then I shall be home for good,' Rafe promised, masking the fury which rose up inside him.

'If you return,' the woman said soberly.

'Don't worry, Mamma, the bullet hasn't been moulded that can penetrate my thick skull. You should know that.'

'Maybe, Massa Rafe, but I was not thinking of no Yankee bullet—closer at hand perhaps? Take care.'

'At least here I have someone to watch my back for me.'

Rafe's answer was intended to imply that he was in no way concerned about such an occurrence, Shanna thought, but she did not miss how his eyes darkened with thought as they continued to ride. Who was there to harm him at Wildwood? He did not get on with either his father or brother, but neither would surely resort to bodily harm against him. Only Hanson might do that, although she doubted if he would have the courage to show himself at Wildwood again. He was a coward and a bully and without the power he had possessed and maintained through the use of his whip—he was nothing!

* * *

'A ball!' Shanna echoed disbelievingly. Wayne had brought her into the study where he told her his father wanted to tell her something of great importance. 'For my birthday! I cannot believe it. It is so long since I have danced. . .but do you think it proper, sir, with my father dead but a few short months?'

'My dear child, your father would not have wanted you to grieve over him forever. He was a brave soldier, who accepted he could become a casualty of the war. He was also my friend and when he gave you into my keeping he did so because he knew I would make you part of my family. And you are a part of it, you know,' Alexander declared, patting her hand and then bending low to bestow a light kiss upon her forehead. 'I intended to keep it a surprise, but Wayne thought you might like to go into Savannah and buy yourself something pretty.'

'Indeed, I do not have anything suitable for the occasion. I do not know how to thank you, sir.' Shanna was overwhelmed, deeply touched by the offer.

'To start with, my dear, you can be less formal. I soon hope you will be able to think of me as more than just your father's friend.' Alexander turned to his younger son to ask casually, 'Why don't you have Leon drive you into Savannah tomorrow? Wine and dine Shanna. Show her some Amberville hospitality.'

'You have shown me that since the first day I set foot inside your door,' Shanna replied with a warm smile. A day in Savannah would give her the opportunity to see the lawyer. It would be just as painful a month from now so she saw little reason for delaying it as she had decided to do at first. And then she could start repaying the Ambervilles for their generosity.

'You will allow me to escort you, then?' Wayne asked. Out of the corner of his eye he was aware of Rafe entering the room and crossing to the sideboard to help himself to a snifter of brandy before the meal—aware too of how Shanna's eyes followed him; but his apprehension was short-lived. When he chose he could be a perfect gentleman, and was confident that after one day alone with him she would not give his elder brother a second glance.

'I shall be delighted.'

'I shall tell Leon after lunch.'

'I need Leon here with me, you will have to take one of the other boys—or drive yourself,' Rafe declared, relaxing down into a chair beside the open window. 'There are a hundred and one things to do in the few short days I am here and I need him with me now that Hanson is no longer working for us. I fired him this morning,' he added as Alexander's face turned as dark as thunder. 'He was no good. If you had not allowed Wayne to take over Wildwood you would have realised that long ago. How long is it since you have ridden over the place? A month? Two? Maybe six. . .'

'That is none of your damned business,' Alexander thundered, fists clenching at his sides. No more than a minute in the same room together and already they were at each other's throats. 'I am master here. Neither of you do anything here without consulting me first. And we have managed very well without you. For the second year we have a good cotton crop. We supply the army hereabouts with fresh vegetables and salted meats.'

'And maintain your position of power in the community by hiring an overseer who has put the fear of God into our workers,' Rafe said contemptuously. 'What good will your precious cotton be when the bluecoats come riding through South Carolina and trample it flat, burn the barns, free those you have beaten and half starved to death? What will you think of Wayne when you watch Wildwood burn to the ground and he lifts not one finger to do anything about it? It has already happened in New Orleans when negroes were freed. Plantations were overrun, looted, destroyed out of hatred and revenge, and now they lie derelict, perhaps never to be restored. When the South loses this war—and it is going to—we shall also lose our way of life. I, for one, do not intend to allow that to happen here at Wildwood.'

'Yankees here!' Wayne scoffed. 'They are hundreds of miles away, heading towards Richmond, and Joe Johnston's men are holding Sherman back outside Atlanta.'

'Were.' Rafe corrected coming to his feet, eyes blazing. 'You both sit here in your little cocoon and ignore what is happening in the real world. Ask Miss de Lancel if you don't believe me, which you don't. Ask her to tell you how many faithful negroes remained to protect her when she needed them. Sherman and Sheridan are two of a kind; they enjoy war. Don't you think they want to crush us, humiliate us for daring to stand against them, or have you conveniently forgotten South Carolina was the first state to secede? If we fall, it will be a harsh lesson to others.'

'We are safe here,' Alexander declared. He had drawn close to Shanna's chair at Rafe's outburst and laid a hand on her shoulder as if to comfort her. 'Shanna is safe here, Wayne and I will see to that, and I would be grateful if you keep your talk of war out of my house. We have no need of it to remind us what some of us have suffered.'

'Believe me, the suffering has yet to begin,' Rafe warned, turning towards the door. His appetite had gone. He needed to be with people he could trust, who would listen to his words because they were as much a part of this place as he was.

'I humbly apologise for my brother's behaviour,' Wayne said as he closed the door. 'And for dragging you into his talk of war. Nothing is going to get to us here. Not Sherman, not Sheridan—not one single blue uniform will ever set foot on Wildwood soil.'

'I share Wayne's opinion that Rafe over-exaggerrated,' Alexander added, drawing her to her feet. 'Let us go and enjoy our lunch and forget all this wretched talk of things which will not happen.'

As Wayne took Shanna's arm and led her out on to the shaded veranda where a long table had been prepared for lunch, Shanna wished she could have been as sure as the two men with her that the horrors she had already seen would not be repeated in this beautiful place.

## CHAPTER THREE

'AIN'T you eating upstairs with the family and that nice young lady?' Hannah was surprised when she brought down the last of the dishes to find Rafe sprawled in a chair beside the open window. 'That ain't none of my lemonade you is drinking. Shame on you—and no food in your stomach.'

Rafe put down his empty tankard with a smile, but his thoughts were far away, and she set to washing up, calling for her youngest son to come and dry the plates and glasses piling up beside her.

'Are you to stand there all day, boy?' Abraham came into the kitchen some time later, removing his black coat and relaxing down into a chair opposite Rafe. Benjamin, his youngest and the most troublesome of the three sons he had brought into the world, stood beside a mound of finished dishes, a disgruntled expression on his face. 'When you've finished here, Massa Wayne needs you. He and Miss Shanna are going into Savannah. He has clothes that need pressing, shoes to be cleaned. You know how fastidious that man is about his appearance.'

'A strutting peacock on a wasteland,' Rafe said as if to himself, and Abraham almost choked on his first swallow of the ice-cold lemonade Hannah had placed in his hand. 'Well, isn't he? He'll probably go out to meet the Yankees when they arrive, in his best suit, and invite them in for a brandy. I can't see him lifting a finger to protect the place.' His eyes came to rest on the old man's face and Abraham was disturbed by the coldness lurking there. 'How many do you think will stay? If the Yankees get nearer?'

'You really believe they will?' Hannah sliced the peach tart she had just taken from the oven and placed two large slices on separate plates which she gave to each man. No one ever went without food in her kitchen. After a moment, sensing they wanted to talk, she also fetched a fresh bottle of corn whiskey, knowing Abraham would only partake of one small glass at this time of the day, and left it on the table between them before returning to her work.

'I believe if South Carolina was brought to her knees, then it would only be a short time before the remaining states capitulated. Our ports are blockaded, we can bring nothing in—get nothing out! The Shenandoah is under siege, our supply routes there threatened by Sheridan and his army. Richmond is their next target, or so the big brass believes. There is more, Abraham, there has to be. My men and I are not the only units to be moved elsewhere. Someone thinks it more important to hold back Sherman than protect the valley. To me that means that he does not intend to stop at Atlanta. If he ploughs his way overland to the sea, we shall not only lose the war, we will be left with nothing—nothing at all.'

'If you lose, Massa Rafe, then we do too. We ain't never known no other home but Wildwood. Abraham and me was brought here when we was children,' Hannah declared from across the room. 'Benjamin and Leon were born here—'

'And Samuel,' Benjamin broke in, flinging down the cloth he held. 'Why does everyone pretend he never was born?'

'Watch your tongue,' Rafe snapped. 'No one has forgotten, least of all me.'

Benjamin slammed the door after him with such violence that it shook the table and spilled some of the whiskey Abraham had poured out. Muttering under her breath, Hannah grabbed up a cloth to mop the spillage.

'You must do something about him, Hannah,' Rafe warned. His father was not the most patient of men and tolerated the presence of the old couple because Rafe insisted on their remaining. The sight of them was a daily reminder for Alexander of the wife who had lied to him on countless occasions and, in doing so, had almost caused him to take a man's life. A reminder, too, of Rafe's mother, whom they had both loved and served devotedly all their lives. 'The young fool has his head filled with abolitionist ideas. Freedom is only a word. . .it means different things to different people.'

'To those who have it maybe, Massa Rafe,' Abraham said solemnly. 'It is different for me than it is for you and you can't tell me it ain't.'

'No, I can't,' Rafe agreed. 'But will you have more freedom in the North? Or if the Yankees overrun this place? Will you stay here? How will you survive with no roof over your head, the fields burned? How many of the others will be here to help you try and till the soil, plant new crops so that you can feed yourselves?'

'Better the devil you know,' Hannah said with a broad grin as she took their empty plates. 'And Massa Rafe will be here. It will be as it was in the old days when Miss Charlotte was alive.'

'Bless you for believing that,' Rafe murmured. 'I know no one could have loved my mother more than you both did. I can't see into the future, I can't tell you for certain what is going to happen, only that no one—no outsider—will ever have this place.'

'You don't have to look that far afield for the enemy, Massa Rafe. He's here, right in our own backyard.' Abraham finished his whiskey before he spoke, knowing the hornets' nest he was about to unleash. When Rafe was gone, he might very well suffer for his actions, but it had to be done. It was only right and proper that he know what was happening.

'I've had the feeling you are keeping something back from me. What is it?' Laughter drifted to him from the patio above and his lips tightened. Shanna had spent all yesterday afternoon in his brother's company and this morning she had gone riding with him.

'It ain't only the Yankees who could deprive us of our home,' Abraham replied, with a significant nod in the direction of the sound.

'You mean my father.'

'More like Massa Wayne. Since you went away he's been in charge of everything. The master don't take an interest in Wildwood or anything else. Just sits in his study staring out of the window most of the time. Rarely goes visiting. Something's wrong with him, Massa Rafe, but me and Hannah can't think what. And he ain't called no doctor, so he ain't sick. At least it's nothing we can see.'

'Maybe his sins have caught up with him,' Rafe said humourlessly. 'So he has turned the power over to my brother, who is naturally abusing it. Is that what you wanted to tell me?' It came as no surprise to Rafe. Wayne had always coveted the prestige and respect that being owner of Wildwood brought with it. He had used it on many occasions to gain credit from shopkeepers, to put a foot inside doors which would normally have been closed to him and seduce innocent young things whose fathers discovered too late what kind of man they willingly entertained beneath their roofs.

'It ain't my place to tell you anything, Massa Rafe.'

'If you get out of line, I'll tell you,' Rafe assured him. 'And let me worry about looking after you. I always have.'

'Very well, but you ain't going to like it. Not one little bit!'

There was nothing in Rafe's attitude at dinner that evening to show the extent of the shock he had received. He had suspected that once in control of the plantation Wayne would take full advantage of his situation, but he had expected his father to hold the purse strings, as he always had, to continue keeping the ledgers which were an accounting of everything that happened at Wildwood, what was bought and sold, for how much and when. Instead he had discovered Wayne now did everything except make out the cheques for payment at the bank in Savannah. This Alexander still did every month, but without argument, and each week Wayne spent a whole day in the study meticulously bringing the ledgers up to date, like a loving, dutiful son!

Abraham had seen the amount of one of those cheques—money intended to purchase new equipment and necessities for Wildwood, including new orange trees, flour and molasses. He had also seen the quantities which should have arrived at the plantation to restock empty barns and not only keep the household in continued comfort, but fill the stomachs of the hungry workers who daily toiled under the menace of Hanson's whip. Less than half ever arrived, he had told Rafe in a hushed voice, often looking around him as he spoke, in constant fear of being overheard.

Massa Alexander and his son never went without; no more did the overseer, who had turned a family out of one of the cottages and installed himself there. Only the negroes suffered. Complaints brought the whip and never reached the ears of the elder Amberville—sometimes not even Wayne. And the final bone-jarring revelation had left him speechless. One night when Wayne had been working late and neither he nor Hannah were allowed to retire before he did lest he required something, the former had gone into the study. His usual knock unanswered, he had entered in time to see Wayne working on a second ledger which he had hastily concealed with a mass of papers. Two sets of books! One for his father and one for Wayne himself, Rafe realised. Obviously Abraham's observations had not been noticed or he would have been removed from harm's way before now.

Rafe knew he had to find the second set and discover for himself how much his brother was milking from the plantation. He gave a good impression of being very tired at dinner and, while coffee was being served in the drawing-room, excused himself and retired early.

Nothing could have been further from his thoughts than sleep. Once in the rooms he had taken for himself, he opened wide the windows, turned down the lamps and sat in a chair waiting for everyone else to go to bed.

He heard Shanna come upstairs, escorted, as always, by Tante Lea. The door of her bedroom closed and moments later he heard the maid go down the corridor to her own room at the far end. But only just. . . If she had been one of the enemy stealing up on someone in the night, they would have been dead before being aware of her presence, he thought. The war had heightened his senses to such a pitch that he was often aware of a movement in the dark before any of his men, and glad he was of it—for his life had been saved on several occasions through his sensitivity. He did not necessarily see or hear—but he was aware.

The long-case clock outside in the corridor chimed midnight. He waited until the echoes had died away before opening the door, paused for another full minute before stepping out and closing it noiselessly behind him. He needed no light to guide him downstairs to the study. As a rebellious boy he had often stolen out of the house and gone drinking with his friends, not returning until dawn.

He stood in the darkness of the study to get his bearings, then, with uncanny accuracy, stepped up to the large desk and lighted the lamp there, immediately turning it down to a muted glow. He doubted if his father would stir again before morning and he had watched Wayne ride away an hour before, wondering as he did so why his brother had not been more angry over the dismissal of the overseer—his chosen man! Had the latter merely been a pawn or did Wayne intend to reinstate him as soon as Rafe was safely out of the way again? He found that thought disturbing. He would be far away and helpless to intervene. Damn the war!

In the second drawer he opened he found the plantation ledgers. He could find no fault in them, not even a mistake crossed through, a figure erased and rewritten. Mathematics had never been Wayne's strong point at school. It was hard to believe that almost overnight he had become an experienced book-keeper—and so careful with his work.

It was as Abraham had suspected, Rafe mused, relaxing back in his chair for the moment. On the surface his brother could not be faulted, gave no reason for his father to complain or investigate one little thing he did. So where was he keeping the second set of books? Not in the study. Their father was an avid reader and spent hours in this room.

They would have been found too easily. Likewise he doubted if Wayne had hidden them in his own rooms. There was only one place—the 'monk's hole'!

Adjoining the drawing-room was a smaller room—the solar which his mother had created and where she had spent most of her afternoons, sewing or writing letters or just enjoying the late afternoon sunshine which flooded into it. It had not been changed after her death. The sofa she had used was still in the same place, and beside it a small table inlaid with marquetry which she had purchased on a rare visit to Charleston. The two oil-paintings of Wildwood, a present from her parents on her wedding-day, still adorned the wall. How relieved he had been that the second Mrs Amberville had not liked the solar and consequently had left it alone. Dull and uninteresting, had been the comment, and not worth bothering about. Not so the rest of the house. She had changed that and would have invaded the sanctuary of his dead mother's rooms if he had not threatened the direst consequences should she do so. And burn them he had been prepared to do, rather than allow her to set one foot inside them.

Beneath one of the pictures was a tapestry sampler in a wooden frame. Rafe slid his fingers down the right-hand side until they connected with one of the tassels hanging there. A slight tug and a whole section of the wall swung back, revealing a recess large enough for him to stoop through. A frown creased his brows as he did so. As far as he could recall, this secret tunnel had not been used in the last ten years, yet there had been no sound as the door opened.

Again his fingers groped in the darkness and came away with the smell of oil on them. He was right! Wayne was using this as his hiding place. The elation which engulfed him at his success was quickly curtailed by caution and the realisation that he must work through the hours of darkness if he was to set into motion the plan coming together in his mind. If it was successful he would deprive his brother of his ill-gotten gains and ensure the safety of Wildwood until he returned.

He struck a match and in the brief glare found the wall torch which had always been positioned just inside the opening. The pitch flared to life immediately, flooding with light a small room some ten feet square. His mother had once told him a story of his great-great grandfather, who had brought his new bride to a new land and built this very house for her. A reformed privateer with letters of Marque who had sailed under the proud flag of his homeland England—not always with distinction—and grown rich on the booty from ships he had plundered, he had soon grown bored with the life of a plantation owner and had taken to smuggling to ease his boredom.

The dark winding tunnel which stretched ahead of Rafe came out in the bayou, near a cabin used by the negroes when they were planting the new rice fields. What came and went along those waters at night he could only guess. As a boy he had used it to leave the house unobserved, returning the same way often in the early hours of the morning. Wayne too had found it useful when he wished to pay his usual visits to the ladies of the town whom he knew would not be approved of by his father. And now he was using it for a more deceitful purpose still — to deprive their father and Wildwood of money and supplies! A sudden thought striking him, he started off down the tunnel. He had gone but a few yards when he encountered the first of the boxes which stretched as far as the eye could see. He thrust the torch close to one of them. Corn. That was fetching more than twenty dollars and there was case after case of it! Coffee. At fifty dollars a pound. . .! A soft whistle escaped his lips. No wonder Wayne always had money. Five barrels of flour. At three hundred dollars that made fifteen hundred dollars clear profit.

He wandered slowly further, examining in detail every new sack or barrel. Green tea! Soap, which had increased in wartime from ten cents a pound to one dollar and ten cents, a tenth of a soldier's monthly pay! His brother was deliberately hoarding vital, necessary supplies and probably selling them above the exorbitant prices that already prevailed. Rafe felt no surprise at his discovery, only sadness. Even anger took second place. One day Wayne's greed would be the death of him.

His first impulse was to tell Abraham of his find and have it all removed to a place of safety and then distributed to the plantation workers, but he realised that should he do that Wayne would know of his visit here and of his discovery of the second set of ledgers which lay quite openly on a table in the room behind him. To thwart his brother he had to leave everything here. A smile touched his lean mouth as he gathered up the books, extinguished the torch and made his way back upstairs. Perhaps there was a way. . . Once he had been to Savannah, his plan executed, there would be nothing his brother could do.

Back in his room, he locked the door. Better safe than sorry. He poured himself a drink from the decanter Abraham had thoughtfully provided while he was at dinner and settled down to peruse the books.

Four hours later, his mind still reeling from the enormity of his brother's fraudulent activities, but his work completed, he returned the books to the monk's hole, and obliterated all traces of his boot-marks in the dust. Wayne would never have dared perpetrate such a blatant conversion of money and goods had he been around. But with Rafe out of the way, the plantation under his control, there had been no one to stop him when greed reared its ugly head.

A fierce expletive broke from Rafe's lips as realisation finally sank home. Wayne hated not only his elder brother, but his own father too! Why else was he stealing from him when he was provided with everything he wanted for the asking? It had been foolish of him to leave details of that other account in one of the ledgers, together with a letter, not yet sent out for local tradesmen. His signature was so easy to copy! Tomorrow, if his luck held, that account would be empty and the money in a place where Wayne would never find it. He had become so confident that no one would ever discover what he was doing or how it would affect Wildwood. No wonder Wayne was unconcerned at the thought of the Yankees taking over. He had converted his paper money to gold and could go anywhere in the world he wanted. Or so he had thought!

Tiredness overcame Rafe as he returned to his room and settled himself in a chair, relaxing for the first time since Abraham had broken the news of Wayne's little game to him. But he knew he could not sleep. As soon as the house was empty, he would himself leave for Savannah on horseback. Luckily his father had been called to a meeting of the local plantation owners, some of whom were concerned by the rumours of the fall of Atlanta. Perhaps they could persuade Alexander of the seriousness of the matter where he had failed, Rafe thought. On Balthazar he could be there and back before he was missed and Abraham would cover for him if questions were asked, which he doubted. It had been made clear by both father and brother that his return was not to their liking. Had he not had Wildwood to return to he knew he would have abandoned them without another thought after the war and made a new life for himself elsewhere.

But he had this place to come back to. His eyes rose to the portrait above the fireplace. He could remember as a little boy of not more than three or four sitting where he sat now, watching it being painted. He had been fascinated by the deft strokes of the artist's brush so that he forgot the long hours in one position. Charlotte, his mother, never seemed to tire and that same soft smile remained on her face no matter how long the sitting.

Patience had always been her virtue. It was mirrored in the gentle eyes, as blue as a cornflower. She had never been described as a beautiful woman, although Rafe, who had idolised her, had always thought her to be the most beautiful in the whole world, for his revolved around her. But there was strength in the face, in the high cheekbones and wide mouth which bore a hint of stubbornness.

She had loved the colour yellow. The colour of the sun, of life, she had once told him. It dominated the sitting-room in which he sat and the bedroom beyond. One room was filled with morning sunshine, the other with the softer afterglow which accompanied the later hours. During his absence Hannah had maintained the rooms to perfection at his request, a reminder to his father that there had only been one mistress of Wildwood—Charlotte—and that he would never forgive him for his treatment of her during their five short turbulent years of marriage.

His eyes closed. He should get up and shave, he thought with a yawn. . .

An insistent knocking at the door brought him back to life with a start. Instinctively his hand reached for the pistol at his belt, only to discover he was not in uniform, asleep on some hard ground and surrounded by danger.

'Who is it?'

'Shanna de Lancel. May I speak with you?'

She stood hesitating on the threshold when Rafe

swung wide the door and motioned her to enter, but, as if reassured by the unexpected brightness and warmth of the interior, she stepped inside.

Although it was very early, she looked a picture! The black hair had been brushed until it shone and curled over the right shoulder, held in place by a dark green ribbon, which matched those on the wide-brimmed hat and tied beneath her chin. Her gown was of green and white check, quite plain, and she carried a matching reticule and parasol. For some reason, into Rafe's mind flashed a vision of her wearing a dress of yellow watered silk, that mass of hair piled high on to the crown of her head and adorned with fragrant magnolia blossoms.

'Is—is anything wrong?' Shanna's eyes flew downwards at his prolonged scrutiny. 'This is the best dress I have at the moment. We could not save anything from the plantation house and in Atlanta I did not see the need to buy new clothes when I spent half my time in the hospital or at committee meetings. Money was too precious. I thought I should look presentable to see the lawyer. . .'

'Forgive me, I just like looking at you,' Rafe returned with unashamed candour and the remark brought instant colour rushing to her cheeks.

'You are beginning to sound like your brother. He showers me with compliments every moment of the day. He is really very sweet. I am beginning to feel as if I belong. But as you are here for such a short time. . .' Shanna hesitated, unsure now that she was face to face with him. He had been avoiding her, of that she was certain, while Wayne had taken every opportunity to monopolise her. She did not mind. She had been alone for so long, it was pleasant always to have someone to talk to, to flatter her and make her feel wanted. 'I was wondering if you would care to come to Savannah with us? I was not looking forward to it at first. . .the lawyer and my father's affairs. . .but I have accepted it will be better done and over with. And then I can go shopping—'

She broke off as Rafe chuckled.

'How like a woman! I shall allow my brother the privilege of carrying your parcels, Shanna, I have too much work to do here.'

'Of course. . . I did not think. . .' Shanna backed away from him, her expression growing cold. Did he have to make it so obvious that she was uninteresting to him? His kisses had meant nothing! A moment of pleasure forgotten as soon as she was out of sight. 'I am sorry to have disturbed you.'

She was gone in a swish of checkered skirt and Rafe kicked the door closed after her with an expletive exploding under his breath. Damn the girl! Why did she make him feel as if she had been hurt by his refusal? She had Wayne to pamper to her every need; after all, it was in his best interests. The sooner he was recalled to duty the better, he thought, as he went into the bathroom. Before he poked his nose into something which did not concern him!

Benjamin had followed Shanna and Tante Lea from shop to shop in her fruitless search for a ballgown or material with which to make one, and his dislike of both women had grown very apparent.

'What is going on?' Tante Lea asked in puzzlement, watching the throng of people approaching them. They took up the whole width of the road and spilled over on to the wooden pavements. And the crowd was made up totally of women. Angry women clutching hammers, rolling pins, axes, and any kitchen utensil, as far as Shanna could see, that could be used as a weapon. A few even brandished carved knives or sharp-edged cleavers which gleamed in the sunlight. The leader—a veritable Amazon—carried a pistol.

'This is unbelievable,' Shanna breathed. She had witnessed a similar demonstration, but on a much smaller scale, in New Orleans before it fell to the Yankees, when food and supplies had dwindled and black marketeers openly peddled their wares for outrageous prices. But then only bread, flour and sugar had been taken, and no violence had been used. Here today there was the smell of death in the air, and Tante Lea looked at her sharply as she shivered.

'This is no place for us. Take us back to the carriage,' she ordered Benjamin.

'I cannot return to Wildwood without one final present,' Shanna said, looking around her for a side-road to escape into as the throng moved closer. The sound of breaking glass, of laughter which bordered on hysteria filled her ears as she did so. 'And I have nothing to wear for the party.'

Tante Lea looked at her as if she had taken leave of her senses. Here they were surrounded by mad-women and all she could think about was a dress!

Shanna did not like what she saw moving around her, was afraid of the undercurrent of violence she felt radiating from the grim-faced women, but she understood the frustration that drove them. She had experienced hunger and fear herself. She had lost all of her family and knew what it was like to be alone . . .to have her whole world turned upside-down overnight.

She felt a tug at her sleeve and found a thin-faced woman at her side, clutching a well worn carpet bag against her emaciated body. As Tante Lea opened her mouth to shoo her away, Shanna shook her head. She recognised desperation in the eyes which looked at her, pleaded with her silently, pathetically.

'Help me, please, lady. You look as if you have a kind heart. My husband was killed last year and I have five youngsters to support. . .and no money. I can't even afford a loaf of bread. That's what this is all about. The government put up the price of everything again last night. Bread, flour, tea—and my children haven't seen meat in eighteen months. My youngest has the colic and I can't afford medicine.'

'Take this. . .' Shanna opened her purse and pressed a coin into the woman's palm. She recoiled at the sight of it indignantly.

'I don't want charity. Look!' She opened the bag. It contained a pistol and a black leather belt with a large brass buckle such as was worn by soldiers. 'It belonged to my husband. It's all I have left, but it is yours. Give them to your man. Look at the belt. . . the finest leather.'

She held it out to Shanna with a pride that was touching.

'I shall buy the belt, but not the pistol. . .you may need that to protect your family. I shall give it to someone. . .who will be returning to the war shortly, and I know he will treasure it,' Shanna said softly. She did not give the belt to Benjamin, but folded it away in the small valise carried by Tante Lea. The woman stared dumbfounded at the gold coin pressed into her hand. Then, with tears running down her cheeks, she grabbed Shanna by the arm and kissed her on both cheeks.

'God bless you and your man. I will pray he comes back to you.'

'I am sure Rafe Amberville will be very impressed with such a gift,' Tante Lea said, one eyebrow rising sceptically, knowing instinctively who would receive it.

'He is accustomed to the best, and the belt happens to be made by Magee, Horter and George of New Orleans. The same place that Father and James my brother always used. But I was thinking only of that poor woman. . .how much longer can this suffering go on?'

She gave a cry as women converged on them from all sides. For a moment she was caught up in the mass of bodies surging forward, then Tante Lea was holding on to her arm, dragging her to one side. A hefty woman bumped into her and she lost her balance. She fell to one knee, the breath knocked from her body momentarily. Someone pulled her roughly to her feet and tried to propel her along with the crowd and, as much as she fought to extricate herself, she could not get free.

A man came pushing his way through to her side, caught her around the waist and with apparent effortlessness propelled her to safety. She sagged in the arms which held her, fighting for breath, unable to put any weight on one knee which had begun to throb maddeningly. She found her cheek resting against a dark blue broadcloth coat, which bore the faint aroma of sweet tobacco smoke, raised her head to blurt out thanks for his timely intervention—and then the words died in her throat as she found herself gazing up into the berry-brown face of Rafe Amberville. The look of incredulity which spread across her features brought a chuckle from deep in his throat as he drew her off the main thoroughfare and into a deserted alleyway.

'People will begin to talk if we continue to meet in these strange circumstances,' he drawled, his voice full of mockery at her reaction.

'You have already intimated that to be seen in your company is sufficient to start the tongues wagging,' Shanna returned, drawing away from him, but the moment she tried to put full weight on both legs one buckled and she pitched forward against him again.

'You are hurt!' Immediately the mockery vanished from his expression as he saw the pain mirrored in her eyes. 'We must find a place for you to rest. Can you walk at all, or shall I carry you?'

'That will not be necessary,' Shanna gasped, biting her lip as red hot needles sank deep into her knee.

'Where is Tante Lea? We were separated. And Benjamin? Those women. . . Dear heaven, what was that?'

'Rifle fire. I saw the army making its way in this direction,' Rafe said grimly, urging her further down the alleyway. After only a few steps it became obvious she was unable to go far, so great was the discomfort. 'That mob of unfriendly women—although I sympathise with their predicament and the desperation in them all to have resorted to such extreme means—have wrought havoc this afternoon. Eight shops wrecked and looted and two unfortunate men, one an innocent bystander, rushed off to hospital. As if they are not full enough as it is.'

'They—they would not fire on women,' Shanna said aghast, although secretly she had to admit that, confronted with such a frenzied crowd, she doubted if they would be given an alternative.

'Probably not. But they will put the fear of God into them. As, I think, *they* did into to you.'

'Yes. . .' Shanna could not deny it. 'They made me remember a time when I was so desperate, I would have done anything. . .'

'Yes, memories do have the unpleasant habit of intruding upon you without warning.' Rafe's blue eyes searched her face, so intent, so serious, that she felt, without knowing why, that they shared some bond of suffering between them. Memories. . .he would have many, as she had, which neither could bring themselves to discuss in the light of day. 'Damnation,' he ejaculated as he saw her wince in pain, 'I shall have to send someone back for the carriage. Where did you leave it? And where is my brother? He should be with you.'

'I wanted to go shopping alone. . .to buy presents for everyone. Your family has been so kind to me. We arranged to meet back at the carriage at four-thirty. Benjamin left it on Delaney Avenue. Is that far from here?'

'Far enough. Carrying you that distance would be a most enjoyable experience for me,' Rafe said—but one he knew he would have to postpone.

'You are impossible, Rafe Amberville.' Shanna tried to look indignant at the thought of being paraded through the streets in his arms, but found herself smiling instead at his audacity.

'I have a reputation to maintain—remember,' he teased.

'Would the gentleman care to bring the young lady in here to rest for a moment? Perhaps I have something to soothe the pain she is experiencing,' a quiet voice remarked behind them.

The face of the enormous negress who stood in the open doorway grew quite amused at Shanna's reluctance to accept her invitation. She moved back, motioning them to enter, and reluctantly Shanna allowed Rafe to help her over the threshold. The small room was illuminated solely by candles which cast eerie shadows over the strange-looking objects suspended from the walls and roof.

A shrunken head, what was left of the features contorted into a wizened grin, spun in the breeze above her head, alongside locks of different-coloured hair. There was a layer of thin grey smoke spiralling around the occupants, which, she saw, came not from the fire but the bowl set in an alcove beside something which looked suspiciously like a shrine. Alongside this were masks of every description.

'We cannot stay here,' she protested as Rafe reached for a stool for her to sit on.

'Gently, Shanna, you don't really believe in Voodoo surely?' he chided, easing her down on to it. Her hand trembled in his and his grip tightened as he turned on the negress, his eyes sweeping the shadows from force of habit. He did not believe in the mumbo jumbo which he knew was widely practised—well out of sight and hearing of his father and Wayne—at Wildwood, but there was no harm in being cautious in strange surroundings. The eyes which encountered his were like pieces of jet and challenged his scepticism.

'You have something to ease her pain? Mind you, no rubbish, like Mountain Herb Bitters or some concoction you bought from some quack peddler.'

'I am content to rest a few moments, then I shall be able to walk back to the carriage,' Shanna assured him, though she very much doubted it.

A clay pot was held out to him containing a white cream.

'Roll down the young lady's stocking and apply this to the knee joint. You should know where that is, being a soldier accustomed to dealing with wounds.'

Shanna froze where she sat. There was nothing about Rafe's appearance to give away the fact that he was a fighting man. In fact she had never seen him looking so elegantly clad. Since he had arrived home, she had grown accustomed to seeing him dressed in well worn trousers and a casual shirt. Today he looked every inch a gentleman.

The unruly hair had been combed back beneath his wide-brimmed hat. The snow-white ruffles at his wrists and the jabot at his throat accentuated the darkness of his skin. Both his jacket and trousers were impeccably cut and on his right hand she caught a flash of candlelight on a large diamond ring.

And then, as his fingers reached for the hem of her skirt, she snatched it away, cheeks flaming. He had refused her invitation to join her and Wayne in their visit to Savannah, yet something or someone had brought him here in record time. Only a woman could have done that!

'The salve will take away the pain,' the negress said in a patient tone as if she were addressing a small child. 'Take it with you if you would prefer. And ask your maid, the one who carries the Tarot close against her heart today. She will tell you there is nothing harmful about it.'

'Tante Lea! She will be frantic with worry. . .'

'She is here now,' the woman said, glancing towards the doorway. Barely were the words uttered than Shanna's maid stepped inside, her face flushed from the exertion of running. Her gaze swept the dimly lighted room and, when it came to rest on the negress standing beside her mistress, a moment of awe registered in her eyes. Like Shanna, she too recognised that they were in the presence of a high-ranking priestess of a primeval cult which held thousands of negroes in fear throughout the South.

'I am Mamalou.' The name was supplied with dignity and pride, as if, by her revealing it, they were assured they were in no danger. 'Your mistress is quite safe and in good hands.'

'I am Lea. We are grateful for your kindness.' Tante Lea did not recognise the name, but she knew the symbols of high rank which dominated the room and demanded great respect be shown by all who stood beneath this roof. '*Mignonne*, what has happened to you? The crowd swallowed you up and someone said a man—' She broke off as Rafe rose from Shanna's side and inclined his head slightly in her direction. He looked so different that she had not immediately recognised him. Her mistress was not safe in *his* hands—far from it—and the sooner she realised that the better.

'Mr Amberville came to my rescue, but I have injured my knee again. The one I hurt at Baton Rouge. I shall not be able to finish my shopping,' she added ruefully. 'I can hardly stand on it.'

'I sent Benjamin for the carriage the minute I found out where you were. The wretched boy dropped all your parcels when the soldiers appeared and if I had not soundly boxed his ears he would have left them in the street to be trampled on.'

'It seems I have been deprived of the pleasure of carrying you after all,' Rafe murmured, a gleam in the depth of his blue eyes, although secretly he was relieved, for he had been wondering how to extricate himself from a potentially explosive situation. It had been his intention that no one should know of his visit to Savannah, but when he had seen Shanna being swept along in the mêlée, with the possibility of her being rounded up with the other women when the army arrived, the only thought uppermost in his mind had been to snatch her to safety.

And now, because of his gallant gesture, his whole plan was in jeopardy.

'I am sure you will find some way to compensate for your loss,' Shanna returned. 'Will you be accompanying us back to Wildwood?'

She knew at once from the way he stepped back from her that the suggestion was unacceptable—as her earlier invitation had been. It confirmed the lingering suspicion that he had ridden in all haste to Savannah to see an old flame.

And yet why should he not make the most of what little time he had left? He was free to spend it as he chose—with whom he chose. And if he wanted to keep the identity of his ladyfriend a secret from his family, it was no business of hers. She had no claim on him, no right to pry into his life. Why then did she feel rejected when her company was refused?

'Unfortunately that is not possible, and, if it is not too great a favour, I would like you to keep the fact you have seen me from my father and brother. May I ask that of you, Shanna? I have very good reasons for the deception.' The whole success of the day depended on her answer.

'If you choose to keep your comings and goings a secret, that is entirely your affair,' Shanna replied with a shrug of her shoulders to indicate she did not care one way or the other what he did. She saw Tante Lea's eyes narrow; the latter sensed it was a lie and was disapproving of her agreement to his demand.

'I shall take my leave, then, before Benjamin arrives.' Rafe took one of her hands and touched it to his lips, his eyes bright with mockery, as he caught the withering look directed at him by Tante Lea. He'd be damned if they didn't believe he had a woman hidden away in Savannah. Nothing could have been further from the truth, but it served his purpose admirably. 'I am sorry your day has been curtailed in such an unpleasant manner.'

'I have survived worse calamities,' Shanna replied, withdrawing her hand when he appeared in no great hurry to release it. Even through the thin fabric of her lace glove his touch burned her skin. 'I am just disappointed that I could not find a gown for my birthday party—nor even material to make one. That does sound so selfish, does it not, when some people do not even possess a change of clothes these days? The gown should not be important—the party is and the friendship your family have shown me. I must not complain; I am one of the fortunate ones.'

She spoke of being fortunate when she had lost the man she loved, a father and a brother. She had a pride and dignity such as he had encountered in few women. As he stepped back and turned towards the door, Rafe remembered the trunks lying in the attic, untouched since the day his mother died, gathering dust, unwanted, forgotten. . .until now. . .

# CHAPTER FOUR

'I MUST confess I am dying of curiosity to see what is in all these parcels,' Wayne said, nudging one of the cartons at his feet. 'Have you bought up the whole of Savannah? Let me guess. . .breathtaking dresses to turn the head of every man in the county. Perfume, so that your presence will linger in every room in Wildwood. Am I right?'

She had not money in her possession when they left that morning, he knew, for his father had told him she had refused the offer of a loan. And she had insisted on seeing the lawyer alone, while he waited restlessly in an outer office. Even when she emerged, her cheeks glowing with colour, he could only guess that the undercurrent of excitement he sensed in her meant she now had money of her own. And a great deal of it from the look of her purchases.

'Obviously you have not purchased very much in Savannah lately,' Shanna replied ruefully, 'or you would know that even the smallest items that we once took for granted are considered luxuries—if they can be bought at all. There was not a single decent gown to be had anywhere—nor material. I am afraid I shall appear like a poor relation at my own party.'

'Looking after Wildwood is a full-time job,' Wayne said, with the air of someone who was accustomed to sacrificing all his spare time for the good of the family plantation.

Nothing could have been further from the truth. Most of his time was involved with the very lucrative black market trade in which he had become deeply involved. No matter how high his price, there was always someone willing to pay it. By the end of the war he would be richer than he had ever thought possible—doubly so with the prospect of marriage to Shanna.

He had decided on a course of action, difficult though it would be at times to control himself: charm and restraint in the face of his brother's constant verbal attacks. After all, in a few days he would be gone and then he would have all the time in the world for his act of seduction. She had led a sheltered life, protected first by mother and brother and then by her father. His success was assured and once the marriage had taken place he felt confident he would have little trouble getting her with child. After that. . .

His father would have his grandchild, Wayne would have her money, and she could go to the devil for all he cared. Yes, he told himself, as he settled more comfortably in his seat, watching the breeze stir loose strands of Shanna's hair about her face, he could afford to be patient.

'I think your father has guests,' Shanna remarked, as the carriage slowed in its approach to the house. The sun and the pleasant journey home had made her drowsy and allowed her to forget the pain in her knee.

In front of the wide sweep of steps which led up to the front door were two horses. One was Balthazar, the other a white-stockinged roan mare. Rafe had beaten them home! Had she been mistaken in her suspicions?

'Dammit!' Wayne ejaculated and she turned to look at him in astonishment. 'I am sorry, Shanna, but unless I am mistaken that horse belongs to the wife of one of our close neighbours. She and Rafe . . .well, just before he went away they were more than friends, if you understand. The whole county was scandalised by his activities—nocturnal ones, that is—but somehow he managed to keep this relationship a secret from everyone. I only discovered it by accident on his last night here.'

The lies slipped from his lips with such ease. Not one woman, but several! Shanna was shocked, yet also puzzled. Why then had he been so insistent that they should return home that day by the riverbank? That had not been the act of a man who considered every woman a potential challenge to his prowess as a man as Wayne seemed to be intimating.

'Considering the fact your brother will be called back to the fighting at any moment, I do not think it fair to judge him too harshly,' she said, choosing her words with care. She did not want to offend Wayne, who had been the most perfect companion she could have chosen throughout the whole day—who, when he had learned of her unfortunate experience in the women's riot, had insisted she remain in Savannah and take tea with him before making the journey home, to soothe her nerves and make up for the fact he had been elsewhere when it occurred—but she did consider his comments more than a trifle unfair. She, too, had judged Rafe solely on what she had heard about him, and that she now knew to be a mistake.

He was an enigma, a man not to be taken at face value, nor categorised, as she might have done with others. And, apart from that first meeting when he had so outrageously kissed her, he had behaved with her as a perfect gentleman.

'Because he is a soldier!' Wayne ejaculated, looking hurt by her words. 'I wanted to fight too, you know, but one of us had to stay here, my father insisted. When I refused, he talked to friends of his—friends with influence—and my application for a commission was refused point-blank! The excuse was that any planter or overseer who owned more than twenty slaves was exempt from duty. My father convinced everyone that with Rafe gone I would have to run Wildwood. . .'

'I am so sorry, I did not realise. . .' Shanna murmured, allowing him to lift her down from the carriage. Somehow she could not imagine Wayne as a man of action. The cologne he used with abundance filled her nostrils and she quickly disengaged herself. 'But even so. . .'

'You feel sorry for Rafe. So many women do. He has that effect on them and the next thing they know they are in bed with him! Damaris LaFontaine, the woman I am sure is with him, is the wife of a very influential man in this county—a very jealous man. He has killed more than one admirer that she had been foolish to flaunt under his nose. And still he remains married to her! The man is a blind fool, which is, of course to Rafe's advantage, although I have often wondered who would be killed if those two faced each other on the field of honour.'

'What a terrible thing to say,' Shanna said, paling. 'Do you dislike your brother so much that you want to see him hurt—killed?'

'Of course not.'

'Tante Lea, help Benjamin with the packages and take everything up to my room,' Shanna said. 'I shall join you in a moment. I have enjoyed myself very much,' she added, as Wayne took her arm and they moved towards the front doors and the couple who had just appeared. Instantly she was aware of how possessively the beautiful woman at Rafe's side held tightly to his arm. Behind them Alexander looked uncomfortable, as if the visit had not been to his liking. 'I do hope the little gifts I have purchased please everyone. You have all been so kind to me.'

Wayne would have felt better had he known his brother was not included in the statement.

'You should not have spent money on us, Shanna. We are delighted to have you here for as long as it pleases you.'

'My father's will. . .' Shanna swallowed hard, absorbing the pain and allowing it to fade into the past where it now belonged '. . .has left me quite well off. . .' Tante Lea had warned her not to reveal the extent of her good fortune, and she could not understand why. Such news was to be shared with friends and loved ones and the Ambervilles were her whole world now. 'Perhaps soon I can do something to repay your father's kindness to me.'

'He would not hear of it.' Wayne pressed her hand with a smile. But *he* would not be averse to a loan or two. . .for the good of Wildwood, of course! The girl would never know the difference.

The woman who stood at the head of the palisade of steps was more than just beautiful—she was exquisite. Flame-red hair and eyes the colour of emeralds, which considered the approach of Shanna and Wayne with something near to derision in them. The riding habit she wore was of emerald-green and clung to her in all the right places, accentuating a tiny waist, neat hips and full breasts straining against the tightness of the fitted jacket. She was perhaps in her late twenties. Shanna thought what a handsome couple they made as Rafe inclined his head in her direction, not one flicker on his face to betray what they had shared earlier.

'Shanna. Wayne, I hope your visit to Savannah was an enjoyable one. I rode over to the LaFontaine plantation today to tell Damaris and Claude about the party. They have, of course, both accepted.'

'Thank you, our day was very pleasant,' Shanna replied politely. 'I am so glad you and your husband are able to come, Mrs LaFontaine.'

The green eyes narrowed at the underlying tone of hostility which Shanna was horrified to find she could not keep out of her voice. One look at this woman and she disliked her immediately! What was wrong with her?

The outing had tired her and the pain in her knee

was returning. It had nothing to do with Rafe or the woman at his side, she told herself strongly as Wayne helped her into the cool interior of the house. After a rest and a bath she would feel herself again.

'I must go home or Claude will send out a search party for me. You know what an old worrier he is,' Damaris LaFontaine declared, turning to bestow a kiss on each of Alexander's lined cheeks. 'I am so looking forward to the party. Rafe, until Thursday.'

She raised a ringed hand and Rafe touched it to his lips. The look which passed between them baffled Shanna. A challenge from the green eyes which met his. . .but almost indifference in the returning gaze. He had used her as his alibi and had therefore avoided awkward questions from father and brother, but was he as deeply involved with her as Wayne hinted? Or just extremely adept at concealing his feelings?

'And how was your trip to Savannah, my dear?' Alexander asked, following Shanna into the house.

'I managed to purchase most of what I wanted,' Shanna returned with a smile. She was so looking forward to giving them the presents she had bought. She noticed Rafe still lingered on the steps. Was he afraid she would give away his secret? 'But I did not realise so many things were in short supply.'

'I can do nothing about a ballgown, although it would give me great pleasure to buy you the loveliest creation Savannah has ever seen,' Wayne murmured, 'but I have managed a few surprises for you. I hope it will be a day to remember.'

'You should not have gone to any trouble for me,'

she protested, touched by his words. 'I know how difficult things have become for you.'

But perhaps that was something she might be able to alleviate in time, she thought, as she excused herself and went upstairs. Her money could help buy so many things for Wildwood, to make life more comfortable for the Amberville family and ensure the continued running of the plantation until the war was over.

She did not realise how exhausted she was until she fell across the bed with a sigh and found her eyes beginning to droop immediately. Tante Lea fixed the pillows comfortably behind her head and proceeded to roll down her stocking, frowning as she saw the knee had swollen.

'If you do not rest, child, you will not be dancing on Thursday,' she warned. 'You should go to bed immediately.'

'Tomorrow I shall rest. All day if necessary,' Shanna said, smothering a yawn. 'Tomorrow.'

When she awoke after a deep sleep, untroubled by the usual dreams, Shanna was relieved to find the salve provided by Mamalou had worked wonders. The redness around the swollen joint had disappeared and she could walk on it again without pain. But she knew Tante Lea's advice was sound and that only rest would continue the improvement.

Over dinner she related to Alexander and Wayne — the latter had explained most apologetically that he had been several streets away and knew nothing of what was happening, or he would have come looking for her without hesitation—her involvement in the women's riot.

Rafe, of course, could not comment on the incident. Wayne was, again, apologetic for abandoning her and allowing her to go off alone. Shanna wished he did not try so hard to be nice. She liked his company and that was all she wanted, yet she sensed he was trying to push their friendship too far too soon. It had been a long time since she had been paid attention by three men. Well, two, she thought, as coffee was served and Rafe refused any and excused himself from the room.

Tomorrow she would spend the whole day with Tante Lea trying to renovate one of the dresses she had brought with her. She had become friends while in Atlanta with a young girl whose fiancé had recently been killed and in desperation, when her mother became seriously ill, had found it necessary to sell off most of her belongings, among them the wedding dress she would never now wear.

Although she had no use for it, Shanna had bought it and immediately packed it away in the one trunk she possessed, thinking no more of it until today. It was far too small for her, but perhaps Tante Lea's ingenious mind could find some way to solve the problem. Otherwise what would she do. . .?

'I want you to put these in a safe place,' Rafe said, pulling a bulky envelope from inside his jacket. 'I suggest an excellent one would be your favourite place to hide that extra bottle of corn whiskey which always seems to appear when needed.'

'You know about that?' Abraham said, his mouth gaping visibly, and from across the room Hannah gave a soft laugh.

'There ain't nothing that boy don't know about what goes on in this house. Did you think you could keep anything hidden from him? Used to prowl around this place all hours as a youngster—especially in my kitchen. I ain't found nowhere yet that my preserves were safe.'

'You shouldn't make them so tempting,' Rafe chuckled. Then the amusement died from his voice, and both knew the envelope handed to Abraham was of vital importance. 'You were right about my brother. Without your sharp eyes and ears I would never have discovered what he is up to, so you deserve to know what you are going to look after for me. In there are copies of the inventory from the second set of books Wayne is keeping, unknown to my father. Also a bank book. I have transferred all of his assets into another account—not in my own name, I might add. He is in for one unpleasant shock when he finds out, but there is nothing he can do about it. There is no way he can trace his ill-gotten gains even though he will find out I am behind it as soon as he talks to the bank manager. And do you know what I found in the monk's hole? Enough supplies to keep us going here for months. I was thinking of clearing the whole place out as well, but when I'm gone he'd turn on you and the others, I'm sure of that. So we will syphon just a small amount off—a case here and a case there from the back of the pile. Thursday night will be a good opportunity while everyone is in the house enjoying themselves. There will be a little more celebrating than my father has planned. Tuck the envelope away, Abraham, and forget it is there until I come home again.'

He watched with a great feeling of satisfaction at the day's achievements as Abraham carefully eased out a large piece of the stonework some two feet from the right of the stove to reveal a large cavity behind. Rafe smiled as he reached inside and brought into view a half-full bottle of whiskey, and grinned sheepishly as he put it on the table between them. The envelope was pushed far to the back of the recess and the stone replaced, leaving no trace that it had ever been disturbed. Only he and Leon and his two companions knew of this place, so Rafe felt confident neither his brother nor father would discover the envelope and what it contained before he returned again.

'Now to lighter matters. . .did you see to that trunk?'

'Had Benjamin take it up while Miss Shanna was at dinner. Ain't you going to join them in the drawing-room? Her maid says she's brought presents back for everyone.'

'I hardly think I am included among them,' Rafe replied with a tight smile. Shanna was the only flaw in his plans. She knew too much already, but he had no other choice but to trust she remained silent. Presents. . .yes, she was soft-hearted enough to want to repay his father's kindness, ignorant of the future he was planning for her. How could he warn her?

Did he have the right? She seemed to like Wayne's company. . .

'My dear, these are exquisite. I cannot thank you enough. Come and kiss me!' Alexander exclaimed, visibly moved by the six snifter glasses embossed with the initial 'A' in gold on each one. Shanna went into the outstretched arms with a smile, pleased by his reaction.

Such luxuries were still available for those who could afford them. She had found Wayne's gift—a pearl-handled walking stick—in the same shop. Only Rafe had presented a problem. At the time she had hoped the belt would suffice, but now she was not so sure and even less certain she should give him the good-luck talisman that Mamalou had handed to her before she left.

'Shanna, there is something I have been meaning to ask you. . .' Alexander began. 'My dear, you have been here for only a short time, but I must tell you how wonderful it is to have a woman about the place again. Already I—both Wayne and I are beginning to feel that you are one of the family. I know it is too soon for you to make any plans, but I have a suggestion I would like you to consider.'

Shanna found the breath catching in her throat at the way he looked at her—such affection in his eyes, as if. . . She knew he was a very lonely man, despite his manner which indicated otherwise. Lonely—and, she suspected, in need of a family again.

'Would you find it possible to think of this house as your home? I want you to stay here with us,

Shanna, become part of our family. I am getting old and, at times, my temper gets the better of me. Abraham and Hannah think I am a cantankerous old devil and they are right. This house needs a woman to run it, to take care of the everyday problems. To make it a home, which it has not been for many years. Could you—would you take on this responsibility. . .for as long as you decide to remain?

'Run the house?' Shanna's voice was a trifle shaky with relief. For a moment she had been seized with the incredulous idea that he was after another wife! 'Why—yes. . . I mean. . .if you really think me capable. I would be pleased to.'

It was a large house, but much of it unused, and only three indoor servants. She had managed perfectly well for her father, both in New Orleans and at the plantation house where the staff had been over a dozen. And it would keep her mind occupied. These days she was not accustomed to being idle.

'Splendid. I will tell Abraham he is to speak with you in the morning.' Alexander was obviously delighted at her acceptance and even Wayne, still examining his walking stick in great detail, managed to divert his attention away from it long enough to add his relief that the house was once again to run smoothly. 'But the arrangements for Thursday are still my responsibility,' he added as he escorted Shanna to the door. 'We do not want to spoil the surprise, do we?'

It was not until she was outside the door of her room that Shanna realised she had not taken into account Rafe's reaction to his father's offer. She doubted if Alexander had even bothered to mention it to him, although she was sure it had been discussed at great lengths with Wayne. How sad that lack of communication was—and he did deserve to know. Besides—she looked down at the package in her hands—she still had to give him this!

There was no answer to her knock. Rafe appeared in the corridor as she was turning away, to enquire, 'Are you looking for me?'

'I—yes, I have this for you.' She held out the present and would have turned quickly away had he not caught her by the arm and held her fast. 'I bought something for everyone. . .'

The colour rose in her cheeks as his eyes met hers, questioning why he had been included in her generosity.

'I cannot remember the last time someone gave me a present—without some strings attached,' he drawled, opening the door and ushering her firmly inside. 'I am intrigued. . .'

'It is only a small thing. You were the most difficult of all to choose for—nothing seemed right,' she added lamely as again those blue eyes pierced her soul.

As the wrapping paper fell away, an expletive broke from Rafe's lips as he recognised what he held in his hands.

'You do not like it. I knew you would not!' Shanna declared.

'On the contrary, you could not have given me anything more suitable. Let me show you.' Turning away to the closet, he opened the door and reached inside. The belt he produced had been dusty and scratched when last Shanna had seen it; now it had been cleaned and polished, although it still showed the signs of wear. He showed her the back of it, almost cut in two. 'A Yankee sniper tried to put a bullet in my back as I was leaving the Valley, cut it almost in two. Leon gave it to me the day I left here in my new grey uniform, gleaming boots and shining sabre. Everyone thought the trouble would be over in a few months. . .and we all rode off like young gods to do battle with the enemy, thinking we were invincible. My God! What a mess!'

'Our boys fight with their hearts and souls; that is why we shall win this war,' she said, unable to ignore the cynicism which had crept into the quiet voice. He spoke as if he believed it was all in vain. 'These past years have been brutal—callous—and we have discovered we are not invincible, nor are we cowards who turn tail and run when faced with a foe greater in strength than our own army. The South will not lose. It cannot!'

'If Sherman takes Atlanta, it is lost, and there's nothing anyone can do about it.'

'How can you even think such a thing? He will be stopped—he has to be. . .'

'Because if he is not then he will be heading in this direction and people are going to have to start believing what I have been telling them. Richmond is pouring men into the countryside around Macon to try and block him if Atlanta falls. They have even resorted to calling up young boys, cadets from the military colleges and old men who should be sitting in front of a fire, peacefully puffing away at a pipe instead of sighting up on a blue uniform that most of them won't be able to see until they are under their very noses.'

'You are very cruel,' Shanna whispered, afraid of the implications he had planted in her mind.

'War has the habit of making men like that. It is not a time for sentiment—nor does it bring out the best in a man.' He was thinking of his brother as he spoke. 'In a woman, perhaps, and it has made us men realise just what versatile little creatures you are.'

If he thought that then he would not mind her being in charge of the house, Shanna thought, watching him return both belts to the closet. He had not found the talisman which she had placed there at the last minute, and when he did he would probably be hundreds of miles away, unable to question her about it.

'Your father has done me the great honour of asking me to make Wildwood my home,' she said a trifle tentatively and instantly she had his full attention.

'And have you made a decision?' Step one, install Shanna beneath his roof. Step two, subject her to all Wayne's many and devious charms. Step three, courtship, marriage and a fortune within the family grasp.

'No.' Why was she lying? Of course she would stay. There was so much she could do here for people who had shown her kindness and hospitality. 'There is something else. . .whatever I decide, he would like me to take over the running of the house for him. He says it has been too long without a woman's touch.'

'Did he, now?' There was a mocking undercurrent in the softness of Rafe's voice as he moved towards her, pale eyes glittering at the news. It was difficult to stifle the anger which engulfed him at the image of this wan creature taking the place of his vivacious, capable mother. He had never considered his father's second wife to have been mistress here—and had never considered the day there would be another woman in charge. And then he controlled it, for, after all, she was being used as a pawn in a greater game for very high stakes. She was not to blame.

'I see no reason why the arrangement should not work out to the advantage of everyone,' he murmured, his hands coming to rest ever so lightly upon her shoulders. 'So long as you remember one thing, little Shanna. When you are giving orders beneath this roof, remember *I* am the real master here. Not my father, not Wayne and certainly not you. But I feel confident I can leave my domain in your charge.'

He was laughing at her, challenging her competency!

'Do you know, you look at me with the eyes of a child, but in my arms you feel like a woman? Too much of a woman for Wayne to handle. You need a real man.'

Shanna's gasp of indignation was stifled beneath the lips which crushed hers, bruising them with a relentless pressure that rendered her weak and incapable of thinking. It would be so easy to surrender to the fires this man ignited in her, enjoy what she had found for as long as it lasted. She might never know such moments again—with anyone! And then a coldness settled over her so penetrating that it chilled her bones and she shivered. At once she felt the fierce grip on her shoulders lessen and tore herself free, two bright red spots of anger burning in otherwise ashen cheeks. Without thinking she drew back her hand and slapped Rafe hard across his face.

'That is so you remember I have had enough heartache in my life, Rafe Amberville, and I want no more. If you need company why do you not seek out Mrs LaFontaine as you did this afternoon when you needed someone else to lie for you?'

'And what little stories has my brother been whispering in those shell-like ears?' Rafe's fingers momentarily touched the spot where she had struck him, then he moved backwards to perch himself on the edge of the desk beneath the French windows, apparently unperturbed by her outburst.

'Always Wayne. Always you blame your father or your brother,' Shanna scathed. '*I* saw you together! I saw the way she looked at you.'

'And did I look at her the same way?' Rafe enquired, one blond eyebrow rising sardonically. So there was fire beneath the ice. Wayne would not like that. His mistresses he liked to have spirit, but a wife. . . No, she would have to be docile and obedient. . .and, deprived of her inheritance, what else could Shanna be once she was tied to him? Perhaps the plans being made would not progress as smoothly as was intended.

'You! You are incapable of caring for anyone. You say your father is devoid of feeling, but I believe you are colder.'

'Well, at least we understand each other. I want nothing in my life but Wildwood. I was quite honest about that with you as I am with any woman. And you?' The blue eyes narrowed as they stared across the room at her. 'What is it you want? Security? A safe husband?'

'I see nothing wrong in that,' Shanna returned defensively, although it was the last thing she wanted. Her freedom, her independence and a life free from pain; that was what she wanted.

'What a waste.' The contempt in the words cut her like a knife. With as much dignity as he had left her, she picked up her skirts and left him.

So she wanted a husband who would give her security, did she? Nothing more, Rafe thought bitterly; then she was welcome to Wayne and he had no more reason to feel guilty about riding away and leaving her to be seduced and married off to a man who did not care a fig for her. They deserved each other!

'Did he like the gift?' Tante Lea asked as Shanna threw her shawl across a chair and went to stand by the windows, her arms folded, her lips compressed into a tight line. She had seen that obstinate stance before. It meant Shanna had given way to an outburst of temper which she always immediately regretted. Only James, the brother she had idolised, had ever been able to rouse it in her—until now. . . 'Did you hear me, child?'

'Yes, Tante. I do not want to discuss Rafe Amberville. . .he is insufferable! I wish I had not left that wretched charm in his belt. When he finds it he might be conceited enough to think I harbour some foolish feelings about him,' Shanna replied through trembling lips.

'And of course you do not,' the maid said quietly, and her words brought Shanna wheeling around to face her.

'No, I do not. I shall never love anyone again. . . it is too painful. Life is too cruel.'

'You are still a baby and life has not dealt kindly with you,' Tante Lea soothed, 'but somewhere there is the right man for you and when he comes into your life there will be nothing you can do to alter what has been written for you both.'

He was in her life already! She lifted fingers to touch lips still bruised from masterful kisses that both thrilled and frightened her and then, aware of Tante Lea's curious gaze, quickly withdrew them.

'I have some news. We shall make our home here for a while—until the war is over perhaps. . .then I might be able to think about going back to Baton Rouge.'

'Here?' In a house where death lurked in the most mild manner awaiting the opportunity to strike?

'Mr Amberville has asked me to take charge of the house and I have agreed. Don't you see, Tante, it is just what I need? I need to be useful. . .in Atlanta it was the hospital or those awful women's committees. I don't think I want to go back to knitting socks or rolling bandages, but here. . .here

*I* am needed and perhaps in some small way we can do something about the deplorable conditions of the negroes. I know Abraham and Hannah will help me and Leon too if I ask him.'

'So we stay here—and you wait for him to come back—to turn your life upside-down the way he is doing now. Or perhaps you prefer the other one should do that. He has fine manners, but when he smiles my skin crawls.'

'Am I to be forever plagued by people intent on deciding my life for me?' Shanna snapped. 'I am tired. I shall go to bed and I want to hear no more talk like this. We shall stay.'

'Yes, child. I never doubted it for one moment.' Tante Lea turned away to lay out Shanna's night-clothes, then straightened with a soft expletive. 'I think you should come and look at this. I almost forgot about it. It was brought up here while you were at dinner.'

Mystified, Shanna followed her into the other room. An enormous trunk, well worn with age, its lock broken and one hinge dangling precariously, had been set down behind the sofa, which was why she had not noticed it immediately she came into the room.

'Benjamin and Leon brought it, with the compliments of Mr Rafe Amberville. He hopes you may find something of use to you in it,' Tante Lea said, a smile spreading across her face. 'Well, open it and satisfy my curiosity.'

Shanna could not resist, even though she knew she should have sent it back to him immediately unopened. She wanted nothing from him—no charity, and that was all it was to him.

'Oh, look! Clothes! Tante. . .how beautiful!' Shanna exclaimed as she threw back the lid and brought out a gossamer-soft dress in the palest lilac, sewn with stones of the same colour. Beneath, another, saffron-yellow, a mass of lace beneath the single tier of silk. 'Who do these belong to?'

'His mother. They have been stored in the attic since her death. Abraham said he is very protective about anything she owned. Threatened to burn her rooms, he did, rather than let the second Mrs Amberville take them over.'

'I know. He told me.' His mother's clothes! And she had just accused him of being without one iota of emotion. She was swept with shame as she recalled those heated moments. She had to swallow her pride and thank him.

There was a light beneath the door as she approached, but as she raised a hand to knock it went out. She tapped once, louder a second time, but heard no sound from within. She returned to her room knowing she had been deliberately ignored.

## CHAPTER FIVE

'I'M SURPRISED you decided to put in an appearance, but I suppose with the opportunity for a stroll in the garden with Damaris the effort was worth it.'

Wayne was annoyed to find his brother looking cool and debonair—something he always failed at miserably—and dangerously attractive, helping himself to a glass of punch, and it showed both in his tone and in the daggered look he directed at Rafe, who chose to ignore not only that, but the gibe connecting him with Damaris. The only person in the whole county who did not know that she and Wayne had been involved in an affair for the past year was her long-suffering husband, Claude. And Shanna, of course. . .

Rafe had taken particular care with his appearance, knowing it would be a long time before he felt the sensuous touch of a silk shirt against his skin again or enjoyed the luxury of a leisurely bath and a shave with hot water, not to mention clean towels! Such comforts did not extend to the battleground.

He wanted to keep his mind away from the war and what he would be returning to and as he allowed his gaze to wander around the crowded room, at the men and women he had known all his life—sadly few friends of his own were present for most had ridden away with him—he realised here, at

Wildwood, time had stopped. The war did not exist inside the plantation boundaries. There was dancing, drinking, laughter as if not one person had a single care in the world. Southerners had an inborn talent for survival, but would it suffice in the face of William Tecumseh Sherman and his foraging army? He prayed it would. Everyone had so much to lose – and he was no exception.

He swallowed his punch and refilled the glass, determined not to allow Wayne to annoy him. Although he had told no one yet, this was his last night of leave. As he was dressing, Benjamin had brought him his orders which had arrived by military courier. Tomorrow he would head for Atlanta to join General Joe Johnston's forces in the defence of that town. God help him, he had thought as he folded the paper and placed it inside the pouch of the belt Shanna had given him. God help them all. It was then his fingers had encountered the hard object he had not known was there. He had seen Voodoo talismen many times since his childhood. Many negroes on the plantation wore them or hid them beneath the paliasses on which they slept.

'I would not have missed it for the world,' he replied mildly now and saw at once that he had confused his brother with his refusal to retaliate. The time was not right. This night belonged to him more than it did Shanna and he was going to enjoy it.

'Don't think you can get her into your bed with something as mundane as out-of-date clothes. Even though the girl is desperate to get rid of her mousy appearance,' Wayne sneered in a low whisper as other guests moved alongside the table.

'Is that how you see her?' Rafe's gaze was drawn to something over his brother's shoulder. The pale eyes narrowed, filled with amusement which bordered on derision as he drawled, 'You are in need of spectacles, brother, if you think the apparition coming downstairs bears any resemblance to a mouse.'

Rafe felt the breath catch in his throat as he watched Shanna descend the stairs. She had chosen the cream gown. It had never flattered his mother's colouring, although it had been among her favourites, but it did wonders for Shanna, accentuating the black tresses coiled on to the crown of her head and adorned with two creamy pink magnolia blossoms, the perfection of the flawless skin.

The watered silk, cut low across the fullness of her young breasts, curved downwards to a tiny waist which, he suspected, would be the envy of half the women in the room. A long, delicate lace shawl in white was draped over one shoulder in such a way that it diverted no attention from the beautiful gown and, in fact, drew attention to the slender line of shoulder and arm.

A bitter taste rose in his mouth as he saw the pride which registered on his father's face as he drew Shanna close to him and began to introduce her to his guests. Pride for a stranger, but not his own.

She was his future, the realisation of the dream that Rafe refused to bring to fruition, as was expected of him, being the eldest son. An heir for

Wildwood. And, as much as he hated himself for acknowledging it, he was forced to admit that he could not have made a better choice. If he had wanted a wife and family, of course. And yet, in the deepest recesses of his mind where he dared not allow his thoughts to wander, was that not what he did desire? Ached for—and feared?

He had learned enough from his mother's unhappy life to know he could not have both. Love or Wildwood, that was the choice he had to make. A woman would demand all of his time and he would have none to give. When the war was over, whether the plantation survived the onslaught of Yankee soldiers or not, there was much work to be done to make it the home he had once known.

There was the posibility that given the chance the negroes would leave and seek the freedom President Lincoln in the North had promised them, which meant his wife would find herself doing every little menial task herself without help. Such a woman did not exist, he told himself, as he turned back to replenish his punch glass. His father would single him out in his own good time, making it plain to everyone present that he was not in favour.

It was a full ten minutes before Alexander turned in his direction.

Wayne had joined the group around his father almost immediately, needing to bask in the limelight that Shanna provided. He intended himself to be a part of her life and with their father's blessing, Rafe realised as they approached him. She looked exquisite! He would snatch her for a dance from under his brother's nose. . .and then the smile on his face slowly died as his eyes fastened on the pendant around her throat, the earrings adorning her lobes. His mother's jewels! The final insult his father could have thrown in his face. *Her* emeralds on a stranger!

'Rafe. . . I cannot thank you enough for this. . .' Shanna's cheeks grew quite pink as the pale eyes bored into her. There was not one iota of friendliness in them. He looked at her as if he hated her! 'What is it? Is something wrong? I thought you wanted me to wear something—' She broke off, confused, embarrassed.

'Where did you get those?' He gave a curt nod in the direction of the huge emerald nestling between her breasts.

'This?' She touched the stone with a hesitant smile. 'Why, from Wayne. And the earrings from your father. All three of you have done so much to make this day perfect for me. I shall be forever in your debt.'

'There will be no talk of debt here, Shanna,' Alexander said, frowning at his elder son. He knew that look and sensed Rafe was sinking into one of his dark, dangerous moods. It was something they shared in common—unacknowledged, but part of them both. 'You are happy and that was the intention of us all, was it not, Rafe?'

'There is not a woman alive who deserves to wear those jewels,' Rafe said between clenched teeth, the blackness descending on him obliterating all else. 'Not even her!'

Shanna gasped at the cruel words and turned pale

as he spun around on his heel and strode across the room. As she fought back the hot tears which pricked her eyes, he led Damaris on to the floor and began to dance with her.

'Why did you not tell me?' she asked Alexander, and he patted her hand reassuringly.

'The jewels are mine to do with as I please, my dear. It is true that they once belonged to his mother, but they were part of her dowry when we married and became mine upon her death. Rafe is wrong, you know. I believe if there is another woman alive who can wear them with the grace that she did, then it is you.'

Shanna looked at him disbelievingly. He spoke as if he had loved Charlotte, yet everything Rafe had told her had led her to believe that had not been so and that they had shared a miserable existence.

'Perhaps I should not accept them. . .' she began.

'They were given in love, Shanna,' Wayne said quietly, convincingly. 'Accept them, wear them. Will you allow Rafe to spoil this evening for you—for all of us? Come now, dance with me. Let me show you that one Amberville brother appreciates beauty and can remember his manners in the face of great provocation. Please,' he entreated as Shanna hesitated, loath to go in the midst of the dancers, where Rafe and Damaris were dominating the floor.

The woman looked stunning in a flame-red dress. With her red hair loose about her shoulders, she was aflame from head to toe and drew every eye in the room to her. She had eyes only for her partner, totally ignoring the husband who watched her with a frown upon his face. A very jealous man, was Shanna's first thought as she passed him by.

'This is how it is every time,' Wayne murmured, following her gaze as she continued to follow the progress of Rafe and Damaris. 'I have always lived in the shadow of a brother who is irresistible to women. They flock to him like moths to a flame—a destructive flame. His moods do not deter them, or his indifference. Am I to lose you to him too, Shanna?'

'I am not yours to lose,' he was reminded quietly. 'Nor your brother's to insult.'

'I am glad to hear that for I am hoping you will come to look on me as someone who will always be at hand if you need advice or help of any kind. I have none of Rafe's aggression, but my word is my bond and I will never let you down. I would like to be more than a friend. . .'

'Let us begin with friendship,' Shanna said, with a cautious smile. After all, it was all she wanted from any man. But, as the thought crossed her mind and Wayne led her into the midst of the dancing, she kept her gaze averted from the couple close by, knowing it was a lie. With one man she would want more—much more—and it was the one thing which was impossible.

'At last the party girl is alone and I am claiming her for a dance.' Shanna had danced until her feet ached and had turned down the last offer from an elderly gentleman with long white whiskers who had proved himself to be surprisingly agile on the floor despite his years. And now, the moment she found herself a vacant chair to rest for a moment, Rafe was at her side.

'I think I am too exhausted to dance another step,' she said, fanning herself with the beautiful ivory fan that her brother had brought her back from a visit to Paris before the war.

'Nonsense. The night is still young and so are you. One dance is all I ask and then I will take my odious presence elsewhere.'

There was a smile on his face as he spoke, but she sensed the offer was genuine, as if he was attempting to make up for his earlier rudeness.

'I shall return these jewels to you tomorrow morning. Or rather to your father,' Shanna said as she allowed him to take her hand and lead her back on to the floor. 'I shall be the cause of no trouble between you.'

'You will be trouble to any man, little Shanna,' Rafe chuckled as he drew her closer. He had seen Wayne and Damaris slip away some while ago so he knew he had Shanna all to himself. The perfume she wore filled his nostrils and sent his mind spinning back to other balls that had been held at Wildwood, other women he had danced with, made love to. But none had been like her. She smelled sweeter than any other, felt softer, danced better. 'Keep the damned things. They look good on you. I had no reason to take out my foul temper on you. Them—but not you.'

'You make it sound as if the pair of them had conspired to hurt you in some way.' Shanna looked up into his face and further words died on her lips.

The music softened in her ears, the hubbub of voices about her died away. There was no one else on the floor, only her in Rafe's arms, in a dream moment when the war did not exist and she was happier than she had ever been in her life before. Tante Lea had known from the very beginning what *she* had been afraid to acknowledge. She had fallen in love. Two short weeks during which they had been more like sparring partners and yet had this man asked it of her she would have followed him anywhere.

And then, as he had done so often in their short relationship whenever this air of intimacy leapt unbidden between them, Rafe shattered the spell.

'It's surprising how money can make people do the most unpredictable things. What will my brother do next, I wonder? Propose on his knees?' And what would Damaris say to that? She liked her men to be always available. Once married to Shanna, he suspected Wayne would sadly neglect her.

'What are you saying?' Shanna stiffened in his arms, the smile fading from her features. 'That the presents were some kind of bribe. . .? Are you so jealous that you cannot believe either of them capable of a decent gesture? Are you sure you are not judging them by your own standards?'

'My goodness, perhaps Wayne has made more of an impression on you than I realised,' Rafe replied, his eyes narrowing slightly as he contemplated her indignant face and the quivering mouth that was—oh, so tempting. . . 'I am going to give you a word of advice, little Shanna. Whether you take heed or not is up to you. You are being used. You are a pawn in a game being played by my father to get himself a grandchild.' He heard her sharp intake of breath and tightened his arms about her as she tried to pull free of him. 'He knows he may never see the day that I marry or sire children and he has grown impatient. Wayne is his last hope—and you, my sweet, would grace any man's bed. Unfortunately once you have done your duty you will probably find yourself sleeping alone. By that time you may or may not prefer it. Father will have what he wants, Wayne will have your money—and you. . .'

'I think you are insufferable to suggest such a thing!' Shanna gasped. He was holding her too tight for her to break free without drawing unnecessary attention to them both. 'That dear, sweet old man. . .'

'He would eat you for breakfast if it suited him,' Rafe drawled sardonically. 'Get out while you can. As far away from here as possible.'

Shanna became still in his arms, understanding dawning in the depths of her eyes. No woman would ever rule Wildwood in the place of his mother! That was the reason behind all his lies, not concern for her welfare. Well, two could play at that game.

'I like your father and I am growing to like your brother more each day. What more could I ask than a fine house, and two people who care for me? I am sorry to disappoint you, but I like it here and I am going to stay. Who knows? When you come back again, Wayne and I could be married.'

The words hung in the air between them. The blue eyes became chips of ice piercing her very soul.

Without a word he led her from the floor, but his tall frame blocked her path when she turned towards the open French windows, seeking an escape from him.

'When I return—and I shall—it will be to take back what is mine and to deal with those who have taken it from me. Do not be here. For your own sake—do not be here.'

As Shanna stood inwardly trembling from the threat, he wheeled away and was lost in the people milling around them. What could he do to her? Nothing! Alexander and Wayne would protect her, but how would she protect herself against the love she had discovered and must reject? If anything destroyed her, it would be love of Rafe Amberville!

Rafe wandered back to the refreshment table and helped himself to some of the cold delicacies there. Abraham filled up the empty glass held out to him and said in a voice too low to carry beyond the two of them, 'Leon has just returned. Everything is well hidden. Massa Wayne won't know anything is missing for months.'

'Unless he gets a bulk order, and I very much doubt that at his prices,' Rafe replied humourlessly. 'Is he still outside?'

'Taking the air with Miss Damaris,' Abraham said, and a huge grin crossed Rafe's features at the comment.

'That's not all he's taking—and under Claude's nose too. He likes to live dangerously these days—or his new-found power has gone to his head.'

'What has gone to whose head?' Alexander

enquired as he came to his son's side. 'Is it possible you have decided to enjoy yourself after all?'

'With such a magnificent spread, how can I not do so?' Rafe said with a shrug of broad shoulders.

'This is all thanks to Wayne.' There was a pride in his father's voice that made Rafe grit his teeth. 'His trip to Savannah was most successful, although he did not tell me what he was doing until everything arrived. Flour, coffee, sugar, molasses and French champagne. I had to pay through the nose for it all, of course—black market prices—but it's worth it to see Shanna looking so happy.'

Rafe pretended to be engrossed in the sliced chicken sandwich he was holding, momentarily lost for words. Fool! He should have realised all these things had come from Wayne's secret hoard in the monk's hole. His father had paid a second time for goods already his! If he had ever doubted his suspicions that Wayne hated his father, they vanished now. It justified all he had done to deprive his brother of his ill-gotten gains.

'Have either of you seen Damaris? She was dancing with Wayne a few moments ago.' Claude LaFontaine came to join them as they stood in an awkward silence, further polite conversation impossible between them.

'Perhaps she has gone to rest for a moment,' Rafe suggested. 'It has become exceedingly warm in here and she has not missed a single dance.'

A fact Claude would not have missed, any more than he had her absence.

'Come into my study, old friend. I have a bottle of

brandy there especially for the two of us,' Alexander suggested. It would not be the first time Damaris LaFontaine had gone off with a man who was not her husband and he wanted no trouble beneath his roof. Stupid of Wayne to leave the room at the same time; Claude had such a suspicious mind he believed the worst of any man who looked sideways at his wife. But then his mind eased. . . Shanna was also missing. She and Wayne would be together, of course.

Shanna, in fact, had lingered on one of the long verandas which flanked the house on all sides, in no hurry to return to the crowded room until she had fully composed herself again after Rafe's scathing rhetoric. A cool evening breeze fanned her bright red cheeks as she relaxed down into a cane chair, listening to the cooing of the fan-tailed doves on the roof overhead. From the bayou came the sounds of full-throated bullfrogs, crickets and an occasional owl, and from the direction of the slave quarters the soft sound of singing. It brought back a moment of nostalgia for her. The plantation house at Baton Rouge had once been as peaceful as this. Never had she thought she would see the day when anything or anyone could destroy it. If Rafe was right, then soon bluecoats would be trampling and riding over the beautiful lawns of Wildwood, invading the house, desecrating it with their presence. Knowing this, how could she stay?

She would stay for him—Rafe. To try and protect what he loved most in the world, because she loved him.

The unexpected murmur of voices close by caught her attention, followed by a stifled laugh and a not very strong protest from a woman to leave her dress intact.

'I'll buy you a dozen more when you get rid of that fool of a husband,' came the confident reply from her male companion, and Shanna froze in her seat as she recognised Wayne's voice. Wayne and Damaris LaFontaine! But she had Rafe, surely. . .?

'And what would your little magnolia blossom say to that?'

'Who. . .? Oh, you mean Shanna. I shall have her eating out of my hand by the end of next week. I think Father would like a quick wedding. He wouldn't care if I married a woman who had a face like a sow so long as she gave him a grandchild. As it happens she is not bad-looking—and so rich. . .'

'You are a cold-hearted swine, do you know that? With you everything is for money,' Damaris replied.

'Not everything, or I would not be here with you, risking the wrath of your husband,' Wayne chuckled. 'You and I are going to have some good times together.'

'So long as you do not ask me to remain faithful to you; that would be too much of a bore.'

'I shall have enough money to buy all the women I want if you choose to be stupid,' came the heartless answer.

'You may not live long enough to spend any of it.' The third voice brought Shanna to her feet. As quietly as was possible in the half-light, she crept to the corner of the house and tentatively peered around.

Damaris was struggling into her gown. She did not look in the least embarrassed at being found in such an awkward situation. Wayne had sprung to his feet and was pulling on his coat. If anything, he looked afraid, Shanna thought, and with good reason. The fury blazing out of Rafe's eyes would unnerve the bravest man.

'You pair of damned fools! You know how jealous Claude is. He's looking for you, Damaris, so you had better have a good explanation ready.'

'How chivalrous you are, Rafe,' Damaris murmured. Smoothing down the crumpled skirts of her gown, she lightly brushed her fan across one of his cheeks. 'If you drop by the house some time, I am sure I can find a way to thank you.'

'I would rather pay for my pleasures; that way I am sure of satisfaction,' came the biting retort, and this time the fan sliced across his cheek in a savage blow.

Shanna leaned weakly against the side of the house, her mind reeling from all she had heard. Rafe had not lied. Wayne was intending to marry her for her money and Alexander. . .her father's close friend. . .had only been thinking of himself when he'd befriended her. A grandchild, that was what he wanted. He cared nothing for her.

And Rafe! Rafe was not involved with Damaris! Only Wildwood stood between them. How did she fight memories and dreams? A house where she had begun to feel she belonged, yet he considered her an outsider?

She stiffened and was instantly alert again as she heard the heavily accented voice of Claude LaFontaine begin remonstrating with his wife. She knew she should have turned and walked away, left them to argue, shut her mind against Wayne's deception and the blindness on her part which had made her so sorely misjudge Rafe, but she could not.

'It was nothing, old friend,' she heard Rafe intervene quietly. 'A moment of madness in the moonlight.'

'My quarrel is with your brother, not you,' Claude returned coldly.

'If you call my brother out and kill him, then regretfully I shall be forced to call you out also and kill you. I will, but before I do so I will make sure the whole damned county knows what a whore your wife is. Not that it's any secret these days.'

Shanna stifled a gasp behind her hand. Rafe's anger seemed to have disintegrated. He was facing Claude with a half-smile on his face, totally ignoring his brother and Damaris. Was he serious? How calmly he spoke of death, while Wayne, ashen-faced, was visibly quaking at the possibility of fighting a duel.

'If you persist in this stupidity, Claude, perhaps you should have your facts straight or you will be taking the life of an innocent man.' Damaris spoke for the first time since her husband had arrived on the scene. She was in perfect control of herself now and seething from Rafe's personal comments. She had wanted him for years, but he had always ignored her—and pointedly so. When he had sought her out the night before he went off to war she thought she had used him—instead he had used her! No man had ever done that to her before—and then behaved as if she did not exist! He would pay for his insults and for her injured pride. 'I do not know what you think you saw, but once again your jealousy has blinded you to the truth. Did you not see me strike Rafe? It is he who accosted me. Wayne came to my aid and I fear they would have come to blows had you not arrived. It is not the first time Rafe has shown an interest in me, but I have always ignored him. Wayne will bear me out. He knows only too well the lustful nature of his brother. No woman is safe with him.'

'And no man safe with you, my dear,' Claude replied drily. 'Is this true, Rafe? Deny it, for the love of heaven! You are a friend. . .'

'Does it matter which one of us you face as long as honour is satisfied?' Rafe said with a shrug of his broad shoulders. If he denied the accusation Wayne and Claude would face each other in the cold light of dawn and one of them would die—over a worthless woman! He had no intention of killing Claude LaFontaine. If it was at all possible, when the man's temper had cooled and he could recognise how ludicrous his wife's words were, he might even be able to talk him out of the duel. But later—when they were alone. . .

'Very well. I will select my seconds and send them to you within the hour. Come, Damaris, we are leaving.'

'As for you, brother,' Rafe said as the couple moved out of earshot, 'you will acquit yourself at first light as my second. If I don't decide to shoot you before morning, that is.'

There was silence. Shanna risked another look around the corner of the house and found Rafe staring directly at her, hands on his hips. As she emerged into the half-light, she watched his lips tighten.

'I thought I heard a movement back there. What did you hear?'

'Everything. You cannot fight him, it isn't fair,' she protested.

'Wayne is a lousy shot. Claude would kill him and I have other plans for the way my brother will leave this world,' came the grim reply. 'Forget everything you heard—and saw. Tomorrow it will have resolved itself.'

'In a duel! Where one or both of you could be hurt? Killed? Have you grown so accustomed to killing that you have begun to enjoy it?' Shanna regretted the heated words the moment they slipped past her lips, but there was no way of retracting them. Rafe reached into his pocket and brought out a long cigarillo which he lit, filling the space between them with sweet-smelling grey smoke. 'I did not mean. . . I shall go to your father. He will prevent this nonsense.'

'You will do no such thing.' His voice was like ice, cutting through her. 'This is a family matter. Nothing to do with you. Go back into the house and try to act as normally as possible. Claude will not want anyone to know what is happening and so I do not think he has made the event public knowledge. Go back and enjoy your party, Shanna, and stay out of things which do not concern you.'

'What—what are you going to do?' She was loath to leave him, despite his brusqueness and the intimation that despite all his father's plans she did not belong.

'I am going to spend the remainder of the evening as I should have in the first place! With a bottle and a friend!' The mask suddenly dropped from his face and she saw mirrored there fury which made her step back in alarm. 'Damn you! Damn you all!' he added harshly and as she stood, stunned and speechless, he turned and strode off across the lawn and was swallowed up in the darkness.

'He was hurting, Tante Lea. No matter what he said or did, I could feel the pain in him. And I was helpless to help him.' Shanna sat on the edge of the bed while the woman brushed her hair. Rafe had been wrong in his assumption that news of the duel would not become known. It had and, after the first buzz of excitement and speculation had died away, the guests had begun to depart. Shanna had lingered to see the last of them leave before she had retired, taking her leave of a stern-faced Alexander and a very quiet Wayne, who could not meet her gaze as she bade them goodnight. She had spoiled his plans by overhearing him with Damaris. . .would she now see the other side of his character, that which Rafe hinted lay beneath the smiles and politeness? And could she stay at Wildwood now, knowing how she had been used?

'There is nothing you can do. Come to bed, child. Let tomorrow take care of itself. Rafe Amberville surely will,' Tante Lea replied soothingly, leaving her to turn down the bedcovers.

'What do the cards say? I saw you with them when I came in. What did you read in them? I want to know,' Shanna demanded.

'Very well, but you will not like it. Death, that is what I saw there. The death of a man. Now are you satisfied?'

'Rafe! No, it could not be. . .but everyone was saying when they heard how good a shot Claude LaFontaine is. . . He has killed three men already in duels over his wife.'

'Whatever he is, your Rafe is no fool. He knows the worth of his opponent.' Tante Lea pretended to busy herself with tidying the room and Shanna, her arms locked tightly about her, began to pace the floor restlessly.

Lea had seen more—much more—in the cards. One man would die and one would be injured. Who would return to Wildwood? Wayne—alone, gloating over the death of a brother he hated, or Rafe, sick at heart because he had been forced to kill a friend? 'Besides, he will be gone tomorrow. . .'

Shanna wheeled on her, piercing her with a questioning stare.

'Gone! Gone where? What have you heard?'

'It is something not even the rest of the family knows. . .' Tante Lea hesitated, then decided it was better to relate what she had overheard. With the main obstacle to Shanna's peace of mind removed, perhaps they could get back to living normal lives again. 'He has new orders. He leaves for Atlanta in the morning. He has told Abraham and Hannah. . . and Leon, of course. The two of them are out in the stables now with a bottle of corn whiskey.'

'And Rafe to fight a duel at dawn! Is he mad?' Shanna gasped. 'Why has he not told his father he is leaving?'

'Perhaps he thinks he will not care. His brother will not. There is no one else.'

'I care. Don't frown at me like that, Tante. Someone has to let him know they care. Give me my wrap. I will only be a few moments.'

'I am not allowing you to go down there!'

'Sherman's army could not stop me,' Shanna returned, snatching her robe from the woman's grasp and belting it tightly over her nightgown. 'Don't worry. I know you think the worst of him—as I did when I believed Wayne's lies—but he is a gentleman. I shall be perfectly safe.'

'You have not been safe with him since the first day he set eyes on you and you know it,' Tante warned gravely. 'Go on, then. . .cause yourself more pain when he sends you away again, telling you getting drunk is also a family affair.'

'That was cruel, but I will forgive you because I know you are afraid for me. I shall never have Rafe Amberville, Tante. I shall always love him, but he will never belong to anyone. . .not any woman anyway.'

'And can you live with that?' Lea challenged, and saw the flicker of pain which crossed Shanna's face as she turned towards the door.

'I shall learn—in time.'

She heard the murmur of voices and muffled laughter as she drew nearer to the stables. A full moon illuminated her way and a warm breeze stirred the long hair cascading down over her shoulders. Seeking out a man in the early hours of the morning, in only her nightclothes! Her poor mother would turn in her grave. But it was not as if she was in any danger. So long as he did not touch her. . .no. . .so long as she did not allow him to touch her, then she could say what she had come to say and go.

The stable doors were not quite closed. Through the space between them she could clearly see Rafe Amberville sprawled in the straw beside Leon, who had just said something which sent his companion into a fit of laughter. As she hesitated, knowing her appearance would not be welcome, for it would break up what appeared to be a very relaxed moment between them, Shanna saw a bottle pass between them. And from the paper bag alongside him Leon produced two large succulent chicken legs which they both bit into with relish.

'Who needs them, Leon?' Rafe muttered, his mouth full of chicken. 'When you have Abraham's best whiskey and Hannah's chicken you don't need anything else.'

'You speak for yourself, Massa Rafe. Me, I'm still

human. I need other things too. . .' the negro replied, a grin on his face.

'Like a woman to warm your bed. You sly old fox, I've seen the way you've been looking at Tante Lea. Mark my words, you will get nowhere with that one. A dedicated spinster. I wish I could say the same for her mistress. That little fool is heading for real trouble——'

Rafe broke off, his gaze sweeping towards the doors. He knew there was someone outside, Shanna realised. That same instinct that had warned him of her presence earlier had done so again. Taking a deep breath, she pushed open the door and went inside.

Leon came to his feet, brushing wisps of straw from his clothes and embarrassed to be found with his companion, but Rafe remained where he was, intent on finishing the food he held. If her entrance had surprised him, he showed no sign of it. One eyebrow rose questioningly as he said with a hint of laughter in his voice. 'Isn't it rather late to come visiting, little Shanna? Especially like that! I think you had better watch the door, Leon, and make sure we are not disturbed. Or is Tante Lea out there somewhere ready to defend your honour if you scream?'

'I came to talk to you, to try and make you see reason,' Shanna said, ignoring his taunts. Leon decreetly withdrew outside the stable doors, closing them tightly behind him. 'How can you act like this—drinking when you should be resting, preparing yourself for the morning? You are treating it like some game.'

She was beside herself with exasperation. It was obvious her words were having no effect on him. He continued to lounge up on one elbow, the most wicked lights dancing in the eyes which continually wandered over the pale pink wrap she was clutching protectively at her throat.

'Resting? Preparing myself? For what? To kill or be killed? There is no time to prepare yourself when the enemy come at you out of the darkness on a rainy night. Nor do you have time to rest. I have learned to do without sleep. And no, I do not consider it a game. Claude is an old friend and I happen to like him. I shall do my best to talk him out of this crazy idea, but if that fails, then. . .' He shrugged his shoulders '. . .It will be out of my hands. I came back to find a few short days of peace; instead all I have found is hatred and more killing.'

Shanna's anger dissipated as she realised the torment inside him. She did not know why he had not challenged Damaris's lies, but it was clear to her that he was sincere when he said he did not want to take the life of a friend. If only she could speak to Claude LaFontaine. . .

'Are you going to stay and keep a lonely man company?' Rafe asked, his lips twisting into a sardonic smile when she made no move to leave.

'I did not come for that,' she retorted. 'Besides, you have made it very obvious you prefer other company to mine. And you are drunk!'

'Drunk!' He threw back his head and laughed, but

there was no laughter on his face as he stared up at her. 'Unlike Wayne, I can hold my liquor. I am stone-cold sober—and I want you!'

She recoiled back several steps at the unexpected words, her eyes widening in disbelief.

'Want me! You *are* drunk!'

'Then take your damned comfort, or advice, or whatever it is you came out here to give me, together with your damned virtue and go back to the house. You are of no use to me,' Rafe snapped, reaching for the bottle at his side. Then, with an oath that made her blood run cold, he flung it against the far wall where it shattered into small pieces.

'I'm sorry. I'm no fit company for man nor beast, let alone an innocent like you. Between them my brother and father will drain you of every decent emotion if you remain here, smash all your hopes and dreams. They will destroy you if you let them. Go away from here before it is too late.'

She moved back closer to him, suddenly no longer afraid of his strange mood, and went down on her knees beside him. Close, but not too close. She did not trust him that much.

'I have suvived far worse problems. I am not a fool, whatever you may believe,' she said firmly.

'No, you are not, but in matters of the heart, who can tell what a woman will do?' Rafe murmured teasingly. 'Wayne will never care for anyone but himself. My father wants a grandchild. You—lucky thing—have been chosen to supply it.'

'Don't! You make him sound heartless,' Shanna protested. Even though she had overheard Wayne's confession of deception on the veranda she still found it hard to believe that Alexander could be a party to it. He had been her father's friend. He wanted only to protect her.

'He is. He loved only one person in his life—Wayne's mother. When she died he lavished what affection was left—if you can call it that—on Wayne. He smothered him, then moulded him into his own image. Cold, calculating, a user——'

'Is there not some of him also in you?' Shanna asked quietly.

His lips tightened for a moment, then he nodded. 'Unfortunately, yes, but my will is still stronger than his. It is the only thing that has kept me free. Oh, it didn't stop me from trying to please him when I was a child, but he always ignored me. I had no father, just a man whose eyes held hatred every time he looked at me. When I was old enough to work, he tolerated me because I was useful.'

'But Wayne loves him. . .' Shanna began.

'He loathes him. Both of us. He longs for the day we are both dead. Every night I wager he prays to God I die in battle, then this place will be his. She promised it to him, do you know that? His beautiful, faithless whore of a mother who didn't possess a bone in her body capable of affection. Power was what she craved. "One day this place will belong to you," I used to hear her say to him. "One day—all this! Power! Wealth!" And so he waits, bleeding the place dry while he does so. I've seen the books. . .' Rafe hesitated, realising he had gone too far. Perhaps he had had too much to drink after all. . .but once again he felt an inexplicable feeling of protection for her. After all, who was there to look after her? 'With our cotton stored in the warehouse in Savannah for almost two years there is no money coming in to maintain the plantation. But, by God, he's taking it out. And Father lets him do it because Wayne can do no wrong. Is he not out of the same mould? My father never makes a mistake—at least not one that he will ever admit to.'

'Could you undo the damage he has done?' His words made Shanna more determined than ever to use her money to help the Ambervilles—no, Wildwood, because it was Rafe's first and only love. She would not allow Wayne to destroy it, not as long as there was breath in her body.

'I'll die trying. This place means everything to me. She was born here, married here. I was born here, in your room. Wildwood belongs to me more than it does my father. It will belong to Wayne over my dead body,' Rafe told her with such vehemence behind the words that she knew he would stop at nothing to ensure it was so.

'Your room,' Shanna corrected softly, relaxing a little more. 'Where you can be close to *her* at least.'

'Perhaps you understand more than I give you credit for. Then understand this. If I did not have to leave, if there were no more war and for tomorrow and all my tomorrows I knew I would never have to leave here again, I would never allow you to marry my brother.' He rolled closer to her, drew himself up so that his face was only a few inches from hers. His fingers lightly touched her cheek, brushed back a loose strand of midnight-black hair. 'Go out into the world and find yourself a man who will arouse fire in you. It is there, I have felt it, but you are afraid of it.'

'You talk nonsense. . .' Shanna protested half-heartedly. She *was* afraid of the feeling he had aroused in her, but also of him. . .his touch, his kiss. . .

'If I had a sister,' Rafe murmured, his head tilting slightly to one side as he considered her, 'I would want her to be just like you.'

'Now you are making fun of me again. Would you kiss your sister the way you have kissed me?' she challenged, and the wicked gleam in his eyes grew brighter.

'Heaven forbid! Perhaps not as tantalising, then, or I would be forever fighting off would-be suitors.'

'Protecting her? Perhaps she would not want protection.'

'She would have it anyway,' he replied firmly.

'Will you—mind me being in charge of the house . . .if I stay, of course?' Shanna asked hesitantly. He was so close to her now that she could feel the warmth of his breath upon her cheek.

'You have already made up your mind; I can read it in those lovely eyes. When you are angry, they darken until they are like storm clouds. When you smile, I perceive a hint of gold in them. Will you stay, even after all I have told you? All you have heard?' Why did the idea please him? For her to care for his home, be here when he came back.

‘I have weathered worse storms,’ she assured him with a faint smile.

‘Then I do not mind so long as I do not find the place drastically changed. It will be something to look forward to. . .your smile. . .your warmth. . . the softness of you. God, you don’t know how long it has been since I have held anything like you in my arms.’

‘I—I think I should go. . .’ Shanna said as his fingers touched her cheek again, traced the line of bone and mouth down to the slender line of her throat and covered the hand that clutched the wrap to her.

‘I think so too. . .’

Yet neither moved. As Shanna looked deep into his eyes she felt as if she was being dragged down into a bottomless pool. Where was her self-control? Her pride? She felt his hand against her back, burning her skin through the thin fabric of her nightclothes, pressing her close against his chest. The immaculate white shirt he had worn for the party was streaked with dust now and open to the waist. She gasped as her cheek brushed his bare skin. And then her mouth was crushed beneath his and nothing, no one else in the whole world mattered.

He wanted her! The words had come from his very own lips and the passion in the kisses rained on her lips and face left her in no doubt as to the truth of them. The last time he had gone away he had sought solace with Damaris. Was it his intention to do the same tonight—with her?

‘In matters of the heart, who can tell what a

woman will do?' he had teased a few moments ago. What should she do? Follow the dictates of her heart and surrender herself to him? Or deny her love, run from him while there was still a chance?

Run! She could not move. Did not want to. Rafe's lips were trailing hot kisses down over her neck to the rise of her breast where the wrap had fallen away. Her fingers no longer clutched at it, but were entwined in the thick blond hair. Her lips were no longer reticent, but answering kiss for kiss with a fire to match his own. She heard herself whisper his name as she clutched him to her, shutting her mind to the fact that this one moment might be all that they shared together. Tomorrow he would be gone! No, she must not think of tomorrow, only now.

'Rafe. . .' She opened her mouth to say the fateful words—I love you—but they were never uttered as she realised he had drawn back from her and was staring down at her as she lay in the straw, an odd smile on his dark features. Realised too how not only her wrap had slipped away from one shoulder, but the sheer nightgown beneath was revealing far more of her than any man should see before her wedding night. And yet she felt no shame, only a deepening of the excitement he had already aroused in her as his eyes rested momentarily on the firm swell of her breasts.

'I am sending you back to the house, little Shanna, before you make me completely forget myself. I am not going to insult you by using you on my last night, as happened once before with someone else. Nor am I going to allow one very special moment to be ruined forever. I shall have this to remember on some cold, rainy night.'

With impersonal fingers he rearranged her wrap, sprang to his feet and lifted her to hers.

'This is one hell of a time to remember I am a gentleman, but you bring out the worst—and the best—in me, Shanna. One day you will make some man very happy.'

Shanna stepped back from him, colour beginning to creep into her cheeks as she realised how close she had been to giving herself to him completely. He had known it, yet he was sending her away! What could she say to make him let her stay? His brows drew together in a fierce frown as she sought for the right words. His lips tightened and the smile faded from his face.

'You do not belong here—with me, Shanna. Go back to the house and forget this happened between us.'

'I—I will stay if you wish it.' The words fell from trembling lips.

'You deserve more than to be tumbled in the hay.' She winced at his crudeness, stepped backwards towards the door. 'Go, for the love of heaven!'

Shanna turned and left him. She wanted to run, but she knew that somewhere in the darkness outside Leon was keeping watch and she did not want him to see her make an undignified departure, to sense the pain Rafe's rejection had brought her. But as soon as she was out of sight amid the trees she took to her heels and did not stop until she was at the door of her room.

'You want another bottle, Massa Rafe?' Leon stood hesitantly inside the stable doors, looking across at the figure which was leaning against one of the stalls, deep in thought. So deep, in fact, that the question had to be repeated.

'What I want I have suddenly discovered is beyond my reach,' Rafe said, turning to face him. Leon was startled by the bitter lines which twisted his features.

'That Miss Shanna's a nice lady.'

'Which is exactly why I sent her away. Not because I wanted to, but because I cannot give her the one thing she needs, my friend. . .love! I do not know how. . .'

'And what do you suppose the innocent Miss Shanna de Lancel was doing closeted in a stable in the early hours of the morning with my brother?' Wayne mused as he and the ex-overseer Jack Hanson moved away towards the paddocks.

'I'd say he's beaten you to the post.' The man at his side grinned in the darkness.

'A juicy titbit of gossip that she will not want spread throughout the county,' Wayne continued, ignoring the gibe. 'With Rafe gone there will be no one to protect her reputation if I choose to let it slip one day. I think I have Shanna de Lancel just where I want her. . .'

# CHAPTER SIX

'MISS DE LANCEL! In other circumstances I would say this is an unexpected pleasure, but at six in the morning I am not at my best. And you should be in bed,' Claude LaFontaine said in surprise as Shanna appeared beside his carriage. With the thick mists still clinging to the waters of the bayou, he had neither seen nor heard the approach of the boat, nor heard her crossing the open ground from the main stream where it rested.

Shanna had not slept at all. Afraid she would be asleep when Rafe left the house, she had dressed and sat in a chair throughout the hours of darkness. After an hour of lecturing, scolding and cajoling, Tante Lea had given up and accepted that her mistress intended to go to the duelling ground to try and prevent the forthcoming duel.

Abraham had told Shanna that Claude had already killed three men. The thought chilled her as she sat in the small boat in the half-light which came filtering through the Spanish moss trailing everywhere, especially in the trees lining the banks, the branches of which spread out over the water as if to protect her from prying eyes, more so than the cold which invaded her bones despite the warm cloak she hugged about her.

In a few hours the heat of the sun would turn this

place into a veritable paradise of brilliantly coloured flowers, brightly-plumaged birds and small animals seeking food amid the thick undergrowth. But at this time of the morning she thought it a frightening place—a place of death.

'Rafe would not listen to me last night. Perhaps you will.' Shanna shivered as a strange cry came from the depths beyond them and Tante Lea cast an apprehensive look over her shoulder. She had not attempted to make the woman remain behind. She had been glad of the company on the short but heart-stopping journey. 'You cannot fight him. He has done nothing. It is Wayne who has been having an affair with your wife, not Rafe.' Claude's face grew bleak at her words, but she had come too far to give up now. 'I was on the veranda. I heard them—saw them. . .'

'Heard things which those delicate ears should not have heard, I expect,' came the stony reply. 'There is nothing you can tell me, my child, that I do not already know. But you must accept that this is a matter of honour between Rafe and myself. He deliberately provoked me. . .you heard him.'

'To prevent you from discovering the truth. Will you kill him for that?' Shanna cried, near to tears. She fought them back, knowing they would not move him. She was looking at a tired old man who loved a woman who had lied and deceived him and revelled in it. Yet he loved her still and was willing to kill for her. Kill a friend!

'Rest assured I shall not take his life because he has shared my wife's bed, like so many before him—

and since. You are shivering. . . I have some brandy in my carriage that will warm you.'

He beckoned forward the liveried servant standing a few feet away, but Shanna shook her head. He shrugged and instructed the negro boy to bring him a snifter of brandy.

Through the gloom and murkiness came the sound of voices. As they grew louder, Shanna recognised Wayne's plaintive tones complaining of the hour and the cold and his brother's insistence that he should act as his second. How ironic, she thought, for Rafe to make him a witness to the havoc he and Damaris had brought about.

'I must not be seen. Nor must he know I have spoken to you,' she said quickly.

'How much you love him,' Claude replied, his stern features softening as he looked into her distressed face and saw the pain in her eyes. 'As deeply, I suspect, as I love my wife. Each of us is prepared to sacrifice a great deal for those we love. Take care. Do not allow it to destroy you as it has me. Be strong whatever you do. Never commit yourself totally in the name of love or you are lost.'

'Before last night I would have agreed with you,' Shanna said with a sad smile. 'Now it is too late.'

'Rafe does not know how lucky he is to have someone like you to watch over him—to care——' He broke off, suddenly embarrassed at the intimacy of their conversation. She was little more than a stranger, yet he was giving her advice as if she were his daughter—the daughter he would never have because Damaris was too proud of her figure to suffer the disfigurement of a pregnancy. And he had allowed her the whim which deprived him of a family! 'Go now, before you are seen. Go back to the house and wait for him.'

Not until she had retired to the sanctuary of the trees a few yards away did Shanna realise what he had said. Did he intend to call it off after all?

Tante Lea clutched at her arm, motioning with her head towards the boat they had left out of sight at the edge of the water. In it Benjamin glowered in their direction. He had been awakened from a pleasant sleep and was even more grumpy than usual.

As the mists began to roll back, Shanna saw Rafe accompanied by Leon, striding towards Claude. Despite the dampness of the early morning air, he had a coat thrown carelessly over his shirt and did not look in the least worried that he was about to fight a duel with an old friend. But she had begun to understand the depths to which he went to conceal his innermost thoughts and feelings. It was his way out of the dilemma forced upon him by the ashen-faced brother who followed in his footsteps.

She caught her breath and ducked back beneath the cover of the bushes as he paused for a moment and glanced around him as if warned by some sixth sense that what was happening was being observed.

'Claude. I am here, old friend. Can we talk sensibly now? This is damned early to be up and I'm hungry.' He halted before Claude LaFontaine, whose features had grown bleak and unfriendly at the sight of the man he was to fight. Another friend he must abandon, perhaps kill, for love of his faithless wife. No! Not this man.

'It is too late to talk, you know that.' Claude's gaze settled for a brief instant on Wayne and then returned to Rafe's face. 'Are you her lover? Or one of them?'

Shanna clapped a hand over her mouth to stifle a gasp at the audacious question. Rafe did not bat an eyelid. He had come prepared for anything, she realised, even to suffer more insults if it prevented the duel.

'No. We shared a few moments once, a long time ago, but it meant nothing to either of us. The need was there, nothing more. This is not necessary, *mon vieux*. You know that. Let us both walk away from this madness now.'

'For me it is very necessary. Do you think I don't know what she is? How people talk and snigger behind my back? I do this because I have to. I only wish it were not you. You will have to kill me, you know.'

'Over her?' Rafe said contemptuously. 'She is not worth it.'

'At least I would die quickly. Living with her, I die very slowly and in agony, yet I cannot let her go,' Claude returned sadly. 'I will leave you no choice, Rafe.'

'Then I am ending it here and now and walking away. She is not worth one drop of blood from either of us,' Rafe returned, with a slow shake of his head.

He never believed Claude would act once his back was turned. It went against the code of conduct that they both respected and lived by. Only when he heard the muttered oath behind him and the desperation in the sound did he realise how far Damaris had driven her husband to distraction.

He saw Wayne's eyes widen, watched his mouth open as if in slow motion, but heard no sound. None was uttered. The warning, if it had been such, died on his brother's lips. The cry Leon uttered came a fraction too late. Rafe felt the bullet from the pistol Claude had seized from his second tear through his left arm, just above the elbow. The pain enraged him and he wheeled, instinct taking control of his mind and his actions. His right hand snaked down to the tiny derringer nestled in his belt. He had carried it with him throughout the war and had lost count of the times its hidden presence had saved his life. One barrel was all he needed. One shot to end the life of a man he had known since childhood. He knew he would not miss!

He shook off the restraining hand Leon laid on his shoulder, cursing him as he had never done before. Wayne was almost thrown to the ground by the hand which thrust him out of the way. Blood soaking through the sleeve of his shirt, dripping to the ground where he knelt, he cradled the dying figure of Claude in one arm, his face working in agony.

'Why did you make me do this?'

'You have set me free. Now some other poor fool is welcome to her,' Claude said, licking lips that had suddenly grown dry. Rafe looked up at the second standing over them, still shocked into silence by the breach of accepted conduct.

'Brandy, man. Quickly.'

It was the negro coachboy who brought the flask and knelt at their side, moistening a handkerchief with brandy and putting it to Claude's lips. There were tears in his eyes. It should have been Damaris administering to him, Rafe thought, the pain in his arm unnoticed with the fury that swept over him. She had never shed a tear for him in her life, nor would she now that he was dying.

'She is a slut, but I loved her and I will not be the last,' Claude whispered, a strange smile spreading across his features. He looked so peaceful that it startled Rafe. 'It is better this way. Now she can destroy herself any way she pleases. . .'

His head fell back against Rafe's arm. Gently he laid him back on to the ground. He had become so accustomed to death that he thought he was immune to it, but then he realised he was shaking. Leon flung his coat around his shoulders and this time Rafe did not refuse the hand outstretched to help him to his feet.

'You! See he is taken home. You can deliver the body to the widow in person. That should give you great pleasure,' he said coldly to his brother.

'It is the least I can do,' Wayne replied with an indifferent shrug. 'You should not have killed him, you know. Everyone will believe you murdered him to get his wife.'

Too late he saw Rafe's clenched fist moving towards his chin. The blow felled him to the ground and he did not get up. Without a second glance Rafe moved past him. . .

* * *

'And just what do you think you accomplished this morning?' Tante Lea asked in a severe tone. 'Up at the crack of dawn to watch two grown men trying to kill each other. And risking our necks in the process.'

Shanna put aside the hot tisane she had been drinking and laid her head back against the cushioned chair with a sigh.

'Have you never been in love, Tante?'

'Love! You are not in love with Rafe Amberville.'

'Am I not? Why, then, when the bullet struck him, did I feel the pain too?' She jumped to her feet, smoothing down the skirts of her crumpled gown. As she did so, Tante Lea moved in front of the door.

'Do not try to stop me. I am going to say goodbye to him. Scold me if you must, but when I come back. Please, not now.'

In silence the woman allowed her to pass.

The door to Rafe's room was open. As she hesitated on the threshold he broke off his conversation with Abraham and the old man hurried past her into the corridor, his head downbent. She saw he was near to tears. If only she could share as much as a servant did with him.

'Have you come to cheer me off to war again?' Rafe said as she moved into the room. The clothes he had worn earlier were thrown across the bed and he had now donned his grey uniform. Aged though it was, she thought he could never look more handsome in anything else.

'If I had my way I would keep you here,' she said without thinking and as one blond eyebrow rose questioningly added quickly, 'Wildwood is going to need you—and your strength.'

'It has you, little Shanna, and you possess a great deal of strength that no one, myself included, gave you credit for. What were you doing out there this morning?'

The question was asked so calmly that it took her aback, but she knew she had no reason to lie, only tactfully avoid the truth. As he stepped towards the decanter and glasses on the table beside her, she saw how stiffly his left arm hung by his side and was brutally reminded of how close she had come to losing him forever.

'I hoped I could persuade Claude to call it off. I realise now he wanted to die,' she said quietly.

He poured some golden whiskey into two glasses and gave her one.

'I wish to God he had chosen someone else to be his executioner,' Rafe said, a bitter twist deepening the line of his mouth. And then he smiled at her and raised his glass. 'Will you drink with me, little Shanna? To the day I come home and claim what is mine. And how can I not return when I have your talisman to keep me safe?'

Shanna blushed to the roots of her hair and took a larger swallow of the whiskey than she intended, which made her cough violently. He chuckled. It was a sound she would carry with her until he returned, she thought, and remember in the long hours of darkness when she could not sleep. His laugh, the way his eyes watched her, the memory of his arms holding her, his lips inflaming her senses. She would die a thousand times over until he rode through the plantation gates again, but in her heart she knew he would come back. He had to. . .!

'You—and Wayne. . .' Rafe began.

'I shall stay because your father has offered me a home and I happen to like him. Your brother is another matter. I shall be quite happy never to speak to him again, let alone consider a proposal of marriage,' Shanna replied.

'Be careful of him. He's tricky. . .and ruthless. I wonder how many people have underestimated him and paid dearly for it?' His eyes left her face to dwell on the ornate mantel clock across the room. 'Time I was leaving,' he added, gathering up his hat and setting it at a jaunty angle on his head.

'Are you not going to say goodbye to your father?' Shanna asked, as he pulled on his long leather gloves. It was not yet eight o'clock and Alexander would not appear for at least another hour. Since the return of his elder son, she learned, he had taken to having breakfast in his room.

'Why? When he realises I have gone he will probably offer up a prayer of rejoicing,' came the humourless reply.

'But you have to explain to him about the duel with Claude. You heard what Wayne said. Everyone will believe. . .'

'That I killed the husband to have the wife. Let them. I shall not be here and my father has a thick skin. He will weather any gossip. Wayne will revel in it, of course. This will be his chance to turn the knife.'

'And you are prepared to let him do it?' Shanna whispered, disturbed by his acceptance of the situation. He would not be blamed. Not if she had her way.

'When I come home there will be a final reckoning,' Rafe said, heading towards the door. He paused, turned and took a last, lingering look around the room. As his gaze rested on Shanna, the old mocking smile she had come to know so well returned to mask his features. 'And there will be one between you and me. . .if you have not run off and married some rich merchant man in Savannah. No, don't come down with me. Stay here until I have gone.'

She opened her mouth to protest, but the door opened and closed so quickly that he was gone before the words were uttered. She turned blindly to the window, waiting for him to appear outside.

Leon was waiting with a horse. Not Balthazar, she noticed, but another stallion from his stables. One thing he valued left in the care of a trusted slave. The other, Wildwood, in the hands of a girl who watched him mount with tears in her eyes and her heart almost torn in two by the agony of the love she had denied. She could not let him go without telling him!

By the time she reached the front porch steps, Rafe's horse was just clearing the top rails of the paddock. He was out of sight almost immediately and she sank on to one of the cane chairs to compose herself, aware of Hannah and Abraham watching her from a distance.

'Don't you worry none about Massa Rafe, Miss Shanna. He'll be back before you know it.' Leon tried to comfort her before he left, but his words fell on deaf ears.

'Coward!' Alexander said from the doorway behind her. 'He kills one of my oldest friends and then rides off like a thief in the night unable to face me.'

Shanna looked up into the lined face and saw something there other than anger. There was pain. Great pain. But for whom? Himself? Rafe? Or Claude LaFontaine? She rose, a hand outstretched towards him, then froze as into view stepped Wayne, the look on his face so smug that she was seized with the urge to hit him.

'Good riddance, Father. He has brought enough shame on our name and this house. We can get back to normal now he has gone. I shall reinstall Hanson tomorrow.'

'If you must,' Alexander replied with a shrug. His gaze was still centred on the direction Rafe had taken and the pain in his eyes was intensifying as the minutes passed. He *did* care, Shanna realised. Cared, but could not show it! And Rafe had ridden away believing his father hated him. It was not hatred she saw mirrored there, but longing, regret—almost desperation. And if she did not intervene Wayne would benefit from this new development which had estranged father and son still more. 'Tomorrow I shall be going into Savannah to see my lawyer. We have things which need to be discussed. Your brother is no longer a part of this place. He has disgraced us for the last time. When I am gone Wildwood will belong to you, Wayne. And your wife.'

'I shall not be his wife, Mr Amberville,' Shanna said coldly. 'I would rather wed the devil than marry such a shallow, devious creature as Wayne. He is not half the man his brother is, nor ever will be. You have sadly chosen to lavish your affections on the wrong son. A liar and a cheat!'

'I have asked you to make my home your own,' Alexander replied stiffly, 'but that does not mean you can slander the only decent human being left here. If it had not been for Wayne we would not have survived this long. You will apologise to him, girl. This instant.'

'I will not!' Shanna stood her ground, her grey eyes darkening with anger as she considered how Wayne had so successfully deceived his father. 'I am aware that it was your intention to throw me at him like—like some saleable item on Galatin Street, and he would have taken me as his wife, even if I had possessed two heads. You want a grandchild and Wayne wants my money. You will have neither. If that means you wish me to leave here, then I will.'

'You make it sound so—sordid, child.' Alexander was immediately contrite at her outburst. To hear his intentions actually put into words, falling from *her* lips and not Wayne's, made the idea quite obscene. 'It was not like that. Rafe. . .will never marry. What woman in her right mind would have him? I only wanted——' He broke off, his shoulders sagging. Suddenly he was a tired old man with nothing to look forward to.

'Perhaps Shanna would have him,' Wayne suggested. 'After their little tête-à-tête in the stables last night, she might have to. You may have your grandchild after all, Father, although it will be a bastard.'

'That's enough,' Alexander snapped disbelievingly. 'Shanna would not. . .'

'Rafe would,' Wayne sneered. 'If he was prepared to kill Claude to get Damaris, he will do anything. Hasn't he always made his own rules? And it would amuse him to seduce the girl I intended to ask to be my wife.'

'And once married you would have me eating out of your hand within a week? Was that not what you told Damaris on the porch last night while you were making love to her? That it would not matter to your father if you married a woman with a face like a sow so long as she gave him a grandchild?' Shanna threw his own words back at him with a vehemence she found startling. Not until this moment had she realised how deeply she detested Wayne Amberville. 'Yes, I was with Rafe last night. I went to ask him not to fight the duel. A duel you and your affair with Damaris provoked. Rafe did not betray you because he thought he could talk Claude LaFontaine around and make him see sense, but he failed. And when he did he turned his back and walked away.'

'You. . .how do you know that?' Wayne felt his forehead begin to grow moist with perspiration. 'It's not true. Don't listen to her, Father. I caught her out last night and now she's trying to get back at me.'

'Be quiet; you sound six years old again, Wayne. Sometimes I think you will never stop whining when someone speaks out against you,' Alexander said in a tone that defied argument. 'Go on, Shanna. What is it you know that I do not?'

'I was at the bayou this morning. I went there to see if I could do something to prevent two men from trying to kill each other. I too failed. When Rafe turned and walked away, refusing to fight, your friend seized a pistol from one of the seconds, Mr Amberville. He shot Rafe and wounded him in the arm. What happened next was so swift I scarce recall it. Only that Rafe turned. . .he had a derringer in his belt. . .'

'It belonged to his mother. . .' Alexander muttered. 'He has carried it since he was a child.'

'Had there been any other way he would never have fired,' Shanna said, fighting to keep back a rush of tears at the memory of Rafe clutching at his injured arm, the bright red life blood soaking through the sleeve of his white silk shirt. 'He is a soldier. . .trained to kill, and Claude LaFontaine wanted to die. It was so deliberate. . .'

'And he rode away letting me believe the worst of him.'

'Had he stayed and tried to explain, would you have believed anything else, the way things are between you?' Shanna asked boldly. She knew by the dazed look on Alexander's face that he believed her. Had he too secretly guessed at the desperate condition of his friend's mind?

'Let him go,' Wayne insisted. He did not like this unexpected display of sentiment on his father's part. 'He has never been anything to you. Before you start wallowing in self-pity, remember who has stood by you all these years and kept this place going. Whom you still need.' He knew that if he was to retain control over his father and Wildwood he must act quickly. 'I am going to find Hanson and give him his job back. The sooner this place gets back to normal the better.'

As he strode off across the lawn, bellowing for Leon to saddle a horse well before the stables were in sight, Abraham stepped forward. He had been a silent spectator until now, with Hannah hovering well out of sight behind the living-room drapes.

'Perhaps you could catch up with Massa Rafe, Massa. I know the road he has taken,' he suggested in his usual quiet manner.

For a moment the hope of father and son coming together without rancour rose in Shanna's mind, but were dashed as Alexander shook his head.

'It is too late. I shall be in the study. Bring me coffee.'

'I tried, Miss Shanna, I surely did,' the man said as he stood with her on the porch, the memory of the way Rafe had ridden away with the devil in his horse's hoofs still vivid in their minds. 'It's going to be as it was before Massa Rafe came back. Hanson will see to that.'

And once more Wayne would be in control—the

master. It would be impossible for them to reside beneath the same roof. The thought of him watching her, trying to touch her as she suspected he would, turned her stomach. And although Alexander now knew it had been Wayne and not Rafe with whom Damaris had been cheating her husband she doubted if it would make any difference. Wayne was here, Rafe was not!

'Shall I pack?' Tante Lea removed the tray of untouched food from Shanna's lap. 'We are leaving, I hope? You know we cannot stay here—not now. Hannah says that Hanson is coming back with his whip. That means trouble and you don't need that, child.' No more did she. Since her first encounter with the overseer in the stables, she had felt uneasy. The tarot cards had predicted danger—and this time not for Shanna or the man she loved, but for Lea herself. And the cards were never wrong!

'I know it would be wise to leave.' Shanna raised her head and Lea was shocked at how drawn and tired she suddenly looked. 'No, that is a lie. I want to stay—for him! I promised. But Wayne. . .'

'Will rule the roost and crow about it every moment he can,' the woman warned. 'There is nothing you can do here.'

'With my money I can keep the plantation going until Rafe comes home,' Shanna insisted.

'If he comes home. If Hanson does not kill off all the help with overwork or the Yankees don't come and drag everyone off to fight or dig trenches. Or Wayne does not persuade his father you and he are still a good match! What will you do if the Yankees come? Run and hide like last time? Then we were lucky.'

'You have seen something in those devilish cards,' Shanna challenged. 'They rule your life. I have a good mind to burn them.'

'That will not erase what I have seen,' she was told gravely. 'If we remain here we are in danger. We are surrounded by it. . .'

'Miss Shanna! Miss Shanna! He's gone. Like a wild man before I could stop him.' Leon came bursting through the door without knocking, Abraham panting in his wake. 'Massa Alexander. . . made me saddle a horse and then he rode off as if possessed.'

'Rode off,' Shanna whispered, the fires of hope once more rekindled. 'Where?'

'After Massa Rafe. Said he'd find him or not come back. I've never seen him this way before. . .what do I do?'

'Do? I do not understand?'

'Massa Alexander ain't been on a horse for months. Never rides these days, and he's on one of our fastest mares. Looks to me as if he intends to ride her into the ground if necessary. But he won't do it. It's not in him any more. Shall I go after him? I ain't got no one else to ask.'

'Yes, Leon, as quickly as you can. Stay with him and bring him home safely,' Shanna instructed. She had given her first order as mistress of Wildwood.

Alexander Amberville was brought back to his home late the following evening. Slaves grouped in silence to watch the carriage that Leon had procured from one of the neighbours to carry his master pass by. He was not dead, but barely conscious after sustaining a heavy fall while trying to force his mount to climb a steep hill. In attendance was the county doctor who had been collected on the way to administer to him.

'What is we to do?' Hannah whispered. 'Massa Wayne will make life hell for everyone with his father confined to bed for the rest of his life.'

She could shed no tears for the man who lay upstairs and who, they had been told, might never walk again. He had been a harsh master, disliking her and Abraham because of their closeness to his first wife. But she *feared* Wayne and his unstable outbursts of temper, his vindictiveness. One wrong word or a look and he was capable of selling them both without a qualm.

'Miss Shanna is mistress here now,' Abraham said. 'It's what the master wanted and Massa Rafe too.'

'I am sure the doctor will have more cheerful news for us soon,' Shanna told them. 'I shall stay, of course, and take care of Mr Amberville for as long as he needs me.'

'I ain't going back into that room again. That man is a devil!'

Mimosa, the young maid newly introduced into the house since Shanna's arrival, came bursting into the kitchen, terror written all over her features. She was a quiet girl, over-awed by her new elevation to the household and eager to please. Her words made Hannah's mouth gape visibly.

'What's wrong with you, girl?'

'Massa Amberville, that's what. Wanted a bottle of whiskey, and when I told him Miss Shanna's instructions was that he could not have strong liquor until he was better he said to get into bed with him and he'd show me there was nothing wrong with him. I ain't going back.'

'You will do as you are told, you foolish child,' Abraham chided, frowning across the table at her. 'The doctor said no liquor and no liquor it is, although I'm beginning to think a couple of bottles might improve his temper.'

'He was only teasing you, Mimosa.' Shanna rose from the table where she had been enjoying a few moments of quiet with Hannah and Abraham, while Tante Lea sat in a chair beside the stove, sewing. Such moments were few and far between since Alexander had sustained the fall which had confined him to bed for over two months now. June had slipped away without her noticing it and now the countryside was sweltering in July heat. 'He is a lonely, frustrated old man and he has no one to take out his anger on. He is not accustomed to having to rely on anyone.'

'You are right about that,' Hannah said, relenting enough to pour Mimosa a glass of fresh milk. 'Sit down and calm yourself before you take up his supper.'

'I will do that,' Shanna said quietly. 'He will want to know the latest news. I hardly know what to say. None of it is good these days.'

Two months and no word from Rafe. No letter

either to say he was wounded, or missing, captured – or killed. Two months during which Wildwood had once more reverted to the whip and fear to control the black workforce. Wayne justified his actions to his father by saying the news of more Union victories was making them restless, that several had tried to escape and go North.

There was a very determined expression on Shanna's face as she opened the door to Alexander's room and went in. It was in her mind to tell him how she felt about Hanson and his brutality. To her surprise Wayne rose from a chair beside the bed. He rarely visited his father and when he did he nearly always left the old man in a mean or despondent mood.

'Here comes your angel of mercy, Father. I wish I had someone as pretty to look after me.' He made a compliment sound like an insult, Shanna thought as she put down the tray she held and went to draw the curtains across the windows. 'Perhaps you could stop by my room later on, Shanna?'

'Leave the girl alone,' Alexander growled, swearing under his breath as he tried to pull himself up in bed and failed. Shanna saw the gleam in Wayne's eyes as she brushed him aside and went to help. He wanted his father dead! He was nothing but a nuisance now, for, although confined to bed, he still held the purse strings. Her suspicions were confirmed as Alexander added sourly, 'Tell Abraham to bring up my personal box. You shall have the cheques in the morning.'

'One short letter to our bank would take all this

out of your hands,' Wayne told him. 'You should not have to worry about such little matters at a time like this.'

'Your concern for my health is most touching,' came the bitter retort which made Shanna draw back in surprise. Since his accident she had noticed how a rift had developed between Alexander and his youngest son. There were times when they were barely polite to each other. 'But while I can still draw breath, which I intend to do for many years to come, I shall remain in charge of all money matters.'

'It's a wonder you haven't handed everything over to your ministering angel,' Wayne sneered. 'You'll have her inspecting the plantation next or taking over Hanson's job.'

'That might not be a bad idea from all I've heard that is going on.' Alexander glowered at his son, then checked his anger and dismissed him with a wave of his hand. 'Leave me. My supper is getting cold.'

'And it's time for telling tales.' Wayne looked at Shanna as he spoke, a warning in his eyes. 'Remember there will also be a time for settling things between us.'

'I am sure I have no idea what you mean,' Shanna replied politely, wondering how she managed to be so in the face of his provocation. 'You go your way and I shall go mine as we have been doing and everything will progress as smoothly as always.'

The door slammed behind Wayne so violently that it shook the room. Alexander gave a snort of disapproval as she placed the supper tray before him.

'Creamed corn again! And underdone pork cutlets. Damnation, I'll have Hannah's hide if she doesn't give me a decent meal.'

'This is exactly how the doctor ordered it cooked and you will eat it, please, without further complaint. Food is not to be wasted these days,' Shanna said, seating herself in a chair.

One hesitant mouthful of creamed corn and the fork was dropped back on to the plate. Her brows drew together into a fierce frown.

'No supper, no news. I shall take the papers back downstairs with me.'

'There's food to be wasted at Wildwood.' Alexander cut a piece of cutlet that had been cooked in butter and decided it was not as bad as it looked, although he did not tell Shanna that. 'We shall never starve here.'

'Then why does Wayne need more money?' she ventured to ask.

'Why, to pay for that last grain shipment two weeks ago. We were lucky to get that. I'll say one thing for that boy—he has his contacts.'

'He has indeed. If there was a delivery then I know nothing about it and the day before yesterday when Abraham and I checked the storeroom we were out of almost everything. I am sending Benjamin and Tante Lea into Savannah at the end of the week to try and replenish what we can.'

'You've made a mistake. Must have. Wayne tells me we have plenty of cotton seed, bacon and beans, and he can lay his hands on the essentials of life like a little smuggled brandy, if we pay the black market price.'

'I am sure he can.' Now, more than ever, she was convinced that Wayne was somehow stealing from his father. 'You must allow me to help. I hope you do not object, but I have sent orders of my own to your suppliers and instructed the bills to be sent direct to my lawyer who will settle them for me. Men can work better and faster if they have full stomachs and know their families are provided for.'

'You will be giving the women curtains to hang at the windows next,' Alexander said, with a reluctant smile. 'I'm not asking you for help; you understand that, don't you? I just feel better knowing someone with a sensible head on their shoulders is caring for the place. Wayne seems so. . .distant these days. . . and I don't help matters. . .' He pushed the tray away and, knowing he would not eat more even if she bullied him, Shanna removed it. 'If only I could have caught Rafe. . .'

She almost fell back into the chair again at his words. Had she really heard him utter them? How he had changed over the past months. He was much thinner, unshaven—he refused to have his whiskers removed more than once a week and then complained incessantly throughout the whole procedure. And for the first week or so he had lain with the room in darkness until Shanna had thrown open the curtains and taken him in hand.

This was the first time he had mentioned his elder son and the wild ride which had made him a cripple. She waited patiently for him to continue.

'If you are waiting for me to bare my soul, forget it,' he said with a frown. 'You could not understand these things.'

'What things? Pride? Stubbornness? Because I was born a woman that does not mean I am blind or oblivious to pain—the pain you and Rafe are causing each other because you are both too pigheaded to admit the blood you share is far stronger than anything else in the world,' Shanna retorted, deciding to take the initiative. If only she could make Alexander admit he cared, Rafe would return to a far different house from the one he had left, and the next time he would be made welcome. 'Why have you never been able to tell him you love him?'

'Love!' Alexander gave a bitter laugh. 'I purged myself of that weakness long ago.'

'Before or after his mother died?' The words were uttered before Shanna gave them thought. The oath unleashed at her made her wince.

'Damn you, girl. Who gave you the right to judge me? What do you know of love when no man has ever bedded you? Or was Wayne right after all. . . you and Rafe in the stables that night?'

Bright colour stained Shanna's cheeks as Alexander brought back to mind the turbulent encounter with Rafe which she had tried so hard to erase from her thoughts. During the daytime, when she kept herself busy, it was possible, but at night, lying alone in bed, she could feel his arms tight around her, the warmth of his body, and more than once she had fallen asleep with his kisses still tingling upon her mouth.

'Would you be pleased if he had done so?' she challenged. 'After all, you want a grandchild. That was the only reason you wanted me to marry Wayne. An heir for Wildwood, to satisfy your dreams. Is no one else allowed to have their dreams? Wayne has them—to be rich and powerful, master of this plantation no matter what it takes.' The colour surged more strongly into Shanna's cheeks and she was unaware of the gleam which had crept into Alexander's eyes at her passionate words until he ejaculated,

'Damnation! You are in love with Rafe! That's why you stayed. Not for me. Not out of the goodness of your heart. For him! You little idiot, he will never love you. He cares only for this place.'

'And knowing that you would still try to deprive him of his birthright?' she countered, and the lined features deepened into a sullen expression.

'I answer to God for my actions and no one else,' came the dour reply at length. 'Now, are you going to read those papers to me or not?'

'As you wish.' Shanna unfolded the first of them without protest. She had touched a nerve. It was a beginning. 'Some of these are over two weeks old . . .and the news is not good. This one says the Yankees are only twenty miles from Atlanta.'

'Read on. I want to hear everything, mind.'

For the next hour Shanna scanned the newspapers. If she hesitated, Alexander was upon her immediately, pressing her for more.

Atlanta would fall. Nothing could save it now. Sherman had crossed the Chattahoochee river with the main force of his army after defeating General Joseph E. Johnston and his brave army who had withstood a devastating pounding from ten miles of entrenched Union artillery in torrential rain for over two weeks. He had crossed the river ahead of his enemy, destroying railroad bridges, trestles and pontoons behind him, but it seemed as if nothing could stem the flow of blue uniforms converging on Atlanta.

On July the seventeenth, the Confederate president Jefferson Davis ordered Johnston relieved of his command and replaced by General John B. Hood. The army turned over to the new commander in Atlanta amounted to a little over forty-eight thousand men. The strength of the enemy numbered over one hundred thousand well fed, well trained fighting men.

'This is too depressing. Perhaps Tante Lea will bring back better news when she comes back from Savannah.' Shanna folded the last of the papers with a heavy sigh.

'Tomorrow Wayne wants more money. Money I can ill afford to pay out, the way things are. Damn these useless legs! I need to get out and see for myself what is happening around here. But why am I complaining now? Even when I could walk I allowed someone else to run the place for me. Everyone's sins come home to roost, do they not, Shanna?'

'Don't talk like that. With rest. . .who knows. . .?' she replied softly, touched by his helplessness.

'Don't pity me, I can't stand that. Bring me the

plantation ledgers and tell Abraham and Hannah that I want them here promptly at nine in the morning. If anyone knows what is going on in this house it is those two.'

'You bitch. I'll have the pair of you for this!' Wayne came out of his father's room as Shanna approached, grabbed her by the arm and swung her back against the wall so violently that the breath was knocked momentarily from her body. 'Got the old man twisted around your little finger, haven't you? It won't do you any good. He's crippled, confined to bed and I'm still running the place. For the trouble you've caused me, you and that smooth-tongued cat of a companion will rue the day you ever set foot here.'

'I do—not know what you mean,' Shanna gasped. Her arm was growing numb beneath his cruel grasp. He thrust his face close to hers. It was not yet ten o'clock, yet she could smell the aroma of brandy on his breath. And not just one small snifter!

'The books are in order, my nosy little Shanna. He can find nothing there. Rafe didn't and I'll warrant he spent hours looking. But your loose-mouth Lea has started him thinking and he hasn't done that in years. The old fool's actually started taking an interest in the place. Nothing to do, I suppose. But it's too late; he'll never get back control now. It's mine, do you hear? Lock, stock and barrel. Everything beneath this roof.'

Shanna gasped at the implication and, with an effort, wrenched herself free. He was including her in that statement. Was he mad?

'That's right, even you,' Wayne drawled, gaining a great deal of satisfaction and something more—yes, pleasure—from the apprehension which registered on her face. He would teach her to be so high and mighty. 'If you know what is good for you, you will pack your bags and leave. If you stay. . .' he lifted immaculately clad shoulders as he stepped back '. . .you do so at your own risk, my dear. Who knows? I shall have so much to offer, I may even appeal to you. . .'

'The devil would appeal to me more.' Shanna spat the words at him in disgust.

'But you already know my brother,' Wayne chuckled. 'I am a far different proposition. By the way, did I tell you Hanson has taken a fancy to your Lea? He's welcome to her as far as I am concerned. . .'

'If he dares to lay one hand on her. . .'

'What will you do? Run to Father? There is no one else, is there? And he cannot help you. I am sure you and I can come to some understanding. . .'

He left her leaning against the wall, faint and sick with fear. Lea and Hanson. The idea was too ghastly to contemplate—as were his last words. An understanding. She knew only too well what that would mean.

As there came the sound of Alexander's voice raised in anger from the other side of the door, she opened it and went in. Hannah, for all her huge stature, stood at the end of the bed shaking like a leaf. Abraham clung to her arm, trying to comfort her. A few feet away were Leon and Tante Lea. As she approached the latter said in a hostile tone, 'I am not one of your slaves, Mr Amberville. I belong to Miss Shanna and I have no fear of being flogged or sold because I speak the truth.'

'Tante, be quiet,' Shanna said sharply, horrified by her blatant disobedience. The woman had always had a mind of her own, but she had never deliberately, to her knowledge, gone behind Shanna's back. 'You were to come to me with any information.'

'What difference does it make, child, so long as the truth is known?' Lea replied with a shrug of her shoulders. Leon was gazing at her in awe. He had never heard anyone of their colour or status speak out so forcefully to the master of the house.

'This—this creature of yours tells me my workers are starving and haven't seen a decent piece of meat in months. That there are no vegetables for them to cook, no rice.' Alexander almost choked over the words. He did not want to accept it was the truth, because if he did it meant all that Rafe had told him was also true. Wayne was deceiving him! Had been for years. Growing rich on the discomfort of others. The condition of the slaves was of secondary importance to his purse, but he had always considered himself a fair man and provided adequate rations for them to survive on. He did not overindulge them, except perhaps at harvest time when the cotton pods had been picked and stored safely in the sheds. Then it was a time to relax and think of the next spring and more cotton. At such a time he had been known to open the storehouse and have Abraham issue extra food.

'She is not a creature,' Shanna returned indignantly. 'Tante Lea is a friend. And she does not lie. You can believe whatever she has told you, however unbelievable it may seem to you now.'

'Then why won't these two confirm her words?' Alexander thundered, flinging a hand out towards Hannah and Abraham. 'Or him!'

Leon opened his mouth to speak but received a sharp jab in the ribs from Tante Lea and remained silent.

'Because they know they will suffer for it,' Shanna replied, seating herself on the edge of the bed beside him. 'They are afraid. All your people are afraid—of Hanson and his whip. Of Wayne depriving them of what little food they are given as punishment for speaking up. Threatening anyone who tries to make life easier for them. . .'

'Anyone?' Alexander picked her up immediately and watched her mouth tremble as she sought to find words which would not hurt him more. 'He wants you. He's made no bones about that, but I've made it very clear you will have nothing to do with him and that you are to be left alone.'

'And he made it clear to me not a few minutes ago that he is in charge of Wildwood and will remain so. And that everything beneath this roof belongs to him. I am in no doubt I was included in that statement.'

'If he dares to lay a finger on you——' Tante Lea began. Shanna silenced her with a single look. Unless Alexander believed all he had been told and curbed his son's power, none of them would be safe.

'I spent all last night going over the books.' Alexander frowned at the ledgers beside him as if angry that they had not immediately revealed something to him. 'I found no flaws in them. Wayne has maintained them with meticulous care. Do you want to tell me something, Abraham——?' He broke off, staring at the old retainer. 'Speak up, man.'

Shanna's eyes flew to Abraham's face. It was clear he wanted to speak, but was having trouble in finding the words. And now it was Hannah clinging to him, reminding him of his place. They both knew a great deal more than they were willing to reveal, she suspected. They had Rafe's confidence, would do anything for him no matter what the risk to themselves. As would Leon. What had he discovered and entrusted to them before he left? If only she had their trust too.

'No, Massa Alexander. I ain't got nothing to say.'

'Then don't stand there with your mouth open catching flies. Find me some clothes and you—Leon! Have the buggy outside the front door in half an hour and then come back up here and help me. You can put those muscles to good use.'

'What do you mean to do?' Shanna asked, half afraid of the answer even though it would solve the immediate problem of who was telling the truth. 'You cannot mean to go out.'

'That is exactly what I intend to do—and your Tante Lea is going to come with me.'

'I shall come too,' Shanna insisted. 'This is sheer foolishness. Dr Matson would never allow it.'

'No, you will not. I am sure she is quite capable of

showing me what I need to see. I want to hear from other mouths that Alexander Amberville abuses his coloureds. Mark me well, all of you. If I find this to be a tissue of lies—though why you, Shanna, should be a party to such fabrication after I have taken you into my home and made you one of the family I cannot imagine—I shall sell the lot of you forthwith. And you, my girl, will leave my house immediately.'

'I have every intention of being here when Rafe returns. You see how confident I am that you will discover everything I have told you is true?' Shanna said with a faint smile. 'Besides, who else will put up with your bad moods and complaints? I am the only one in the house who is not afraid of you.'

'What I do today is out of anger,' Alexander told her. Already he was wondering if he had not overstepped himself. For him to be seen carried to the buggy. . . 'I have no illusions that I will ever walk again, but by God I won't lie here and rot!'

'You are very brave and I am proud of you.' Shanna bent and kissed him on both cheeks.

'And still sure of your facts?' he challenged. What grandchildren she could have given him. Strong, yet with her gentleness in them.

'Such as they are—yes. Please—please take care. Leon, you are not to leave him for a moment. Nor you, Tante Lea. Stay with Leon at all times.'

'I understand, Miss Shanna.' How Shanna had discovered Hanson's unwelcome attentions Tante Lea did not know, only that she was being warned. 'I'll stick to them both like molasses.'

## CHAPTER SEVEN

'DON'T you agree that Mr Amberville should have been told what is happening here?' Shanna asked Hannah as they paused in their stocktaking of one of the linen closets. The woman had barely spoken a word to her since Leon had driven off with Alexander over two hours before. 'Did I do wrong in your eyes?'

'It ain't for me to say one way or the other, Miss Shanna,' Hannah replied, with a shrug of her shoulders. 'But I'll tell you now, there ain't nothing anyone can do or say that will make Abraham or me speak out against Massa Wayne.'

'Because you are afraid of what he will do to you. I understand that, but unless we all stand together against him our lives, such as they are, will be made miserable. He frightens me too,' Shanna admitted, 'but he's only one man. . .'

'One mean, vicious man. He was a spiteful child and he hasn't changed. Besides, Massa Rafe wouldn't want us to do anything that might——' She broke off as if afraid she might say too much, and Shanna seized on her words immediately.

'Might indicate you and Abraham know more than you say? I know you do. I only wish you would trust me.'

'It's best you stay well out of it,' Hannah warned

in a low tone. Even though they both knew Hanson and Wayne were closeted together in the study she spoke as if the walls had ears. 'There's bad things been going on here for years, Miss Shanna. Things only Massa Rafe can put right when he comes home.'

But Rafe had gone off to war, leaving her in charge! What a joke that was, Shanna thought bitterly as she completed the inventory. She had no real say in what went on. The power was still in the hands of a crippled old man who even now might be persuaded to believe that his youngest son had the interests of the plantation at heart—no matter what methods he used.

'Why don't we go down to the kitchen and I'll make you a nice cup of lemon tea? I'll put some honey in it too. You are looking quite peaky this morning.'

Hannah believed her lemon tea to be the answer to all problems, Shanna thought with a smile as she followed her downstairs. How she wished it were. The sound of voices as she neared the study slowed her footsteps. Wayne's voice, sounding very satisfied and smug. Hanson's low chuckle that always sent a shiver down her spine when she heard it. For him to even consider himself good enough for Tante Lea made her blood boil. She had heard enough tales since she arrived to know the kind of man he was. He used and discarded women without conscience. He abused them when he was drunk and men and women alike often bore the marks of his violent temper.

'Don't linger,' Hannah warned. 'Heaven only knows what those two devils are about now.'

'I smell burning,' Shanna said in a low whisper. She edged tentatively towards the door, which was partly ajar, and the acrid smell grew stronger. Despite Hannah's muttering, she eased the door open a fraction more until she could see into the room. Wayne and the overseer were standing by the fireplace where flames were still licking hungrily around a mass of papers and something which looked more substantial—books. No. . .ledgers, like the ones she had seen Alexander examining in his room. She knew those to be still upstairs—so what were these and why were they being destroyed? She motioned Hannah to come and look also, but the woman shook her head and stayed well back.

Identical ledgers. . . The words Rafe had spoken that night in the stables came slowly back into her mind. Something about Wayne's mother promising him that one day the plantation would belong to him. And Rafe had said he was waiting for that day, bleeding the place dry. 'I've seen the books. . .' One set for Alexander and one secret set which Wayne kept, probably the true accounting of what went on, and now he was destroying them. There would be no proof of what he had done. Nothing to present to his father when she made the accusation.

Hannah gave a gasp of disbelief as Shanna flung wide the door and stood on the threshold, confronting the two men within. The alarm that spread across Hanson's face confirmed her suspicions that they had been engaged in something no one was supposed to witness. Wayne's expression was murderous as he turned to consider her. The smile which spread across his pink face caused a flicker of fear to run through her body.

'Come in, Shanna. I was wondering if your curiosity would get the better of you. A little late, I fear. The damning evidence has been destroyed. You can prove nothing, no more can Rafe, and when I have finished with the old man I shall have him eating out of my hand again. And unless you behave yourself I shall persuade him that you are a bad influence here and should be sent away. Where would you go?'

'Wherever it is I would live in style and comfort, on the money left to me by my father,' Shanna reminded him confidently. 'Money I intended to use to help Wildwood get back on its feet after you have drained it dry.'

'So you did know about the monk's hole. The two of you probably planned it together and laughed at how you were putting one over on me,' Wayne sneered, and the innocence of her expression only heightened his anger, his desire for revenge on the two people who had robbed him of his very profitable sideline. 'What makes you think my brother will be returning? From the war news that has been reaching us I should expect him to be dead by now. If he isn't and he's caught in Atlanta when the bluecoats take it, then he'll never get out alive. A pity. After what he has done to me, I wanted the pleasure of killing him myself. You may have to consider second best after all, Shanna.'

'I would not consider you if you were the last man

on earth,' she replied, her head tilting proudly, and as he stared at the long slender line of her throat Wayne's longing to possess her returned. What had Rafe done to provoke this increased hatred? she wondered.

There was nothing she could do if he chose to keep her at Wildwood, Wayne mused. She had no friends or relatives who would worry over her and if his father became difficult, not open to his persuasive charm, then a few well placed threats would keep him in his place. Tante Lea was no problem; Hanson would take pleasure in dealing with her. At that moment as the wild idea raced through his brain Wayne began to believe his mother's promises might come true after all. He had never felt close to her. He had considered her vain and silly and hated the way she used to dress him up in his best clothes to show him off to her equally empty-headed friends. The only thing he had ever cared about was the promise she made to him, that one day the plantation would belong to him—not his elder brother.

To that end he had spent years fawning over a father he despised, giving only a pretence of affection in return for all the attention and love lavished on him by Alexander. And now this chit of a girl was conspiring with his brother to take away his dream. . .

'What are you burning?' Shanna moved closer to the fireplace curiously. The flames were dying now and she could see only a fraction of the ledgers were reduced to ashes. For one mad moment she had the thought of trying to grab them from their fate, but, anticipating her, Wayne grabbed up a handful of papers from the desk, crumpled them and tossed them down on to the red hot bed. Immediately they were consumed and the intensified heat rekindled the untouched pages of the ledgers. Dismayed, she watched flames flicker and roar around them, consuming them totally.

'Nothing will stop me, Shanna,' Wayne sneered. 'Not you, not my father and certainly not my brother. How Rafe knew about the monk's hole was a mystery at first, then I realised that old man Abraham has probably been spying on me all along. I shall have to have a word with him. No. . .perhaps Hanson will persuade him to tell me what I need to know.'

'What is the monk's hole?' Shanna questioned. It was the second time he had mentioned it as if expecting her to understand what he meant.

'Don't play the little innocent with me. Rafe has told you about it, I know he has. When did you spirit away my merchandise, Shanna? On the evening of the ball for your birthday? It was the only time, wasn't it, when everyone was otherwise occupied? Why didn't he take it all? No, that would have been too easy and I would have known immediately. He wanted me to go on believing it was all there and for months I have.'

'Merchandise?' Shanna was beginning to have a horrible suspicion that she knew what he was hinting at. She had several complaints from Hannah about the very same thing. Cash or perhaps goods—or both—finding their way into Wayne's pockets.

'My little store of things which makes life so much more agreeable in these hard times,' Wayne said, a stony glint creeping into his eyes as he again contemplated the enormous amount of money he had lost. Somehow he had to make up that loss.

'Do you not mean necessities?' Shanna challenged. 'Things that could make life here so much easier for us all, black and white.'

'Be careful, or anyone hearing that kind of talk could take it that you share the views of some abolitionists in these parts. And Father would not take kindly to such talk either. Without the negroes this place would be a ruin in six months.'

'You must be very proud of yourself.'

Her scorn did not even touch him. 'I am, Shanna. And I know I shall weather this setback and still come out on top. It is time you accepted I am master here and there is nothing you can do about it. If you continue to get in my way, then. . .' He stepped forward, lashing out with his open palm. It caught Shanna a vicious blow across the right cheek and she fell backwards on to the sofa. 'That is nothing to what I shall do to you. I hope my message is clear?'

'It is to me. Have I been blind all these years or just stupid?' a voice thundered from the doorway.

When he was roused Alexander's voice sounded like the roar of an enraged bull. It was no less on this occasion and the room reverberated with his furious bellow. The sight of Shanna nursing a bruised cheek was like a red rag to him. His bushy eyebrows drew together even more as his gaze switched from her to his son and then to the remnants of the ledgers in the fireplace. If he had needed more proof of Wayne's treachery after his inspection of the plantation—which he did not—this was it. The final straw which threatened to break him, yet somehow he managed to quell his disgust as he looked at his youngest, to hide the disappointment that was crushing him; most of all, to allow none of the disillusionment he was experiencing to be revealed on his face. He had lost both his sons, he realised. One because he had loved him too much, the other because he had not loved him enough. But he *did* love Rafe.

'Father. . .' For a moment Wayne's self-control faltered. Then he was himself again, and the agile mind which had extricated him from so many difficult times sprang into motion with a brilliant lie. 'Did you hear? I hope you did. I need a witness to this woman's treachery! And after all we—you—have done for her! Look!' He flung out his hand dramatically in the direction of the smouldering ledgers. 'Hanson smelt burning and called me and we found her trying to destroy these! I tried to save them when I realised what they were. . .a second set of house ledgers. I have suspected Rafe of double dealing for some time and I have been proved right. In the monk's hole—send Leon to look. Supplies, a hoard of them. God knows how long they have been there. He must have used Abraham to continue his little business while he was away. If you question the old man I know he will talk.'

'And how were these supplies—signed for?' Alexander queried. Shanna was horrified that he was even listening to such lies and started up, but

Alexander motioned her to remain silent and a smile curved around Wayne's lips as he took the gesture as an acceptance of his story. 'Abraham cannot write. None of the house staff can.'

'Leon can. Rafe taught him years ago,' Wayne said, his confidence returning.

'I did not know that.' There were many things he did not know about both his sons and more about the plantation he owned, Alexander realised. Until Rafe returned he could trust no one but Shanna. 'Are you suggesting Leon ordered and signed for goods which never found their way into this house?'

'Exactly. Look at his face. There is guilt written all over it. He and Rafe have always been close.'

'Rafe is a man now. A man I have sorely wronged. And you, sir, are a liar and a rogue and if you were not my son I would have you whipped for your impertinence. You will be saying next that Shanna and Rafe were in this plot together.'

Wayne gaped at him for a moment, the outburst totally unexpected.

'Of course.' The strength of his voice began to weaken. 'She is still here, isn't she? And you have given her management of the house? It's what they planned. She can do anything she wants. They are all doing everything they can to deprive me of what is mine.'

At those words Alexander signalled Leon to set him down. During the whole conversation the tall negro had been holding the old man in his arms on the threshold without a sign of strain. Behind them stood Tante Lea and Abraham, silent spectators to what was taking place.

'Yours,' Alexander echoed scornfully. 'And what do you consider yours? This plantation? Because that scatterbrained mother of yours promised it to you? This place is mine and I shall give it to whomever I please. It will not be you. You are not man enough to step into your brother's shoes, let alone run this place. Save me more pitiful lies,' he snapped as Wayne began to speak again. 'I have seen for myself the condition of my people —'

'Your people,' Wayne broke in with a sneer. 'You have never given a damn about them so long as they did their work.'

'That is true. But for their work I always gave them adequate food. You have not. Nor have you supplied them with a decent roof over their heads. Sick men do not do a full day's work. Starving women and children are liabilities. I am relieving you of all responsibilities for the plantation. I shall give the orders from now on and Shanna will ensure they are carried out, and she can choose anyone she wishes to aid her.'

'A woman running this place!' Wayne could not believe his father had spoken such foolhardy words. 'You will be the laughing-stock of the county.'

'A young woman I believe to be far more capable than you could ever be and who has my complete trust. I shall never trust you again, son or not. And that fawning ape at your side can pack his things and get off my property within the hour.'

The look Wayne threw at Hanson warned him to

stay, but the man was no fool. The negroes at Alexander's side had no reason to like him any more than anyone else on the plantation and he valued his skin more than even the money Wayne had been providing for him. But like the man he worked for, who had promised him not only wealth, but the softly skinned woman who stood in the doorway, he too burned for a way to get back at those who had spoilt the prospect of an easy life.

Tante Lea saw the look in his eyes as he headed towards her, but stood her ground, daring him to utter a word. She was afraid of him, of what she knew he wanted to do to her and would do to her if he ever caught her alone, but she did not show it. Hanson hesitated for a moment only before stepping around her statue-like form and hurrying from the house.

'You can do the same. It is of no concern to me,' Alexander said stonily, and a vulgar expletive exploded beneath Wayne's breath.

'If I didn't know you would come crawling back to me, I would. And you will, Father, believe me. How is she going to run this place without an overseer. . .?'

'I was thinking Leon would step into his shoes very nicely,' Shanna put forward the suggestion, knowing she was breaking all the rules. A black overseer! That would set the county back on its heels too. 'When Rafe was at home, was it not Leon who helped him? And he can read too, an added advantage. Of course people will ridicule such a decision, but it is, after all, Wildwood that you are concerned about, not silly gossip. The house will run itself; Abraham and Hannah have looked after it very well all these years and need no interference from me. And Benjamin can take over the stables. . .'

'Wait. . .wait. . .' Alexander protested, holding up his hand to stem the excitement rising in her voice. 'I agree. I do! And to hell with the county. We are going to put this place back on its feet any way we can for when Rafe comes home.'

The mention of his brother's name was too much for Wayne, who swore at them again, this time aloud, and stormed out of the room. He would never admit defeat in front of them and they would not enjoy the victory for long.

'Now, there are things to be done.' Alexander was silent for a while and Shanna did not speak, knowing his silence was his way of absorbing the pain of the discoveries he had made today. He gave a long, heavy sigh, straightened his drooping shoulders and continued, 'Leon, take as many men as are needed and go to the monk's hole. Remove everything you find there and store it in one of the packing sheds. Shanna, I want you to make a list of what there is and bring it to me. We shall decide what is to be distributed and what is to be stored. And then we must do something about the slave quarters before the rains begin again. We shall probably need supplies from Savannah.'

'If you care to do a list for those, I can give it to Benjamin. He and Tante Lea are going there tomorrow morning,' Shanna told him. She had a long list of her own and she had written a letter to her bank asking them to release funds to Tante Lea.

'You are an organised little thing, aren't you?' Alexander replied, a smile returning to his face. 'I am tired. I shall rest for a while, but bring me the list as soon as it is done.'

Shanna did not ask him what he had been shown on his guided tour. She knew he would speak of it when he was ready. His day out of bed had been a memorable one!

Wayne caught up with Hanson on the edge of the perimeter of the plantation. Together they rode to a nearby inn.

'What now?' Hanson demanded sourly as they dismounted. 'You promised me money. . .and Lea. . . Now I have nothing.'

'You've had enough from me in the past,' Wayne snapped. 'Don't whine, you make me sick. And you liked my ideas well enough with the prospect of money coming in. My father has his pride; he will not tell his friends that he has appointed a black man to run his plantation. I shall remain at home, retain my circle of friends, and no one will know I am not the devoted son I have always been, caring for my father's interests. At the same time we might deplete the workforce a little. Prime bucks are selling well further downriver. As for the woman. . .' Wayne called loudly for the landlord as they seated themselves and the man appeared beside them immediately, knowing full well the temper of this customer when he was ignored. Wayne ordered large jugs of ale for them both. 'I overheard Shanna making arrangements with Abraham to send that idiot son of his and the woman into Savannah. She is delving into her own purse, doubtless to insinuate herself further into my father's good books. The cart will probably leave tomorrow morning and not return until almost dusk. The opportunity is there. The woman is yours for the taking. You have your reward. Shanna is mine.'

'And what will your rich widow say to that?' his companion asked.

'Once I have my hands on Shanna's vast fortune, she will like it. Besides, I satisfy her in other ways.'

Rafe knew that for the remainder of his days he would retain a vivid memory of his superior officer on that last afternoon before they retreated to Atlanta. A quietly spoke man, never given to raising his voice or to uttering profanities, he had often exasperated officers and men he commanded by his reluctance to do anything other than follow orders. 'By the book' Benton was the nickname he had been given. But the morning fresh orders came down the line, Theodore Isaac Belvedere Benton forgot the book, sent all the idiotic generals and the general staff supposedly running the war to hell—and far worse within Rafe's hearing—and tore the paper he held into tiny fragments.

'Retreat to Atlanta! Damnation, Amberville, do you know what that means? Every man is needed here to block Sherman. If Atlanta falls—and it will if our men fall back now—the whole of the South will be wide open.'

It was a prophecy Rafe was to recall time and time again in the following weeks. Brigadier Benton had put into words what he feared—dreaded. The South, deprived of manpower save for a few old men and boys: plantations, run mainly by women and negroes who might or might not turn on them, at the mercy of the Union army. It was not a pleasant thought. For several nights he had dreamed of the bluecoats rampaging through Wildwood, looting, destroying the only way of life he had ever known.

His commanding officer charged into the battle which raged like some avenging angel, determined to right all the wrongs done to his beloved South. Rafe saw him disappear into the smoke and debris caused by the Yankee bombardment of their position and knew he would never see him again. As the next most senior officer, Rafe found himself in command of the survivors. He regrouped them as best he was able and ordered them into Atlanta. There they would find food and lodgings and be able to gather their strength for the assault which would now surely be launched upon them.

His hopes of finding a decent bed were shattered. The city was crammed with refugees, every hotel and private home full to capacity with them or the wounded. But, although there was rationing of food products, he and his men did manage to get a substantial meal, their first in months, and at length found some kind of accommodation in a shed.

In the first grey light of dawn he awoke from a restless sleep to the chorus of his companions snoring lustily beside him, and remembered the letter he had received the day before, from Wildwood. It had taken a full month to reach him. He had only glanced at it then, for other more important tasks had arisen. Leon had written it in his large scrawl, and Rafe could feel the hatred the man felt as he wrote. Damn his father! Damn Wayne!

> Hanson is back. He works everyone until they drop and there is nothing we can do about it. People have disappeared too. Hanson says they are runaways, but Tante Lea is convinced they have been sold to other plantations and the money pocketed by Hanson and Massa Wayne.
>
> Your father is recovering slowly after a bad fall from his horse. He came after you like a wild man, tried to catch you. He is crippled, Massa Rafe. Miss Shanna looks after him as best she can. Massa Wayne calls her a ministering angel, only it ain't nice the way he says it. She is a treasure in these hard times.

His father crippled, following him! Rafe could not believe what he had read at first. What had he wanted to say that he rode so recklessly? Until he was home again he would never know, Rafe thought as he folded the letter and placed it in his belt, alongside the talisman Shanna had given him. Perhaps he would never know.

'Miss Shanna, wake up! Please wake up.'

Shanna came out of a deep sleep with a start to find Hannah at her side. For a moment she did not remember where she was and then it all came back to her and she leapt up from the chair in which she had slept through the hours of darkness, relief flooding into her tired face.

'They are back. I knew it. What happened?'

When the last vestige of light had faded from the sky and Tante Lea and Benjamin had not returned she had grown more than just a little worried. There was so much talk in the county of runaways hiding in the bayous, deserters preying on lonely horsemen that she began to fear they had been waylaid. She had refused to go to bed and had seated herself in a chair by one of the study windows where she could watch out for the returning cart. She had fallen into an exhausted sleep around two-thirty.

Hannah shook her head, her features strained. Tears trembled in her eyes and Shanna knew something terrible had happened.

'The cart came back an hour ago, but there ain't no sign of my Benjamin or Tante Lea. Leon took some men to search, but they've come back without finding hide nor hair of either of them. What's happened to my little boy, Miss Shanna?'

And to Tante Lea! On legs that felt like lead Shanna hurried out into the early morning sunlight. It was barely seven o'clock, but already temperatures were soaring, and she felt perspiration rise instantly on her forehead.

The cart stood alongside the veranda, Leon beside it, Abraham and several of the field hands behind him. As she neared the cart the former moved in front of her as if to stop her seeing something in it.

'What is it?' she demanded. 'What has Hannah not told me?'

'We don't know what has happened to them, Miss Shanna,' the negro replied gravely. He knew how close she was to the woman he himself had come to love, and wanted to spare her more pain. But the stubborn look directed his way told him she would know it all. He stepped to one side and Shanna recoiled in horror at the sight of the blood which streaked the seat. Tante Lea's or Benjamin's?

'We searched all around,' Leon told her gently. 'We really did.'

'Then search again. Take more men. They must be found. . .' She was beside herself with fear. 'Who would want to harm a woman and a boy?'

Who indeed! Leon had his own suspicions, but knew it was not wise to voice them—not at this moment.

'They must have been on their way home when it happened or the cart would have been here sooner. That means they had the supplies you ordered.'

'And money,' Shanna whispered. Dear God, she had placed Tante Lea in danger by asking her to carry money back. Had someone seen her coming out of the bank, or paying cash for the goods, followed her. . .?'Please, Leon, search for them again. Find them.'

'I'll do my best, Miss Shanna,' Leon promised. He knew of only one person who wanted them out of the way and he was standing on the veranda a silent eavesdropper to the conversation.

As Leon sent an accusing look his way, Wayne asked with a lifting of his shoulders as if to indicate total ignorance of what was going on, 'What is all the commotion this early in the morning?'

'Tante Lea and Benjamin have disappeared.' Shanna turned slowly to face him, still stunned at what had happened. 'The cart came back without them and the supplies they were fetching have gone too.'

'Then there you have your answer. The roads are not safe these days. Deserters, of course. Only last week old man Fielding was robbed in his own house by three of the scum. Nearly broke his skull with a pistol butt. You won't see either of them again—alive, that is——' He broke off, afraid he had said too much, but Shanna was too dazed to read any implication of guilt into his last words.

Not so Leon. His eyes narrowed dangerously as he stared into the pink face. Deserters? Perhaps, but he was beginning to believe the culprits were closer to home.

'You may have to consider the possibility that they have both run away,' Wayne suggested smoothly.

'Never!' Shanna declared, anger gathering in her grey eyes.

'Benjamin has thought of nothing else since Father whipped his elder brother and then sold him. He hated it here. Hated us. He would seize any chance to run——'

'But Tante Lea would not,' Leon interrupted. 'We had an—understanding. She would not leave Miss Shanna—or me—and my brother would not let her come back alone. He would protect her with his life.'

As Leon feared he had!

* * *

A week passed. Seven long days and long, tortured nights without sleep until Leon came back from another search, the lifeless body of his brother held in front of him, the boy's face covered with his shirt. He would not allow Shanna to look at him. He had been beaten to death, his features left almost unrecognisable, he told her, and then he had been hastily buried in a shallow grave which had been unearthed by one of the accompanying dogs. Of Tante Lea there was still no trace and no second grave could be found.

They laid him to rest the same evening, as the light was fading, in a quiet spot on the edge of the river. Many of the women openly wept. The men stood sullen and silent, so different from the negroes Shanna had grown accustomed to dealing with of late.

'One day we will find out who did this,' she promised Leon, knowing her words were of little comfort. 'They *will* be punished.'

'That ain't going to bring back my baby,' Hannah said through quivering lips. 'There ain't anybody who can do that.'

She turned blindly away and the crowd opened up to allow her through. Many followed Abraham as he went after her, head downbent, leaving Shanna and Leon alone at the graveside.

'I feel so—helpless,' she said at length.

'There ain't nothing you can do, Miss Shanna. There ain't nothing any of us can do—right now.'

She left him alone with his thoughts, knowing she

was not wanted, and returned to the house. She had never felt so alone!

On the twenty-eighth of July, seven days after the Confederates were dislodged from Bald Hill, overlooking Atlanta, and the latter came under fire for the first time, General Sherman, in an attempt to encircle Atlanta and sever communications to the south and west, moved his army to the extreme right of the battle line. the Confederate general John B. Hood had no choice than to deploy his men in the same direction.

Fighting went on throughout the whole day, both armies knowing this battle would decide the fate of Atlanta. The Confederates fell back from a brave stand at Jonesboro and a bloody retreat from Ezra Church, to the Chevaux de Frise—the breastworks of armed beams of square timber or whatever strong materials could be found which defended the approach to Atlanta. Changing his tactics once again, Sherman moved his main force six miles to the southwest, and the army of the Ohio was redirected to Decatur, destroying thirteen miles of important railroad tracks as they went.

Sherman's doctrine of 'total war', of dividing the ever-weakening enemy and defeating each separate segment of it before pushing on, was producing results. By the end of the day Hood had withdrawn his depleted force of men within the confines of the city—among them Rafe Amberville, exhausted and suffering from a bullet wound in his left shoulder.

The siege of Atlanta, which was to last almost two months, had begun.

'Why have you sent for Tobias Bartholomew?' Wayne demanded, storming into Alexander's bedroom without even the courtesy of knocking first.

Shanna, who had been reading to her patient before his afternoon nap, closed the book and stood up to leave, but Alexander waved her back to her chair.

'This concerns you as much as it does my son,' he told her. 'I want you to stay.'

Reluctantly Shanna took her seat again. These days father and son were barely civil to each other. Wayne spent half of his time roaming the plantation, complaining and threatening. . .in that respect he would never change, she accepted. The other half was spent seeking solace with Damaris LaFontaine, so Hannah told her, and from the rumours circulating through the county she knew this to be true.

When he was at home she avoided him as best she could, for his constant criticisms of everything she did made it hard for her to keep her temper. She hated the way his eyes followed her and the way he smiled as he watched her working, as if he knew something she did not. She had long ago ceased to be annoyed by his suggestions that she and Rafe had become lovers.

He had waylaid her on two separate occasions since Alexander had given her control not only of the house but of Wildwood itself, but she had managed to extricate herself from both potentionally dangerous situations, although the second time had not been without difficulty. Leon, who had witnessed Wayne trying to drag her into the stables one afternoon when he arrived back the worse for drink, was fully prepared to fight on her behalf, and it had taken all Shanna's persuasion to prevent the encounter. She wanted nothing to happen that would deprive her of Leon's continued help and support. Had he struck Wayne, she had no doubt that the man would have had him hung for his audacity and there would have been nothing she could have done to prevent it.

Her belief that Leon would be an excellent overseer was proving correct. He obtained the best results from the negroes and, acting on a suggestion from Shanna, had given them the necessary tools and paint to do whatever repairs were necessary themselves.

'Well?' Wayne snapped, slamming the door after him. He had just discovered that Damaris was having an affair with a six-foot-tall riverboat gambler and he was in a foul mood. Not so much over the competition—he was beginning to tire of her anyway—but because she had given the man jewellery that Wayne had bought for her with money stolen from his father. Money, he realised now, which could have been put to better use. 'I am waiting, Father.'

'I suggest you alter your tone if you wish us to talk. What I do is no concern of yours.'

'If he is here on Wildwood business, then it does concern me,' Wayne retaliated.

'You are remaining under my roof only because of the blood we share,' Alexander said, pulling himself up in bed, eyes blazing with anger. 'Remember I tolerate you for that reason only. Bartholomew is coming here because I have come to my senses. I am making a new will.'

The colour, such as it was, fled from Wayne's cheeks, then returned to stain them a bright red. The narrowed gaze which turned on Shanna made her inwardly quake.

'What has this bitch made you do now?'

The brutal, unexpected words caused her to flinch visibly and Alexander's features grew bleak as he saw the reaction.

'Shanna has nothing to do with this——'

Wayne interrupted him with a savage laugh.

'Liar! I know why she's still here. Not to care for you. You want her here for Rafe. For the two of them to produce your precious grandchild. My God, old man, you make me sick!'

Shanna gasped, wishing she had not been a witness to such hatred. For so many years he had successfully deceived his father, but now there was never the slightest inclination of love in his manner, even of caring a little. The mask had been discarded and what lay beneath was ugly—and, she feared, destructive.

## CHAPTER EIGHT

As August came to an end and the gentler September temperatures eased sleepless nights and soothed frayed tempers, Shanna came to accept the enormity of the honour Alexander had bestowed upon her—and the love which accompanied it.

He had asked his lawyer to draw up a new will. In the event of his death Wayne would receive a small yearly gratuity, providing he left Wildwood the day after the funeral and did not set foot inside its gates again. Everything else was left to Rafe. If he did not return from the war, Shanna inherited house, plantation and slaves and whatever money was left in the Savannah bank. She protested strongly at being left anything at all.

Alexander had had Leon carry him out on to the long veranda outside his room. He had taken a late supper there when it had grown cooler and a breeze from the river brought the sounds of bullfrogs and crickets close to the house. He had never enjoyed the evenings so much as he did now, when he could sit with Shanna and talk. Sometimes they did not even do that, for, even silent, they enjoyed each other's company.

It had been a little before ten o'clock before she joined him tonight.

'You look tired, child.' He leaned over and patted

her hand as she sank down into a chair beside him.

Although working conditions had improved under Leon's control and better food was provided from the stores brought from the monk's hole, Alexander still remained aloof from the menial, everyday tasks of the plantation. He did not know how to communicate with anyone any more, Shanna had realised—except her.

She cast a disapproving look at the full glass of Bourbon Alexander picked up and drank straight off.

'I didn't use to enjoy this as much as I do now. There are many things I enjoy since you came here, Shanna. I pray the good Lord allows me to go on doing so.'

'Do not talk that way,' she protested. 'You are getting stronger.'

'I wasn't thinking about that so much as what will happen to me—to you if the Yankees get here. Bartholomew seems to think Atlanta will surrender at any time. How can they hold out with Sherman at the gates, the city half destroyed by his guns and the soldiers and civilians there starving? I didn't believe Rafe when he said Wildwood and the rest of the South could be overrun. I do now.'

'They are not here yet. If they come we shall fight,' Shanna declared with a toss of her head that sent the cloud of loose black hair swirling about her shoulders.

Alexander threw back his head and let loose a

boom of laughter that quite startled her. She had never heard him laugh before.

'Fight,' he echoed incredulously. 'With what, dear girl? There are not more than half a dozen of our people I would trust with a rifle in their hands. The rest would run away—or stay hoping to see this house in flames and us dead. They would enjoy seeing me hacked to pieces.'

'Because of the boy you whipped and then sold. Hannah's son?' The words were uttered before Shanna gave them thought. She was trespassing on very private and painful territory, she realised, as Alexander's face hardened. 'Forgive me, I did not mean to pry.'

'Rafe never did believe the boy had insulted my wife. My second wife, Julianna, I mean. Charlotte, his mother, would never have bothered me with such trivialities and she would have boxed the ears of anyone who sassed her. Julianna was different. Rafe was right, of course, she did lie. Who knows, maybe she took a fancy to the boy and he refused her. . .?'

'No!' Shanna gasped, horrified by the suggestion, and Alexander smiled into her shocked features.

'When I married Charlotte, I was not in love with her. I was young and I resented being tied down, even though the dowry settled on her was most generous and we wanted for nothing while they were alive—her parents, I mean. I suppose that was part of the problem. Don't get me wrong, the fault was all mine. I thought myself rather a dashing figure in those days and the women I fancied I usually had. Charlotte held out for marriage, which I promised her. Only then did she succumb to my charms,' Alexander added with a wry smile. Shanna had never heard him mention either of his wives so openly and now he had begun to unburden himself she did not want him to stop.

'She was two months with child when we married. After Rafe was born, she ran this place better than I did. She loved it so. Rafe began to grow up just like her—stubborn and fiercely independent. I should have loved him, instead I resented him. I ignored them both. Charlotte never reproved me, but there were times when I saw such pain in her eyes. . .but by then things had deteriorated so badly between us that I could not find the words to tell her how much I had come to love her.

'I told her the day I buried her. I whispered it to the wind, afraid someone would hear me. I prayed she heard me and forgave me all those years of loneliness and neglect.'

'I am sure she did,' Shanna murmured. He had loved Charlotte! Rafe had never known.

'I suppose in marrying Julianna I was trying to erase Charlotte from my mind,' Alexander continued. He rattled the glass noisily on the table until Abraham appeared to replenish it. 'Julianna was everything she had not been. Far younger than me, flighty, faithless. She only wanted my money. When Wayne was born she smothered him, but only because he would one day inherit Wildwood. I had shut Rafe out of my life by then because each day he reminded me more of his mother. He tried so hard to please me. He worked all the hours there were in a day, he loved this place too, as much as she had, but I had no time for him. I could not bring myself even to touch him. Eventually he stopped trying to please me. He went his own way and that made it easier for me to tell myself I had only one son.'

'Things will be different when Rafe comes home,' Shanna said, a smile lighting up her tired face. 'You will be able to tell him what you have told me at last. Show him you love him. He is not as distant from you as you believe.'

'I can pray for a miracle, I suppose, but why should he forgive me?'

'Because deep in his heart, although he has never been able to acknowledge it either, he loves you too.'

'Do you realise if you had not come here I might never have made peace with him?' Alexander said, shaking his head. 'You are like his mother and your affection for Wildwood equals that of Rafe. What a pair you will make.'

'I will not listen to that kind of talk. Rafe does not care for me and you will not utter a word about the way I feel about him.'

'As you wish, but you must not leave when he returns. Not now. This place could one day be yours. . .'

Only if the man she loved was dead, Shanna thought as she leaned across to kiss a lined cheek. She did not want Wildwood at such a cost.

Atlanta had fallen. Shanna's eyes flew to the date on the newspaper. It was over a week old. The city had fallen on the second of September and what inhabitants had not already fled before the advancing Union army had been turned out of their homes by Sherman's soldiers and relocated at a railroad station called Rough and Ready, just south of Atlanta. Deserted homes had been instantly looted, of course, and used for accommodating the victorious army.

Allen, Andrews, Ashton, but no Amberville. She continued on, holding her breath until she came to the end of the appallingly long list of casualties. Rafe's name was not there. He was not dead! She put her head between her hands and said a silent prayer, then composed herself a moment longer before she went upstairs to read the news to Alexander.

Several days later the doctor arrived for his weekly visit. There were the usual protestations from Alexander, which always amused Shanna, for she suspected he loved the added attention. The man was an old friend and they would sit and talk for hours. He needed that, she thought as she left them alone together. . .as badly as she needed to hear Tante Lea's voice again. Wayne believed her dead. Why could *she* not accept it?

Wayne came out of the study as Dr Matson came downstairs. He looked pale and worried and the latter, believing that he was concerned for his father, followed him back into the room at his request.

'How is he? Are his legs stronger?' Wayne's face was a picture of a deeply troubled son. 'He will not listen to me any more, or anyone. He has this obsession that he has to walk again and I fear he will do damage that cannot be repaired.'

'I think you should pour us both some brandy and calm yourself, my boy,' the doctor replied soothingly. 'Your father is stronger, but for the walking. . . I do not know. Perhaps in time.'

Wayne gulped back the brandy with an almost desperate air which brought a frown to his companion's face.

'I'm sorry. . .but the way he has been lately. . . trying so hard to walk. . .tiring himself unnecessarily. . . I think he should be made to rest more, but you know how stubborn he is.'

'I do indeed. More than a handful for that young girl he has nursing him, I'll warrant.'

'Shanna is an angel, but even she can do nothing with him and he flies into the most violent tempers. He swears at us both when we try to reason with him.' Wayne supplied the information with apparent reluctance.

'Violent? Alexander? Good heavens, I have never known the man even raise his voice. . . This does concern me. . .'

'I was thinking. . .' Wayne chose his words with care, knowing the delicacy of the path on which he trod. 'Could we not give him something to quieten him. . .so that he sleeps more? He has dreams a lot . . .about this place mostly and what will happen if the Yankees come. . .you know how much it means to him.'

'You mean begin administering laudanum to him

again?' Dr Matson frowned again. 'I am not sure. Your father assures me he is in no pain.'

'No pain?' Wayne echoed. 'Then why have I found him doubled up in his bed, cursing his legs? Believe me, Doctor, he needs something.'

'But I doubt if he would take it, if he does not believe he needs it.'

'No, that is probably true and he would not take it from me either. Wait. . . Shanna. . .she always gives him his medicine and reads to him. There are times when they are quite close despite his ill manners. I am sure she would be able to get him to take it, perhaps mixed with warm milk or something. I fear for his mind if he does not have rest. . .'

Dr Matson opened his bag and took out a bottle . . .

Late in October Shanna, with Leon driving the cart, went to Savannah. The war news had grown more dismal and she was worried that they would not be able to obtain essential supplies of grain for the animals or food for themselves. There had been no word from Rafe. It was her belief that he was still in the thick of the fighting or he would have found time to write to them.

On every street corner, boys held out the latest papers. Each time she obtained one she dreaded opening it and scanning the casualty lists which grew longer and longer.

'The news ain't good,' Leon muttered, watching her face as she read.

'No.'

'What's that about General Hood—there in the right-hand corner? Ain't he in charge?'

'Of the soldiers fighting around Atlanta? Yes, he is. It says here he is trying to operate from Sherman's rear. That means most of his men left Atlanta before the Yankees got there. He's trying to draw him back to the mountains. It does not say how many men he has, only that there are no reinforcements available. I can well believe that.'

She folded the paper and pushed it down beside her on the seat.

'It's no use brooding about things over which we have no control,' she said quietly. 'We have a great deal to do.'

An hour later she emerged from the office of the wharf manager and Leon helped her back on to the cart. She sat in silence, a stunned look on her face until he blurted, 'Miss Shanna, what's wrong? You look as if you have been struck by a thunderbolt.'

'I have, Leon. I know—we all know—Wayne has been robbing his father for years, but this is the last straw. There is no cotton stored here as Rafe told me. Wayne had it removed over a year ago on written instructions from his father. It was sold to a northern agent for forty cents a pound. One hundred and fifty bales he sold, and told no one. He must haved forged Mr Amberville's signature. He has done it before, hasn't he? That's how he acquired all the things we found in the monk's hole.' She raised a shaking hand to her forehead. 'How can I tell his father? Alexander has been feeling so low lately that nothing I do seems to help him. It is as if he has given up again. I do not understand it.'

'It will pass, Miss Shanna. What he needs is to see Mr Rafe riding up to the house and he'll jump out of bed like a two-year-old.'

'I wish I could believe that.'

They moved off again, at little more than a walking pace, for the streets were thronged with people and carts heavily laden with household goods and furniture. The inhabitants of Savannah were already in a state of panic now Atlanta had fallen and nothing stood between them and the army of Sherman, except tired, half-starved Confederate soldiers who would rather have been at home with their families than fighting against the overwhelming odds that prevailed.

What was to come, Shanna wondered as they made their way homewards in the late afternoon, and would she be able to cope with whatever arrived at the gates of Wildwood?

She did not tell Alexander about the missing cotton. In his present condition she doubted if he could fully absorb the news. There was a vagueness about him that disturbed her for she could find no reason, after his earlier recovery. It could not be his medicine, for the doctor had left only a mild sleeping potion which she administered to him in his milk, every evening before he retired. Was he losing his reason?

The first rains came and with it several escapes by a dozen or more of the negroes, who, hearing that the army of Sherman was on the march towards the sea, once more believed all their troubles were over and all they had to do was run and hide and wait. Shanna did not send Leon after them. What was the use?

A day later she called them all together and told them if they wished to remain at Wildwood they could always consider it their home, that when Master Rafe returned he would right all the wrongs and abuses perpetrated by his brother. If he did not come back—and her voice trembled as she spoke—then she would care for them in his place. But if there was anyone who wished to leave, then they were free to do so, although it would be as dangerous to roam the countryside and be caught by some bounty hunter who would sell them again elsewhere as it would to remain at Wildwood and help to defend the place should the Yankees arrive.

Over the next week, twenty went missing. The following week, another eleven, but eight of these came back after starving for more than five days and being chased by dogs and the dreaded bounty men who patrolled the countryside. By her estimation, she had less than fifty workers, Shanna realised, as she went through the books one night. Those who had not returned would have a miserable existence. Those who had did not trust her; they had been driven back by hunger and fear!

On the second of November, General Sherman received permission to march from the city of Atlanta to his ultimate goal—the sea. His soldiers were given twenty days of rations, after which they would live off the land. Each corps, four in all, with mule-drawn ambulances, stretched for five miles along parallel roads. Animals could be freely appropriated, horses, mules, livestock to replenish the dwindling food of the army. Negroes were to be taken along to be used on roadworks or other heavy labour.

By the time the army cleared the city around the fourteenth or fifteenth of November, a large part of it had been destroyed by fire, as the resourceful Captain Poe, the Union army's chief engineer, put the torch to Atlanta's industrial area. The sky was blood-red, the dense smoke choking. The flames consumed oil refineries, ignited shells from the wreckage of the arsenal.

Sherman left Atlanta, passing over two hundred acres of desolation. Atlanta was battered, but the people were not defeated. Within three short weeks newspapers were once more being published, a post office had been reopened and rebuilding was under way.

'Miss Shanna, look!' One of the women touched her arm. Shanna straightened, wincing as a pain tore through her back, and her gaze followed the outstretched hand. She was helping to clear a large expanse of ground behind the stables which could be used for growing vegetables. It was a hot, humid day, with mists floating in from the river. She prayed for a storm to alleviate the unpleasant stickiness which made her clothes cling to her body. 'Ain't he a soldier?'

A soldier! Dear God, it could not be! The last she had heard the Union army was outside Macon. Through the hovering mists it was impossible to see the mounted figure clearly. Then, as the tired horse stumbled and almost fell, the rider swore at it, kneed it forward until it was level with her.

A gaunt, bearded face was lifted to stare down at her. Cold blue eyes raked her from head to toe without a flicker of recognition in them. The grey uniform was torn and open at the front, despite the weather. She saw he did not wear a shirt. Blood had long since dried on the heavy wad of bandages wound around his chest.

'Help me, girl,' he growled ungraciously and began to slide from the saddle.

The shock which had seized her as she recognised him rooted Shanna to the spot where she stood. Then, as he grabbed at his horse's pommel for support, her arms went around him, tears welling up into her eyes. The breath caught in her throat so that she could hardly speak.

'Rafe! Thank God you are alive. You have come back to us.'

The blue eyes lost a fraction of their coldness as he looked into her tearful face and then from his throat rose a deep chuckle.

'You don't know how pleased I am to see that pretty face again. . .' His voice was weak. She suspected he had not eaten in many days. His arms went around her, imprisoning her against his chest. His mouth fastened over hers in a wild, savage kiss that was frightening in its anger and its hunger.

He grunted as she tried to push him away and then he began to slide to the ground, and she, still locked in his tight embrace, was brought down on to the ground beside him. . .

## CHAPTER NINE

'PLEASE lie still or you will start your wound bleeding again,' Shanna pleaded, but she doubted if Rafe heard her and she was forced to use all her weight upon her hands that grasped his shoulders to hold him until he was still again. Upon the left one there was a recently healed scar.

In the space of three short hours he had already made it necessary for her to change the bandages and the heavy cotton wadding she had placed against the ugly bullet hole in his side. No sooner had Leon carried him to his room than a fierce fever began to rage through his body. He did not know who nursed him so tenderly and cursed her when she placed a hand on him, twisting away from her touch as if it was agony to him.

With Hannah's help she had eased the tattered uniform from his body and sponged his skin with clean, cool water before tucking the sheets carefully about him, despite the negress's protests that it was no task for a lady such as herself to undertake. Shanna had smiled, remembering the soldiers she had nursed before, and continued with what she was doing without comment. This was the man she loved; there was no task so indelicate that she would not undertake it on his behalf. But only because he was hovering between unconsciousness and fever, she told herself, and did not know her, or she would never have dared to lay a finger on him!

'How is he, Miss Shanna?' Leon hovered on the threshold of the bedroom, his eyes locked on the man tossing and turning restlessly in the bed. 'Massa Alexander wants to know if you think I should go for a doctor.'

'I don't think that will be necessary. He has lost a lot of blood and that has weakened him; so also has the fact that I do not believe he has eaten in several days. He is so thin! If the fever has not subsided by morning, then you must go for Dr Matson,' Shanna replied with a brave smile. 'I shall go and set Mr Amberville's mind at rest. Ask Hannah to make up a tray for me—I shall be here for as long as is necessary—and make sure she has a supply of her chicken broth on the stove. If anything will put some strength back into him, that will.'

'Is he home for good?' Leon asked, and Shanna turned away from the bed with a frown. Until that moment she had given no thought as to why Rafe had returned home so unexpectedly.

'I do not know. Perhaps he is on his way to Savannah, like those soldiers who passed here last week. We have to accept the fact the Yankees are coming, Leon, and that nothing can stop them. The South has no more men to hold them back.' She turned back and looked into Rafe's unshaven face. Somehow it seemed to her much harder than before he went away. Was it any wonder with what he must have seen, the memories that would be forever imprinted on his mind?

Leaving him in Hannah's care, she went to acquaint Alexander with the details of his son's return. He was seated in a chair beside the window and had seen Rafe being brought back to the house, had sent frantic messages to the sickroom to know what was happening.

As she entered he turned and looked at her and she was startled to see that his face was wet with tears. If only Rafe could have seen it too and realised the love his father bore for him. Alexander opened his arms and she went into them, grateful for the comfort they offered.

'He is home,' she whispered, placing her lips against a wet cheek. 'He has come back to you.'

'He has come back to protect what is his.'

Alexander put her away from him with a smile touching the drawn features. Once he would have hidden his feelings, allowed no one to see him cry, but he had changed. It was good to care again. . . and to know someone cared for him. If only he were stronger. . .

'Go to him. Time will heal his wounds, but I suspect only you will be able to heal the pain in his heart.'

'Rafe has all he has ever wanted now,' Shanna returned. 'Wildwood. I doubt if he will ever share himself with me. I am not important to him. But should he ever need me I shall be here.'

Shanna found Wayne lounging against the wall in the passageway. His eyes were bloodshot and there was an aroma of stale ale on his breath. Quickly she closed the door of Alexander's room so that he would not overhear their conversation.

'Have you taken to listening at keyholes now?' she asked coldly.

'No one ever tells me what is going on here. I have to learn from one of the darkies that my brother is home again.'

'As if that is of any concern to you.' She turned away from him, but he fell in step beside her as she made her way back to Rafe's room. 'He is hurt, but he will recover,' she added quickly.

'The devil takes care of his own,' Wayne said, with a shrug of his shoulders. He stepped in front of her, barring her way, and before she realised what was happening she found herself trapped against the wall, with his body thrust against hers, his hot breath on her face as he jeered. 'How about a little loving care for this brother too? At least I would be grateful. Rafe doesn't want you, but I do. . .'

There were times when her obvious distaste for him made him furious, but there were others, like now, when her aloofness and her unavailability almost drove him mad. It inflamed his desire for her, made him reckless, when he knew caution and patience were what were needed. She tried to pull free of him and the softness of her crushed against him heightened his appetite. He had spent only a few nights over the past month with Damaris and had been forced to seek his pleasures elsewhere. The whores who frequented the tavern were filthy creatures and so he had selected the young negress, Mimosa, to amuse him, frightening her into silence with threats of what he would do to her if she did not obey him.

But she was little more than a child. . . Shanna was a woman and it was her he wanted. His mouth sought hers, wet, clumsy, reeking of drink. Shanna's nails raked at his cheek. He swore at her, one hand instinctively going to the red scratches on his pink skin. With all her might, she pushed him back, flung open the door behind her and almost fell into the room. Leon spun around from the bedside, took one look at her ashen face, and then another at the man who appeared in the doorway behind her, and started forward, but she caught his arm and held him fast.

'No! There must be no trouble. Not now. I am not hurt. . .he is more than a little drunk.'

'Why not let your watchdog hit me, Shanna?' Wayne would have endured the pain and humility of being touched by a black hand so that he could personally have the man hanged for assaulting him.

Shanna's answer was to slam the door shut in his face.

'One day. . .' the huge negro growled, and she frowned at him, aware that each day his hatred for Wayne intensified.

'If you touch him then you will undo all the good we have done so far. Rafe is back now. Wayne can do nothing to hurt any of us unless we allow him to antagonise us.'

Leon nodded, allowing his anger to disperse, at least from his expression. The day would come when he would be able to settle old scores with Wayne

Amberville, the man he fervently believed was behind the disappearance of the woman he loved. Wayne and the overseer Hanson. He would deal with them both and no one would stop him.

For the remainder of the day Shanna sat at Rafe's bedside, constantly wiping his perspiring face, giving him sips of cool water whenever he grew calmer, which was not often. The fever raging through him was violent and in the throes of it he raged at some unknown officer in the most colourful language, and no matter how hard she tried Shanna could not calm him. All that night and the next day she remained at his side, until Hannah threatened to have Leon carry her to her room if she did not take a break.

She slept fitfully for several hours, awakening to find it was dark outside the windows. Quickly she slipped out of her creased dress, for she had fallen asleep across the bed fully dressed, pulled on a robe over her petticoats and brushed some semblance of order into her loose hair. Now she felt recovered enough to return to care for Rafe. The fever had to break soon, she told herself as she settled herself in the chair at the bedside and Hannah went down to finish washing the supper dishes.

'If Massa Rafe wakes up and sees that girl looking at him the way she does, he'll know for sure,' she told her husband, and Abraham grinned at her. He was feeling good now that the rightful master was home again. Now things would get back to normal.

'That's as it should be, woman. Those two were made for each other.'

Dozing in the chair in the early hours of the

morning, Shanna was rudely awakened by a loud curse from the bed. Rafe, eyes wide open, yet not recognising her, was trying to get out of bed, but his legs gave way beneath him and he fell back again, cursing still more.

'Damn fool, you'll get us all killed!' he cried. 'Madness! You damned drunken fool!'

He fought against the hands she laid on his bare shoulders. His skin burned like fire. Who was he shouting at? she wondered, as she fought to calm him. What nightmare had taken place before he came home? It had to have been something awful to affect his mind so. Eventually he quietened, but hardly had she sat down again than he was seized with a fit of shivering. She covered him with the comforter she had placed at the foot of the bed, but he threw it off, caught one of her hands and held it so tightly that she bit her lips in pain.

'Hush, my darling. Sleep. I will stay with you. I promise.' She knew he did not understand her words in his present state, yet he continued to cling to her as if the contact was somehow reassuring to him. The shivering grew more intense. She had to warm him, to comfort him as she had never comforted any man before.

She drew his trembling body against hers, wrapped her arms firmly around him and gently kissed a bearded cheek. It was an hour before she felt him begin to relax. His face close to hers on the bolster became calm, losing some of the fierceness that had been there since he was carried upstairs. She dared not move for fear of arousing him again. In truth, she did not want to leave his side. It was no way for a young lady to behave, but then he would never know what she had done. . . Her eyes closed and she too slept.

She became aware of someone's lips against hers. Her eyes flew open as for a moment, not realising where she was, she thought Wayne had invaded the privacy of her room. But it was not he who kissed her, whose hands had opened her robe and were caressing her through the thin cotton chemise.

'Rafe. . .' she protested in a whisper. 'No!' He did not know who she was or what he was doing. He could have been anywhere. . .with any woman.

As he felt her body tense against his, Rafe slipped the straps of the chemise from her shoulders, laid burning lips against her skin. She shivered as he pushed away the comforter and moved over her and her feeble protests died beneath the pressure of his mouth on hers. Her resistance was stilled by the weight of his body pressing her down into the feather mattress. She should scream, Shanna thought, but she did not want to. She should fight him, but she did not want to do that either. The hands moving over her skin were exciting her, arousing her as he had done that night in the barn. Then he had sent her away. Tonight. . .

'Did you get any sleep at all last night, Miss Shanna? You look exhausted,' Hannah declared when Shanna appeared in the kitchen the following morning.

'A little.' Shanna sat down, refused any food and asked for a cup of strong coffee only. Exhausted?

She still ached from Rafe's lovemaking. Afterwards he had rolled away from her on to his side and slept like a baby for the remainder of the night, while she lay beside him, stunned at the way she had allowed him to use her, yet at the same time acknowledging that she felt no shame. Love had washed away all feelings of guilt. He had shown her heaven. She might never know it again!

'Rafe's fever has broken.' She put down her cup after only one mouthful because she realised her hands were trembling and that Hannah was staring at her. She had been rearranging the bedclothes around him when he awoke and demanded to see Leon. Just like that! As if nothing had happened. He did not remember those moments that had been so wonderful to her. He was clear-headed this morning, and the hardness was back in his eyes. Once more he was a stranger. She did not tell him she had cared for him, only that he had been abed for several days. She was glad to leave him, escape from the coldness in the eyes which followed her to the door.

Perhaps he was aware of what had taken place between them, she thought as she managed to pick up the cup again without spilling the contents all over the table, and was too ashamed to admit it? Or was there something else in his mind that made him a stranger once more? 'I think he might want to get rid of that beard, but take no nonsense from him. He is not strong enough to get out of bed yet.'

There had been strength in him last night. . . Fierce colour suddenly flooded her cheeks as she remembered how she had called out his name at the height of her passion and clung to him, her body arching up to meet his as she surrendered totally to the fires engulfing her.

Hannah gave her another sidelong look, wondering at that unexpected colour, and then went back to preparing a tray to be taken upstairs for Alexander. Two hours later Rafe, leaning heavily on Leon's arms, came downstairs and was installed in a shady spot on the south veranda. Shanna took refuge in the fields, resuming the work which had been interrupted when he rode up. She needed time to regain her composure. Never, never, she told herself, would she mention what had passed between them. If Alexander suspected. . .he would have a preacher at the plantation the next day. As much as Shanna dreamed of having Rafe place a bright gold band on her finger, she would rather be without him than have him that way. If only Tante Lea were here to give her advice. . . She dug more fiercely at the hard ground, but only succeeded in breaking the trowel handle.

'Are you deliberately avoiding me?' Rafe demanded, coming out of the study as she returned to the house late one afternoon two days later. The sky was overcast, dark clouds threatening rain. She hoped there would be a heavy downpour. It would make the ground that much easier to work. 'Come and have a drink with me. We have to talk.'

'I am dirty. . . I need to wash and change,' Shanna protested. His eyes raked her from head to toe, missing nothing. She looked like one of the field hands instead of the competent, efficient young woman Leon had told him had run the plantation since his father's accident.

'Damn it, I mean now!' He grasped her wrist, pulled her into the room and closed the door behind them. 'Sit down; we have much to talk about.'

Shanna seated herself tentatively on a chair in front of the desk, where she saw there was already a decanter of brandy and two glasses, one half-full. Rafe half filled the second and pushed it towards her. 'You look as if you need it.'

He turned away and stared for a long moment out of the windows at the darkening sky. He, too, prayed for rain, but for a far different reason. It would hamper Sherman's army, bog down their wagons and field guns in rivers of mud, slow their progress, if not halt it altogether. Then he turned and looked back at Shanna. He felt as uneasy in her presence as she did in his, she realised as he limped to the leather chair behind the desk and sat down.

'I want to know everything that has happened since I went away,' he said. It was not what he had wanted to say. He wanted to thank her for the way she had cared for him. Had Leon not told him he would not have known. Perhaps that was why he had dreamed of holding her in his arms, as he had done so often in Atlanta on those lonely cold nights before the army retreated and a promising career, although he had never considered the army such, had come to an abrupt end.

'I am sure Leon has told you everything in the greatest detail.' Shanna did not touch the drink and he frowned as if annoyed by her distancing herself from him. But what did he expect? she asked herself. He had made it quite clear that when he returned home it would be to take back what he considered rightfully his—Wildwood. There was no place for her here now except—if Alexander so wished it—as little more than a housekeeper. She could continue to run the house while Rafe assumed all the other responsibilities that she had dealt with during his absence, but would it be enough for her after all she had grown accustomed to, the satisfaction she had felt from being so useful once again?

'You should not be out of bed, you know. You are not strong enough yet,' she added.

The smile which touched the lean mouth told her how amusing he considered her words to be. She had to admit that he had made a rapid recovery since the fever had broken. The following morning he had taken some of Hannah's nourishing soup and by the end of the day was tucking into a large plate of stew, full of meat and vegetables swimming in a thick gravy, accompanied by dumplings and home-made biscuits. He had shaved off his beard, but the gauntness still lingered beneath eyes shadowed with tiredness and there was no warmth in the eyes which considered her.

'Beds are for dying in,' came the dry retort. 'I intend to live for a long while. Wayne has been bothering you while I was away, hasn't he? Did my father try to prevent it or is he still considering the possibility of the two of you marrying and giving him his precious grandchild?'

The question took her completely by surprise and

she floundered for an answer, wanting to say nothing that would antagonise him or make him do something rash. Abraham was of the opinion that he was going to run his brother off the plantation at the first sign of trouble.

'I have already told you I stayed because your father asked it of me. I would have anyway after his accident. He needed someone to take care of him. Did Leon tell you how he rode after you that day, tried to catch you and make his peace with you?'

'Am I being blamed for his accident?' Rafe demanded, bitterness creeping into his voice. He had passed by his father's door four times before summoning up enough courage to open it and go in. Alexander had looked at him as if he were a stranger and had not even spoken. So much for the change of heart! 'He doesn't care enough to follow me to the main gates.'

'Why is it so impossible to believe he loves you?' Shanna said, seized with a desire to slap him. She had steeled herself to keep him at arm's length, yet it appeared there was no need. The intimacy they had shared before he went away was no longer between them. A multitude of conflicting emotions coursed through her as she stared into the hard brown face and without thinking she snapped, 'You are as blind as he is and as stubborn, but then you share the same blood. You feel about Wildwood as you do about your father. You love this place because there are memories of your mother here, the only person ever to love you. Yet I think you resent it too. You give so much to it, but what does it give you in return? Does it warm your bed at night? You are obsessed with it, but do you really love it?'

Rafe stared at her as if she had taken leave of her senses and then a familiar mocking smile returned to remind her of past encounters with him, which she had nearly always lost.

'My, we have grown up these past months, haven't we?' he drawled sardonically. 'Do not presume to know my mind. I was asking about Wayne.'

'He—he doesn't bother me,' she said at length, trying to make light of it, but she could not meet his searching gaze, thus instantly betraying the lie.

There was another long silence between them. Rafe stared down at his glass, finished the contents before asking in a gentler tone, 'Has there been no news at all about Tante Lea?'

He watched the colour ebb from her cheeks at the question. Leon had confided his suspicions to Rafe, who found it easy to accept his brother had been involved in the woman's disappearance and the death of Benjamin—even that he had been the instigator of the episode.

'There is nothing to tell.' Shanna's lips quivered as she spoke. 'She vanished—just vanished. Leon searched and found no trace of her. I rode to our closest neighbours, but no one could help me.'

'A few more days and then I shall be able to ride again. I will make my own enquiries.'

'Will you not be rejoining your company as soon as possible?' Shanna asked in surprise.

'The army and I have parted company,' Rafe

replied. 'It is not something which is open to discussion. The war is lost and I am needed here. Sherman's army is moving fast in this direction. They were outside Macon the last I heard.'

'So close,' she gasped. If the progress of the army was in no way delayed—and she doubted if there were many Condederate soldiers standing in its path—then it would move at the rate of ten miles a day. In no time at all, the soldiers could be at the gates of Wildwood. Rafe watched her digest his words, recognising her train of thought by the alarm which sprang to her eyes, but he had no comfort to offer her.

For almost an hour they sat and talked, he demanding to know everything she had done, seen and heard, she supplying the answers as best as possible, while a thought nagged continuously at the back of her mind. He was not going back to the fighting. . .why? Had he indeed deserted as Alexander believed? He expressed satisfaction at Hanson's dismissal and Wayne's fall from grace with the comment that they would keep each other company in hell, but never once did he compliment her on her achievements. There was only one explanation she could think of—that he had doubted her ability to manage the place. Now he had returned to find it in better condition than when he left, with new fields being prepared for the spring sowing, the workers more content than they had been in years with no fear of a whip descending on their backs if they paused in their labours. . .he resented her competence—perhaps even the close relationship she now shared with his father.

What would he say when he discovered the new will? He would no longer have to fight for what he wanted, it had been given to him, and Shanna's money had sustained the plantation during his absence. It had pleased her to be able to repay some of Alexander's kindness and, despite first misgivings, she had come to look upon Wildwood as her home. Only Rafe could spoil that for her, but she was not prepared for his reaction to her generosity—not that she considered it such.

He motioned to the two ledgers in front of him. Hannah had told her that they had been the first thing he asked for and then he and Leon had remained closeted together in his room, allowing no interruptions.

'I know about Wayne selling our cotton in Savannah and there's been damned little money coming in, except for the rice and produce you sold to the army and six horses, so how have you paid for all the repairs, the new seed. . .how have you paid our creditors? Has my father released his hold on the purse strings to a girl?'

'I have money of my own,' Shanna retorted indignantly, hurt by his sarcasm. 'I have used it whenever necessary and I shall continue to do so.'

'Like hell you will. This plantation is mine and I will take care of it any way I have to. I don't want your damned charity!'

The vehemence in his voice brought Shanna to her feet, colour blazing into the pale cheeks, her grey eyes growing almost as dark as the gathering storm clouds outside the window.

'I hope you wil both be very happy. If you go on this way, it may be all you have.'

She wheeled blindly towards the door, blinking back the hot tears which stung her eyes. The unbelievable pride of the man! The stupid stubbornness! Could he not realise how deeply she too cared for this place? What had happened to embitter him to the extent that he rejected all help—the offer of friendship?

She caught her breath as she opened the door and found Leon standing there. At his side, leaning heavily on a blackthorn stick, his free hand clutching tightly to the negro's arm, was Alexander. His pained expression told her he had overheard the heated words from within the room.

'You—you are walking. . .' Shanna cried, the unpleasantness with Rafe vanishing as Alexander carefully shuffled one foot in front of the other until he stood in the middle of the room, facing the desk where his son sat, stony-faced, unbelieving of what he saw. . .and confused as to why this man with whom he shared nothing, who had not spoken to him when he entered his room, had left his sickbed to come to him.

Alexander looked into the closed features, wincing as more life returned to his stiff legs and pain flashed up and down his spine.

'Damn you, Rafe. I had to come to you, didn't I? I should have years ago. . .' A strange smile crossed the lined face as he motioned Leon away. 'The mountain has come to Mahomet. My son will help me now. It is time we helped each other.'

He tried to take a step alone, but one leg buckled beneath him. Before anyone else could move, Rafe was out of his chair and had caught him as he sank slowly to the floor. They sat on the carpet staring at each other. . .father and son who could not communicate. And then, hesitantly, Alexander put aside his cane and wrapped his arms around Rafe's shoulders and began to cry. As she ushered Leon out and closed the door quietly behind her, Shanna saw the latter bend his head until it rested on his father's shoulder. No words were necessary. . .

'What are you doing with that?' Shanna asked Abraham as she came out on to the veranda the next day and found the man holding Rafe's tattered grey uniform. She had not seen him since he made his peace with his father. She had taken a tray to her room that evening, pleading a headache as an excuse to leave them together, and locked her door for the first time since coming to live beneath Alexander Amberville's roof. She did not want to see anyone!

'Massa Rafe told me to burn it and that's what I'm about to do. Says he ain't got no more use for it. Not that it's little more than a bundle of rags anyway. The coat's so torn he couldn't wear it again.'

'All the buttons have been torn off,' Shanna said, upon examining it more closely, and then she felt herself grow cold as she saw also that the insignia of his rank had been torn from the collar.

'Perhaps he wants to keep them as souvenirs, Miss

Shanna,' Abraham said before moving away to fulfil his task.

Shanna would have been happy to believe the answer was that simple. She racked her brains to try and remember how the jacket had looked the day Rafe returned. It had been gaping open, she recalled, but all she had noticed was the bandage wound around his chest, the hollowness of his unshaven cheeks. . . The relief to see him alive and back home had blotted out everything else.

'I'm going into Savannah tomorrow morning, so if you need anything you had better let me have a list. It is probably the last time I shall be able to do it,' Rafe said. He had found Shanna in the kitchen late one evening enjoying a cup of hot chocolate before she went to bed. She always looked so tired these days, but she never complained. Why did he find it so hard to communicate with her?

'I will go and do it now, then,' Shanna replied as he lowered himself into the rocking chair beside the stove.

'Chocolate, Massa Rafe, or something stronger?' Hannah asked with a broad smile.

'Hot chocolate will do just fine. Abraham, I'll take those papers you have been keeping for me. I shall need them tomorrow, but I want to show them to my father first.'

Shanna watched the old negro cross to the stove, remove one of the bricks alongside it and take out a thick envelope which he handed to Rafe.

'Proof of my brother's double dealing,' he said,

aware of her curiosity. 'I think he's strong enough to accept the whole truth now.'

'He has improved. Your coming home has done that. I was beginning to get quite worried about his state of mind. Will you make sure he has his medicine before he goes to sleep?' she said, rising from her chair.

'I'll be seeing Dr Matson tomorrow. I want to know if it is necessary for him to take anything any more. I think he's better without it.'

'That girl is working herself too hard,' Hannah said when Shanna had left them. 'She's changed since Tante Lea disappeared. I ain't seen her smile in days.'

'There's damn little to smile about these days,' Rafe replied drily. 'With the Yankees cutting their way across country towards us, all I can think about is how we shall defend outselves. That's why I'm going into Savannah. We need guns and extra men to help us fight.'

'Fight!' Hannah stopped stirring the huge cauldron of soup suspended over the open fire and stared at him. 'If you do that, Massa Rafe, they'll burn the place around us. Then what will we all do? What will happen to your father and Miss Shanna? Where will any of us go?'

It was a question Rafe could not answer. He had never considered life without Wildwood and, despite the seriousness of their impending position, he would not start now. None of them had any choice but to stand together and fight!

* * *

Two days later Rafe returned to Wildwood. The news he brought with him was not good. He had managed to obtain some needed supplies such as chickpeas, salt and oats, and, despite the high prices asked for weapons when they could be found, he had managed to purchase four hand guns, two ancient muskets and six rifles. But he had brought no men back with him. Those who had offered their services looked as if they would turn on him or run the moment there was trouble, he said, no matter how much they had been paid.

He conveyed the dismal tidings first to his father and then went downstairs where he knew Shanna would be eating a late lunch with Hannah and Abraham.

'That looks good,' he said with a grateful smile as Hannah placed a plate of vegetable stew in front of him. 'There are people in Savannah who don't eat this well.' He tucked into it with relish while everyone waited to hear the news. 'Food is scarce there now,' he said at length, breaking himself off a hefty chunk of warm bread. 'The army has requisitioned most of everything. There are more than ten thousand men in the city under Hardee and there should be men arriving from Macon. The Yankees destroyed the railroad tracks outside the town, but didn't attempt to enter it, but, from the way the talk is going, they have met little or no resistance.' He finished off the last potato and shook his head as Hannah reached for the empty plate.

He saw Shanna looked at him and knew instinctively that she was wondering why he was not back out there, fighting to hold back the advancing army. She had asked no questions, neither had anyone else, but he had seen the looks in their eyes and still offered no explanation. Perhaps one day he would be able to talk about it, but he was still eaten away with bitterness at the unfair treatment he had received, the loss of so many good men despite his valiant attempts to help them.

'How soon could they come?' Shanna asked, and he shrugged his shoulders.

'A few weeks. . .perhaps less, although this rain will slow them down. But when they come they will take everything, so we had better start thinking of some places to hide what we are going to need throughout the winter.'

'Miss Shanna's bin doing that for the past month,' Abraham said, and Rafe noted the pride in the man's voice. 'Miss Charlotte would have been proud of her.'

Praise indeed to compare her to his mother!

'I have noticed various bits and pieces, mostly the silver, are missing. Where did you put those?'

'Hannah and I buried them beneath the smoke-house floor. We have some grain and flour hidden out at the old landing stage, in the hut there.'

'That's a relief. For a moment there, I thought Wayne was up to his old tricks again. By the way, after today you will not have to supervise the workers any more. I'm putting Wayne to work with Leon. It's time he got off his backside and started to help around here.'

Wayne, working alongside the negro slaves!

Impossible. And now she would have still more free time to sit in the house and wonder what had happened to Tante Lea, worry about the approaching Yankees and try not to imagine what it would be like when they arrived. What did Rafe expect her to do all day long, start knitting for the war effort? Did he not realise how important it was for her to be occupied every hour of the day? Or was this his way of showing her he was back in command, master of all he surveyed?

When Shanna left the kitchen, Rafe followed her a moment later and came up behind her as she stood out on the south veranda, lost in thought. The rain had stopped, but the overcast sky threatened more and there was an unpleasant sultry heat coming in from the river.

'What are you thinking about, little Shanna?'

He had not called her that since he came home, she realised as she turned to look up at him.

'I was praying that Wildwood will not look like my home did after the Yankees overran it.'

'Who knows? They might not come here at all—we are off the beaten track. But if they do we shall be ready for them. I think you should consider leaving here and going back to your home in New Orleans. It might be safer.'

Shanna stared at him in disbelief. He wanted to send her away!

'Safer! You want me to go back there and take that vile oath of allegiance to the very men who burned my home and killed my father and brother?'

'And the man you were to marry. You have never

talked much about him. Is the memory too painful?' Rafe asked, annoyed by his lack of tact. He had not intended to bring up the subject so abruptly, but then he had never found himself in this kind of position before. He wanted her so desperately, but for both their sakes he had to send her to safety.

'Not in the way you mean,' Shanna answered, the surprise she felt at the question mirrored momentarily in her eyes. 'We grew up together; it was always taken for granted that we would marry.'

'Then you did not love him?' Rafe leaned against one of the pillars and lighted a long thin cigar. His eyes were slightly narrowed as he looked at her, waiting for an answer.

'Now I can hardly remember what he looked like,' she confessed. 'How cruel life can be.'

'No, kind, to make you forget the unhappy times. I wish I could forget——' He broke off, drawing heavily on the cigar, watching the grey smoke dissipate in the breeze. 'You intend to stay, then?'

'Your father needs me and I will never return to New Orleans. If the Yankees do come then I will stand and fight with the rest of you.'

'And get that pretty little head blown off,' Rafe said harshly. 'What good will that do?'

'Why should you care?' she challenged, and for a moment a light blazed in his eyes that made her think he might grab her, but he did not.

'Perhaps I am growing too used to having you around,' he said at last.

'And that would not do, would it? After all, you have Wildwood now.'

'Father told me you knew about the will. Did you persuade him to make a new one?' He had been stunned when he discovered what Alexander had done. He had everything he wanted in the palm of his hand for the first time in his life. Only one thing was out of reach and that was of his own choosing, until he knew that he still had something to offer.

'No. He realised how much his pride had forced him into ignoring you. You are both very proud men.'

'The South has always reared men of pride. Perhaps we all possess too much and that's why we are at war. We are so set in our ways, refusing change, the opinions of outsiders. . .' A crooked grin twisted his mouth and he gave a short laugh. 'I had better stop before I convince myself all the killing and death has been for nothing. I am going to ride for a while; will you come with me? Let us enjoy what we have while we can.'

'One moment you want to send me away, the next you want my company. I do not think I shall ever understand you,' Shanna said quietly, 'but yes, I will come with you.'

They had been riding for an hour when the heavens opened and unleashed a deluge upon them that sent them desperately seeking shelter. The rain was so heavy that it blinded Shanna, plastered her hair about her face and shoulders and had soaked her to the skin in less than a minute. Rafe took the reins of her horse, guiding them both with an uncanny instinct that brought them out of the dense undergrowth a few yards from the old landing stage. She almost fell from the horse's back and her riding boots sank into inches of black earth. He took her arm, but she slipped and would have fallen had he not lifted her and carried her into the hut, somehow managing to retain his balance on the treacherous ground.

The landing stage, which had been used to accommodate the small boats that used the river to transport the rice and cotton produced at Wildwood, had been abandoned three years after the war began and the Union blockade made it impossible for the South to sell its merchandise. Two of the sheds were still packed high with cotton, but the hut had not been used again until Rafe had chosen it as a hiding place for the goods he took from the monk's hole. As he gently deposited Shanna on the rickety floor and slammed the door in the face of the driving rain which followed them inside, he realised he would have to move everything back to the old hiding place. The Yankees would burn this place out of spite, the cotton too, but, no matter what they did to the house, anything stored in the far end of the tunnel would be safe.

'We had best get out of these wet clothes.' Rafe dragged his gaze away from Shanna's shivering form, aware of how her saturated clothes clung to every curve and indentation of her body, and shut his mind against the vivid memory of the dream which had haunted him for weeks. It had been so real. *She* had been real as she'd lain in his arms and he had made love to her. 'We need a fire.'

Shanna watched as he snatched up a chair lying at

his feet and broke it across his knee. He threw the pieces into a small recess in the wall which still bore traces of the last fire, cursed as he discovered most of his matches were damp. It was a full ten minutes before he succeeded in his task and by then she was frozen to the bone.

Rafe straightened, pulled off his shirt as he looked around for more wood, tossed it on to a dirty table and grabbed up a handful of branches he found beneath it. The fire roared into life with the dry twigs and Shanna instinctively moved closer to the flames as the warmth reached her.

'Take off those clothes. We can dry them quite easily and it could be hours before we can get out of here,' Rafe said matter-of-factly.

'Hours,' she echoed. Her fingers reached for the buttons of her blouse, then stopped. 'It may stop in a while.'

'You saw the ground out there. The horses would never make it and it is too far to walk.' Rafe frowned at her, and said again, 'Take off those clothes—or must I do it? I don't want you going down with a cold. Hannah would have my hide.'

She recoiled as his hands reached out towards her, said sharply, 'Don't touch me!'

'Then do as I say or I will undress you myself.' His tone indicated he had every intention of carrying out the threat if she did not obey him. Her legs grew weak. She sank down on to the straw palliasse behind her, and slowly began to unfasten her blouse, her fingers stiff, colour staining her cheeks as she peeled it from her wet arms and handed it to him.

Rafe pulled the table closer, spread it over one side, together with his shirt—waited without a word. Trembling in every limb, Shanna undid the fastenings of her skirt, slid it down to her ankles and held it out to him.

She was beginning to feel quite light-headed with the cold and leaned back against the wall, praying the rain would soon cease. The roof leaked like a sieve and several drops fell on to her arm. With a grimace she moved slightly and then her body grew rigid with terror as a rustling at the back of the palliasse arrested her attention and she found herself staring down into a pair of small jet-black eyes and a forked tongue that flickered ominously as the snake drew itself up beside her.

'Shanna, don't move. Don't even blink!' Rafe's soft tones were somehow reassuring even as that tongue flickered a shade quicker. It stilled the panic rising inside her, the desire to try and escape the inevitable. She had learned all about snakes at the plantation outside Baton Rouge and knew this deeply mottled reptile to be one of the most poisonous.

She had the impression of something hissing past her ear—was aware of the sound rather than of seeing anything. A choked-off cry broke from her lips as the long-bladed knife Rafe had snatched from his boot embedded itself in the snake's throat, pinning it to the wooden planks which made up the wall. And then strong arms were around her, lifting her from the palliasse, seating her in front of the fire, holding her against a firm chest, comforting her. . .

Rafe stroked her hair, drew her head against his shoulder as bright tears glistened in her eyes. She was shivering violently in the thin chemise which left little to the imagination—in his dream she had worn even less! Was it solely from the cold—or fear—or was there something more that he had been too blind to see before?

'Hush, let me warm you,' he murmured when she tried to move away.

As she had done for him in the midst of his fever! His arms tightened around her and she became aware, as only a woman in love could be, of her vulnerability in such a situation, torn between the longing to remain in the arms of the man she loved—afraid of being used—allowing the moment to control the dangerous circumstances in which they found themselves.

'Why are you afraid of me?' Rafe asked gently. He stroked the black hair away from her face so that he could see it clearly.

'I—I am not afraid. Why should I be?' Not only her voice but her whole body trembled as she spoke.

'Uneasy, then, whenever we are together. It was not this way before I left.'

'A great deal happened while you were gone.'

'And that has made it difficult between us—why? Did I say something while I was delirious to upset you—shock you even? Anything I did say was not meant to hurt, believe me. . .'

'No—well, you were rude, but you did not know what you were saying,' Shanna confessed with reluctance. He did not remember! 'But you were very angry with someone. . .it had to do with attacking a hill. It was on your mind all the time.'

'It will be until the day I die. But what have I done to cause this distrust between us?'

'You—you dictate to everyone.' It was a lame excuse and the surprise that sprang to his eyes was genuine.

'Do I? Is that what it seems like to you? Then I can only apologise. There is much to be done here and it must be done well. We *must* survive whatever is heading our way.'

'By fighting? Destroying what you love most?' Shanna said.

'Love? You called it obsession. Perhaps you are right. I have lost so much. . .'

'Don't! That look is back in your eyes. It is terrible to see.'

'Yet we are talking again despite that and it is not so difficult, is it?' Rafe's tone softened as he looked down at her. 'You feel it again between us, don't you?'

'Feel—what?' Shanna lowered her gaze. She felt as if he could see into her very soul with those piercing eyes.

'What we shared that night in the barn.'

'We were both lonely. We needed to talk. . .to share our losses. . .'

'It was more and you know it, but neither of us has ever admitted to it. Me because I am proud and you because you are stubborn. Abraham was right; my mother would have been proud of you. The only woman who could ever step into her shoes as mistress of Wildwood.'

Rafe gave a soft expletive as she shivered again, not understanding that the reason was not cold, but the way his hands, as they slid up and down her arms trying to warm her, were beginning to arouse her. She closed her eyes, and was still, aware that after a few moments the gentle movements were becoming more like caresses.

'I've never forgotten how soft you were that night when you came to me,' Rafe whispered, his lips against her hair. His hands moved slowly over her bare back, around to her waist, stealing upwards to cup the softness of her breasts in his hands. 'Soft and mine for the taking, but I was a fool and sent you away.'

'A gentleman. . .' Words died in Shanna's throat as she lifted her head and saw the look in his eyes. No hardness now. . .something that frightened her more. Frightened. . .no, she was not afraid of him, but of herself.

'War has taught me that life is too short not to take what you want—and regret nothing.' Rafe slid the straps of the chemise from her shoulders. 'I want you.' His fingers eased the front of it open, slid inside, burning her skin as he drew it lower and lower until it was about her waist. Then they returned to tease and caress and excite her as they explored her breasts with the expertise of a man who had made love to many women.

He took her mouth, giving her no chance to protest. Her lips writhed beneath his, in part agony, part ecstasy at the uncontrollable fire which was consuming her. Her body was awakened to the love which had lain unrequited within her for so long.

'This time I am not going to be a gentleman,' Rafe whispered as he pressed her down on the dusty floor. Her chemise was swept above her thighs as his hands continued to devastate her body, leaving nothing sacred. 'At night, cold, hungry, not knowing if I would live to see another day, I would think of you. I dream of you, do you know that? The most vivid dream a man could ever have—holding you, loving you. . .'

'Rafe. . .you do not understand. . .' Shanna began, then fell silent.

'Tell me to stop and I will. That or nothing. . .'

'Who was he?'

Shanna roused herself from the drowsy aftermath of lovemaking and stared up into the bleak features a few inches from hers. Stared at Rafe in amazement as he drew back from her, his eyes cold and acusing.

'Who?' she asked, not understanding.

'The man who had you before me. Was it my brother? Or my father?'

Her hand flashed upwards and the blow rocked him on his heels.

'You can dispense with the show of outraged innocence——' he began, and she hit him again with the same force across the other cheek.

'You! You are the only man ever to touch me! I had no say in it the last time. You took me in your fever. . .it was no dream. . .'

The look of horror which crossed his face told her he believed her. He had made love to her and thought it a dream! He had been delirious! Not to remember the wonder of possessing her, the pleasure her body and her innocence had given him! A deep flush stole into his cheeks, darkening the imprints of her fingers where she had struck him.

'You will marry me, of course.' It was not the way to say it—not the way he wanted to say it, and Shanna scrambled to her feet, struggling into her chemise, grabbing her clothes from the table. They were not dry but she did not care.

'I would not marry you if you were the last man on this earth,' she said fiercely. 'Take me home—or do I have to find my way alone?'

## CHAPTER TEN

SHANNA pulled the warmest dress she could find from the closet, wondering as she did so how long it would be before she did not expect Tante Lea to appear to help her to dress and to brush her hair. To reassure her when she was troubled, as she was now.

'You will marry me, of course'! Rafe's words returned to haunt her again as they had done all night. Just like that! As if he did not expect a refusal. Without emotion—without love. A commitment which would make them both miserable for the rest of their lives, as Alexander and Charlotte had been. His pride, the code of ethics by which all southern gentlemen lived, decreed that he must marry the girl he had wronged.

The sound of loud voices drew her to the window before she realised they were coming from outside in the passageway. She unlocked the door and stepped out, then stood transfixed at the terrible scene being played before her eyes. Rafe and Wayne were at the end of the corridor, outside the latter's room. Rafe had his brother pinned against the wall. There was blood on one cheek and one of Wayne's eyes was puffy and almost closed.

'You filthy, sneaking, murdering coward,' Rafe shouted, and aimed another punch at his brother's head.

Wayne threw up his hands to protect his face and the clenched fist thudded into the side of his head. The defiant tones Shanna had first heard had become blustering, now whining as he pleaded his innocence. Innocence of what? she wondered in horror at the ugly scene as she ran to try and stop them.

'Rafe, no! Stop it. You are killing him.' She grabbed at his arm, but he threw her off and she fell back against the wall. He was like a man possessed, eyes blazing, his expression murderous.

'I intend to do just that and save the county a trial.'

'There will be one when they try you for murder,' she cried, but her words fell on deaf ears.

Rafe hauled Wayne upright, sent a crashing blow to his jaw, and the latter was sent reeling backwards towards the staircase. He tried to grasp the banister as he felt himself begin to fall, then tumbled backwards and lay sprawled halfway down the stairs, barely conscious. As Rafe started down after him, Shanna followed.

At the bottom of the stairs stood Alexander and Leon. Abraham and Hannah were behind them and Shanna saw a faint smile on the old retainer's face. Was he enjoying this as Rafe seemed to be?

'Alexander, for the love of God, stop them,' she pleaded.

Alexander looked up at her and she was shocked by the coldness in his eyes, reminding her of the same look she had seen so often in Rafe's eyes since he returned home. The lined cheeks were pale and he was holding on with all his might to Leon's arm.

Without that support Shanna knew he could not have stood. Yet he seemed determined to do so—and to watch his two sons fighting. Shanna started downstairs, paused only a step behind Rafe as he reached down and hauled his brother to his feet and with another devastating blow knocked him backwards. He sprawled at his father's feet, blood streaming from a cut over one brow and from the corners of his mouth.

'Alexander, do you want to see him dead?' Shanna almost fell in her haste to reach the bottom of the stairs. She stepped in front of Rafe as he moved menacingly towards his brother and Wayne, with a cry, slithered forward and grabbed at his father's legs.

'Stop him. He's gone mad! Father, I wouldn't hurt you. . .'

'Liar! Thief! Almost murderer.' Alexander's contemptuous tones made him flinch. He looked into Rafe's face and saw murder there and knew if he did not intervene he would lose both his sons. He lifted his eyes to Shanna's ashen face, said in a calmer tone, 'Dr Matson came to see me this morning. Rafe had asked him to call regarding the medicine you have been giving me. Thank God he did. Wayne has been lacing it with a large amount of laudanum for weeks now—that is why I lost interest in everything . . .was growing like a vegetable. . .'

'And I was giving it to you. . .'

'You were not to know, child. Only because Rafe had seen the effects of it before was he able to make a guess at what was happening. Wayne intended to murder me.'

'That isn't true.' Wayne's pleading tone made Shanna feel sick. The way he clung to his father's ankles, not daring to look up at the tall figure looming over him. 'Why should I? What would I gain? Wildwood was always mine. . . I had no need to kill for it.'

'I loved you so much I blotted out everything and everyone else. But it was not love. Love was what I wanted from you and you could not give it to me. It is what I should have given to Rafe's mother and could not and she was the only woman I have ever loved. And because of that we lived as strangers, with nothing between us. Because of that I ignored your brother all these years, listened to your treacherous, poisonous tongue.

'Had you killed me you would have done me a favour, do you know that? I told you that I intended to make a new will. In the event of my death, the plantation goes to Rafe. Should he have been killed in action, Shanna would have inherited it.'

Rafe swung around to look at Shanna, utter disbelief on his face. As soon as she had reached the house the day before, she had gone to her room and had not replied to his insistent knocking on her door. As their eyes met, a faint blush of colour rose in her cheeks and she quickly looked away.

'No, I did not tell you that, Rafe,' Alexander continued, 'but her love for this place is almost as great as her love for you.'

'Alexander. . .!' Shanna gasped and stepped back,

a hand against her wildly beating heart as Rafe's narrowed gaze remained riveted on her face.

'Forgive me, child. I have been silent about too many things these past years and I know there is estrangement between you. It should not be so. I have to speak what is in my heart now or see the two of you ruin your lives. It is now that counts. Not next week or even tomorrow, but now. Leon, you will help Master Wayne to pack and then you will escort him from our property. Do not come back, Wayne, or the next time I may allow your brother to finish what he has started here today. From now on, I have only one son.'

'Father, have pity, for the love of heaven.' Wayne started to his knees, wiping the blood from his eye and smearing it across one cheek. He looked so pitiful that even Shanna began to feel sorry for him. Then she hardened her heart, remembering all that he had done—and to murder his own father, using her as his instrument. . . She shuddered, realising how close she had come to fulfilling his wishes. Had Rafe not returned. . . He was still looking at her and she watched something stir in the depths of those blue eyes.

'Where shall I go? What shall I live on?'

'I am sure Damaris will accommodate you. Her gambler friend has found another, so I expect she is feeling lonely,' Rafe said without humour. 'Leon, go with my brother and make sure he keeps his fingers off things that don't belong to him. He takes his clothes and that is all. If I had my way. . .'

Wayne came to his feet, swaying unsteadily as

Shanna took Leon's place supporting Alexander, and backed away from the advancing negro.

'Stay away from me. . .'

'I'm only going to help you upstairs, Massa Wayne,' Leon said with a broad smile, and Wayne cried out in pain as strong fingers fastened over his arm and bit deep into the flesh.

'Don't break his arm or he won't be able to pack,' Rafe drawled, turning away to follow Shanna and his father into the study. The anger was subsiding now; he had something more important to occupy his mind. With Wayne out of his way, he could now, before it was too late.

'One day, my brother. . .' Wayne whispered through swollen lips. 'One day. . .'

Rafe restrained the urge to turn back and silence him, shrugged his shoulders and went into the study. He had taken two steps across the room when Shanna began to head for the door.

'Wait. . .please. We have to talk, little Shanna,' he said quietly.

'We have nothing to say, Rafe.' She was perfectly calm now after the shock Alexander had given her. 'What your father told you means nothing to you, I know that. I accept Wildwood is all you will ever want. I shall stay, of course, until we all know what is going to happen, but once this beastly war is over I shall take your advice and return to New Orleans and, as you do not want me spending my money here, I shall put it to good use and rebuild my home at Baton Rouge.'

'And live in it alone with a bevy of servants only

to keep you company. You will become a sour old maid within a year. Memories cannot give you what you want. What I gave you yesterday.'

'You have no right to mention that,' Shanna said sharply, aware of Alexander's interest.

As she tried to pass him, he caught her by the wrist, reached back and slammed shut the door, much to the chagrin of Hannah, who had been listening to the conversation with great glee.

'Rafe, please, do not make things more difficult.'

The light in his eyes was growing brighter, almost wicked. 'Don't you understand? I don't want to lose what I have found with you. I am living in another world at this moment, an unreal world. A father I have never known wants to know and love me and, God help me, I feel the same about him. I saw you . . .and nothing has been the same since that first day. But my pride—my damnable pride got in the way. I do not know how to talk to him—or you. I have been alone too long. . . I need help. Help from you both.'

It was a cry from the heart of a confused, frightened man. Fear of being loved—of loving and being rejected again, as he had in the past.

Shanna took his face in her hands, her eyes glistening with tears which shone like bright diamonds amid the greyness and then drew back as her cheeks became wet.

'Are you trying to tell me you love me, Rafe Amberville?' she whispered.

'Get on with it, boy,' Alexander ordered. 'Ask the girl to marry you.'

'She doesn't want me,' Rafe replied with a grimace.

'Of course she does. She needs to be courted, boy. Wooed.'

'What does an oaf like me know about courting?' A smile touched Rafe's mouth.

'I suggest you learn pretty quick,' his father instructed, and Shanna blushed at the laughter which rose in Rafe's face.

'We have all the time in the world,' he said gently. Shanna came into his embrace and laid her head against his shoulder. Rafe prayed that they would have time for him to say all the things he had never been able to put into words. To show her the depths of his love.

Love! He had never known it before, had not recognised it when it came. Blind fool!

'Massa Rafe. . . Massa Alexander, soldiers. . . soldiers coming up the drive. Twenty, maybe more.' Abraham stood in the doorway, a frightened look on his face. 'What is we to do?'

Rafe spun on his heel and strode to the window, looked out. The others heard an expletive break beneath his breath.

'They are our boys. . .thank God.'

They made the soldiers as comfortable as was possible in one of the larger barns. The captain in charge of them was not more than twenty and half of his men less than that. Six were so badly wounded that they had to be carried. Others limped or hobbled along on crutches or sticks and slumped down gratefully on the blankets provided.

Shanna and Hannah set about cleaning wounds using sheets hastily torn into strips as bandages. Then out came the bowls of steaming hot soup, followed by rice and chickpeas and loaves of fresh bread. They ate like hungry wolves, wiping the platters clean with the last of the bread.

As she moved among them, she was aware of a boy watching her curiously. She had seen the interest he had shown in Rafe too.

'Is this the major's home, ma'am?' he asked.

'The major? Do you mean Major Amberville? Yes, it is. Do you know him?'

The boy nodded, hesitated for a moment then said fiercely, 'It wasn't right what they did to him. He only tried to help his men. They should have given him a medal instead of a court-martial.'

Shanna caught her breath. Rafe had not deserted! He had been court-martialled, but for what? She sat on the ground beside the boy, said quietly, 'I think you had better tell me what happened.'

'You look exhausted. Come and have some coffee and something to eat.'

Shanna turned to find Rafe standing behind her. As his eyes flickered to the boy and recognition grew there, she said, 'He told me about the way you were ordered to take a hill held by twice the number of men you possessed; by a drunken officer.'

'And that I lost control and hit him—tried to stop them getting killed?'

She smiled and went to him and together they left the barn.

'He was right. You should have been given a medal. How could they have been so blind?'

'Did he tell you only four men survived out of fifteen? They had no chance at all, poor devils,' Rafe said, a flicker of pain crossing his face. 'A sergeant knocked me out when I tried to countermand the order and by the time I had recovered it was all over. . .'

'Those four will always remember what you tried to do and think well of you,' she told him gently. 'Have you not told your father?'

'No, and I don't intend to—not yet.'

Hannah was waiting for them in the kitchen. As soon as they appeared so did two plates of spicy chicken casserole. Shanna only picked at the food, disturbed by what she had discovered, the unfairness of the sentence. . .disturbed by the faces she had seen, grown old before their time. Boys in the prime of their lives looked like old men. Each was scarred in a different way.

'Thank you for believing me.' Rafe lowered his voice so that Hannah could not hear. 'I am not an easy man to understand—everything I have said and done lately seems to come out all wrong.'

'As you said, we have all the time in the world to grow to know each other.'

'If the Yankees let us.'

'We will survive. We have each other. You have your father too. So much more than you had before. He is right too, it is now that matters.'

'That makes me want to carry you upstairs and show you how much I love you.' The gleam in Rafe's eyes was dangerous—challenging—and she blushed, conscious of Hannah straining her ears to hear what was being said.

'There is nothing in the world I would like more,' she replied and saw his eyes widen in disbelief. 'But not now. There are men outside who need me more than you do.'

'I need you! My God, Shanna, you don't know how much.' The depth of emotion in his voice stirred her, but she knew she could not think of herself tonight.

'Miss Shanna, they need you outside.' Leon had hovered in the doorway for several minutes, loath to interrupt what looked like a very intimate moment. Hannah shooed him away with a wave of her hand, but he stood his ground. 'One of the soldiers is real bad.'

'I will come at once.' Shanna rose from her chair, her food hardly touched, the coffee cold and forgotten.

'Damn it! I won't leave.' Wayne said, his cheeks, with the influence of too much wine, now a bright red. He stood with hands on hips watching Damaris dress after they had made love. The news had been delivered without warning and he was seized with a wild urge to put his hands around the slender throat and choke the life out of her.

She had taken him back when he had left Wildwood, but it had not been the same between them and to discover she had even enticed Hanson into her bed—not that the man would have needed much enticement—infuriated him. She had sunk to levels that shocked even him.

'The Yankees are almost on my doorstep, Wayne, darling. You will be in the way when they arrive. I intend to see the victorious soldiers of the North are well fed, entertained, and go on their way leaving my plantation intact.'

'And do you really think you can do that by yourself?' he sneered.

Damaris turned and considered him for a long moment. The contempt on her face told him quite plainly what she thought of him.

'You have always underestimated me. The only man who has ever really known me was your brother Rafe. Now there was a real man. And he has your precious Shanna. My, how they must be enjoying themselves now. . .'

'Shut your mouth, yo bitch.' Wayne started towards her and she stood up and laughed in his face.

'A real man. Not like you.'

The insult struck deep. He hit her with such force that she fell backwards across the dressing-table and then rolled to the floor. Her head struck a brass ornament of a dog that stood beside the French windows with a sickening thud. She did not move. Wayne called her name, knelt and lifted her head. His hand came away covered in blood. She was dead! He had killed her!

For an instant he was gripped with panic, fear that someone had heard their quarrel—but no one came. The house staff were used to the tantrums of the mistress and, by now, the men who came and went from her bed. He sat down in a chair, composed himself, then ransacked her jewel case, taking only the pieces he knew would fetch a good price, also several small items of porcelain and jade which had once belonged to her husband.

Then, with great care, he left the house, ensuring no one was aware of his departure. Hanson was out in the fields, using his whip as usual, Wayne mused as he mounted and rode away. He was pleased with himself for getting the man a job here now. Who better to blame for the murder? And when she was found. . . But where could *he* go? Only one place. . . Wildwood, with his tail between his legs, begging forgiveness. But at least there he would be safe. And if Hanson was not blamed, then there was always the Yankees.

He turned his horse in the direction of home with a smile on his face. How foolish of Damaris to think she could throw him out as if he was a nothing. And once back at Wildwood. . .

An hour after he had left, the first blue-coated Union soldiers arrived. . .

Just before six o'clock the following morning, the wounded Confederate soldiers were loaded into the cart. Rafe gave them three of the work horses and, although several had to ride double, it meant they could move faster and keep ahead of the enemy soldiers in their wake.

Shanna pulled her shawl more tightly around her as she watched them disappear into the swirling mists which came in from the river and at this time of the year would not clear yet for several hours. Rafe slipped an arm around her shoulders and she smiled up at him—a sad smile that touched his heart.

'We could do so little for them,' she said miserably.

'We did what we could.'

'I hope that young lieutenant lives to reach Savannah. There will be a doctor there to see to that leg. . .'

'Without your tending he would not have survived the night.' He turned to the silent negro at his side, said gravely, 'Select two men you can trust and take Balthazar and our three best mares into the bayou. They are to stay there with them until someone comes to tell them it is safe to come back. And then gather everyone in front of the house. It is time we discovered who will stand with us.'

There were wild cheers of jubilation when Rafe stood on the veranda steps, looked down at the black faces gathered in front of him and told them that those who wanted to leave could do so—but that they could only take what meagre belongings they possessed. All food was needed to support those who remained. But the exhilaration was not shared by all. Freedom appealed to many of the younger negroes who had been born on the plantation, but not all, and many older ones, secure with their families, were afraid of what was outside the wrought-iron gates. Freedom? Perhaps. Work? A possibility, but would they have a roof over their heads as they had now? Food for their stomachs? A mistress who cared for their needs, nursed them when they were ill? A master who decreed that the whip would never be used on them again?

Rafe could feel the mixture of emotions churning inside them, but could offer no words to convince them either way.

'The Yankees will be here any time now,' he said, grim-faced. 'Those that stay will be expected to stand up here with the rest of us and protect what we have. Protect our future and yours.'

Within the hour there was a steady stream of figures walking down the main driveway. Some looked back; many did not. Out of a total workforce of fifty-five negroes, thirty remained, including Leon, Abraham and Hannah.

'I expected you to go,' Alexander said gruffly as Hannah brought him a cup of hot chocolate. He had been seated in a chair during the whole time, watching his world slowly disintegrate. The plantation could not be run with less than thirty workers. The fields would go to waste, ruined. Wildwood was dying before his eyes and there was nothing he could do about it.

'And who would you take out that foul temper on then, Massa Alexander?' she replied pertly, and he glared at her, aware of the laughter in her voice.

'Remember your place, woman,' Abraham chided.

'I'm a free woman now, Abraham, and don't you forget it. Massa Rafe says so.' She grinned broadly as she passed Rafe and Shanna, pleased with herself even though she knew nothing would change. She did not want it to. This was her home and no one was going to make her leave it.

'Now we all have things to do. Leon, take Father back to his room, gather up all the valuables he has and bring them to me at the monk's hole. Shanna, you do the same. All your jewellery, especially those emeralds. You are going to wear those on your wedding-day. Abraham, you fetch the painting of my mother and her collection of porcelain from the drawing room.'

'What about the grain sacks out at the landing?' Shanna asked. 'And the provisions in the barn?'

'If we hide too much the Yankees will be suspicious and if they start to search they won't be gentle about it, believe me. Best we leave them something to find. Everything you hid out at the landing was brought back last night, and it's in the tunnel.'

He had thought of everything, Shanna thought as she hurried up to her room, conscious that time was running out fast. Had he thought what he would do when the enemy arrived on his doorstep, threatened not only his livelihood, his home, but his life also? She would stand by him. She would shoot anyone who dared violate what had become so precious to her!

'Rider coming fast.'

She ran to the window as a voice rang out from below. Rafe had taken the precaution of placing men to watch the approach road to Wildwood and there were more down by the river in case the enemy tried to sneak in by a back route. Her eyes widened as she recognised Wayne, wheeled and hurried downstairs. They were heading for enough trouble without his return provoking more. Rafe would not send him away with just a few bruises this time.

As she ran out of the front door, she found Rafe confronting his brother, heard him warn, 'Don't get down. You are not stopping.'

'I've come to warn you. Yankees—not half an hour behind me. They've torched Damaris's place. Look if you don't believe me.'

He turned in the saddle, flinging out a hand behind him. In the distance a black pall of smoke spiralled skywards. It was not a small fire.

'And Damaris?' Rafe asked, eyes narrowing sharply. 'You left her there?'

'No, she thought she could stop them. She wouldn't come. . .'

'Then get back and help her. You are not welcome here.'

'Rafe, you canot send him back. He will be killed,' Shanna said. Despite all Wayne had done to them she could not allow him to be condemned to death so brutally.

'Let me stay. You will need another gun,' Wayne pleaded, sliding from his horse's back, his cheeks ashen with fear. 'For the love of God, I am your brother.'

'Let him stay.' From the veranda Alexander surveyed his youngest son with contempt. 'As soon as it is safe he can go on to Savannah. Come inside and find yourself a weapon. If you try to hide when the Yankees come, I'll shoot you myself.'

'You go back inside too,' Rafe ordered Shanna.

'And you?' she asked, trying not to show the fear rising inside her.

'I am not going to jeopardise what I have found with you, little Shanna. I shall be all sweetness and light—unless they push me,' Rafe returned with a faint smile. She could feel him already distancing himself from her, preparing himself for what was to come. She noticed he wore his army Colt and remembered he would have his deadly knife hidden in his right boot and probably a smaller pistol somewhere on his person. He had left her a two-shot derringer in her bedroom with instructions to use it on any soldier who tried to touch her.

'And if they try to burn the house?' She wanted to fling her arms around him, tell him how much she loved him and make him promise not to fight, but knew she must not do so. Nor could she show her own fear. She had to be as strong as he was.

'What is this old place but brick and mortar? It can be rebuilt. I could never replace you, my love, so go inside and stay out of sight.'

He had never called her that before. She felt herself begin to weaken, recovered, and turned back to the house. Alexander, leaning heavily on his cane, said gently, 'I never thought I'd see the day he put a woman before Wildwood. I guess the boy really does love you, child. Quickly now, there is no time to waste.'

Shanna replaced the tapestry sampler and stood back, making sure nothing was out of place. She had deliberately left little pieces of delicate glass and porcelain in their usual places on tables and shelves. Rafe was right in his assumption that the soldiers would be suspicious if they hid too much. Perhaps they would be content with what they found lying about. Some of the things she knew had been in the Amberville family for generations.

Alexander had installed himself in the study, a Colt resting on his lap beneath the rug which covered his knees. A rifle stood against the desk. Abraham had armed himself too, but Leon had refused to allow his mother to have a weapon, telling her, with a crooked grin, that if she was shot there would be no one to cook for them. The comment had made them all smile, easing a little of the tension which was mounting in each and every one of them.

'The barn's afire. . .' Mimosa came flying along the corridor as Shanna was making a last inspection of all the upstairs rooms. 'There's Yankees out by the back paddock and more coming up the road. Hundreds of them!'

'Calm yourself.' Shanna grabbed her and held her fast. For a moment she thought she would have to slap her as she continued to babble on. Then she calmed and looked sheepish.

'Sorry, Miss Shanna. There's everyone acting so brave and me throwing a fit. . .but after Massa Wayne I never want to be touched again that way.'

'Wayne. . .' The words caught in Shanna's throat. 'He forced you?'

'Yes, Miss Shanna. Said he would do the most awful things to me if I told on him. Don't let them touch me, please.'

'I won't. I know a place where you can hide and no one will find you.'

She hid the frightened young girl in the monk's hole with a warning to remain there no matter what she heard. If the house, heaven forbid, was torched and smoke reached her, she would be able to make her way along the tunnel to the exit which came out not far from the edge of the river and she would be safe. She was inwardly seething as she went looking for Wayne. She found him in the drawing-room, a pistol on the table beside him, a glass of his father's best Bourbon in one hand.

'Have you come to join me? A farewell to everything we have known?'

Shanna slapped him soundly across both cheeks. The sounds hung in the air like a whiplash.

'That was for Mimosa and every other poor girl you have ever laid your hands on,' she cried. 'You are the lowest form of life I have ever encountered. Even lower than a Yankee.'

His only answer was to finish his drink and refill the glass to the brim. He would be so drunk by the time the enemy appeared that he would be useless, she thought.

'You will not be so high and mighty when the bluecoats have finished with you. You don't have Tante Lea to protect you now.'

He began to laugh. It was the most horrible sound Shanna had ever heard. Evil. . .full of evil. Picking up her skirts, she turned away and left him, for the first time since her maid had disappeared beginning to wonder if deserters had really been behind it all.

That laugh. . .and the look in his eyes. . . She shivered. . .

'Best you stay inside out of sight, Miss Shanna,' Leon said as she neared the open front doors. 'They're coming fast. Two of the barns are on fire and we can't stem the flames. Seems a dozen of them sneaked in on us from behind. The main force is coming up the road now.'

'Leon. . .' It was on the tip of Shanna's tongue to voice her suspicions about Wayne, but, as the man looked at her and she recalled his deep affection for Tante Lea, she could not utter the words. If he thought Wayne had been behind her disappearance he would kill him without hesitation. 'Please, be careful.'

'I ain't got nothing to worry about. These crazy soldiers think they are liberating me. For what? A better life than I've got here? You take care of yourself and stay out of sight.'

The sound of rapid gunfire almost drowned his last words. Sound advice that it was, Shanna ignored it, ducked beneath the arm outstretched to detain her and ran down the steps in time to see Rafe fall to his knees, regain his balance and stagger towards the house, only to fall face down on the damp grass a few yards away. Blue uniforms came from all directions behind him. There were more shots as she began to run towards the fallen figure, terror in her heart, and she heard the squealing of pigs, abruptly curtailed by more shots, the squawking of hens as someone chased them and they scattered in panic.

From the direction of the slave quarters she heard

shouting, a woman screamed, but she shut her ears against the noise as she fell to her knees beside Rafe, rolled him over on to his back. There was blood on his face from a wound just below the hairline. She pushed back the blond hair and saw the bullet had not penetrated his skull, but glanced of the side, merely stunning him.

Leon's tall frame loomed over her. He held one of the pistols Rafe had brought back from Savannah.

'Is he. . .?' He could not bring himself to finish the sentence.

'No, thank God.' She looked up at him in relief. 'Help me get him back to the house.'

'You ain't taking him anywheres, lady.' A grinning Yankee stood alongside them, a dead chicken dangling from one hand. The other held a pistol pointing at her head. 'Well, go ahead, black boy. Finish him. Ain't that what you want to do? What are you waiting for? Then you can put a torch to this place like them other niggers did at the last place we were at. After we've had a little look around, you understand.'

'What did you do there?' Shanna whispered. 'The woman. . . Mrs LaFontaine, what did you do to her?'

'LaFontaine, now ain't that a fancy name?' The Yankee grinned still more, his gaze raking over Shanna and liking what he saw. He was part of an advance group scouting the immediate area. His commanding officer was somewhere behind with a small troop of men while the main army pushed on to Savannah, and he was under strict orders to provoke no trouble. But there was no officer here to reprimand him. . .'The niggers there say they found her dead upstairs when they ransacked the place.'

'I don't believe you!'

'Don't care what you believe, lady. Somebody got to her before we did. Shame, that. A good-looking woman. The house was an inferno when we arrived and the overseer—well, there wasn't much left of him. They whipped him to death then cut him into pieces, scattered him all over the place.'

Damaris and Hanson both dead! And Wayne alive and safe at Wildwood.

'Well, boy, you take as long as you like killing this here man. Me, I've got better things to do with my time,' the soldier said, reaching down for Shanna. She cried out as dirty fingers coupled her wrist, dragged her struggling to her feet. 'You and me is going to get acquainted, little lady.'

As he began to pull her towards the house, her fingers reached deep into the pocket of her skirt and brought out the derringer she had placed there less than ten minutes before. She levelled it at the soldier, said in a trembling voice, 'Let me go or I will shoot.'

Her voice was not as firm as she would have liked, but the hand which held the pistol was rock-steady and her determined features told him she meant every word. He let her go, still grinning, then took a step towards her.

A voice rang out behind Shanna. 'Leave that woman alone, soldier, or I'll shoot you myself.'

The Yankee major who dismounted a few feet

away was middle-aged and bearded, a seasoned campaigner who had grown weary of war and sick of the atrocities committed by soldiers of the Union army as they carved a path sixty miles wide throughout the heart of Georgia. Sherman's report on the campaign boasted damage to the countryside and military resources at over one hundred million dollars, which he had not found at all satisfactory, remembering all the burnt homes and bitter faces which he had left behind as they marched, nor did he consider it anything to be proud of.

'My apologies, ma'am, for this man's behaviour. Rest assured for the short time we are here you will not be subjected to such treatment again.'

'I am grateful for your intervention, sir.' Shanna slid the derringer back into her pocket, ignoring the major's outstretched hand indicating that she should surrender it to him. 'It is the first time I have encountered a Yankee who was a gentleman. I wish you had arrived earlier. Your men have already begun killing our livestock and burning our barns.'

'Unfortunate, but necessary. I have certain orders which must be carried out, as much as I have grown to regret them. You will assemble your negroes, ma'am, so that I can inform them they are free. Then, I hope, you will stand aside and allow us to do what has to be done without injury to anyone.'

'There are no slaves here,' Shanna said proudly. 'Our people are free. They stay with us because they want to. Ask them if you don't believe me. Leon, tell him.'

She swung around and found a man in uniform

bending over Rafe, ran to him and pushed away the hands that were examining him.

'Leave him alone!'

A young face, a shock of bright red hair showing beneath his cap, smiled into her indignant features. 'Don't fret none, ma'am. I'm a doctor and this man's wound needs attention. If this negro will carry him into the house for me?' He straightened, looking around him as if searching for someone as Leon lifted Rafe up into his arms as if he were a baby and carried him into the house. The lawn was full of horses, trampling over the flowerbeds. A squealing hog scampered past her with two laughing soldiers in pursuit. 'Now, where is that woman? Ah, there she is.'

He beckoned to someone and a coloured woman detached herself from a group of her own people that were accompanying the troop of soldiers with the doctor's medical bag. She looked a pathetic sight, thin, limping, in a tattered dress of drab brown cotton. Long, unkempt hair hung past her face and yet. . . Shanna's heart came up into her mouth. There was something about the way she walked. . . And then she looked up and she found herself staring into the unmistakable features of Tante Lea.

Rafe had been carried to his room and his head bandaged by the doctor who assured her he would recover consciousness shortly and suffer no ill effects from the wound apart from a headache.

She had left Alexander with him to go in search of Tante Lea and Leon—the other woman had run from her former lover the moment she saw him. She could not find them anywhere. Confusion reigned about her. Soldiers shouldered her out of the way as they tramped through the house, pocketing items here and there, appearing with bottles of brandy and Bourbon under their arms, paintings, which disappeared into sacks or bulging pockets before they went back outside. Despite the order she had heard given that there was to be no looting and the occupants of the house were not to be molested, she was accosted more than once as she went from room to room looking for Tante Lea.

Alexander's study was a wreck. Books had been flung to the floor, the desk totally ransacked in the hope of discovering more valuables. Charlotte's solar had suffered less damage and the tapestry had been torn from in front of the monk's hole, but the woodwork behind it had been so skilfully disguised that no door was visible. Had the silken tassels still hanging limply at one side also been ripped away, it would have been a different story.

Shanna fought down the anger and frustration she felt at her helplessness. She wanted to lash out at the grinning faces that passed her, scream back at the innuendoes and suggestive remarks which followed her, but she knew that to do so would jeopardise not only her safety, but that of Rafe and Alexander. Their safety and that of the house was her sole concern. But how her heart ached to see such wanton destruction for destruction's sake.

Rafe was conscious when she returned to the bedroom. He struggled to sit up as she appeared, his features bleak as sounds of laughter floated up to him from below. He had never felt so helpless.

'By God, I've got to do something.' He started up, cursing the pain that momentarily distorted his vision. 'They are destroying all we have.'

'No!' Alexander's hands clamped down over his shoulders with a strength that surprised him. 'I almost lost you once; it is not going to happen again. We will do and say nothing to provoke any further violence. And when they have gone we will start to put our lives back together again.'

'I am indestructible.' Rafe slowly pulled himself into a sitting position and, reaching into his shirt, pulled out the voodoo talisman Shanna had given him, suspended on a leather thong about his neck. 'You see.' Pain flashed across his face again, this time not from his wound but from the visions that came into his mind at the sounds from outside and the floors below. He did not have to ask what was happening: the noise of breaking glass, of furniture being smashed gave him his answers.

'Miss Shanna, I found her.' The door was flung open and Hannah appeared, dragging behind her a tearful, struggling Tante Lea. 'Says she's going with those Yankees when they leave, that she can't stay with us. Talk to her, Miss Shanna. Make her see sense.'

'Yes, I will.' Shanna took the woman's arm and led her to a chair. All resistance suddenly vanished and she sank down into it, staring at the faces before her with dull, vacant eyes. 'Are you all right downstairs? Do you want to bring Abraham and Leon up here? It might be safer.'

'Safer? I'm not afraid of those blue-coated bullies,' Hannah scoffed. 'Came into my kitchen, they did, started stealing my preserves and bread. One of them went away the sweetest he will ever be—I smashed a jar of my strawberry sauce over his head for his cheek! I ain't been bothered since. Abraham's out trying to save some of our livestock, though he's got little chance of that. And Leon. . . I don't know where that boy's got to. He was talking to Tante Lea and then he ran off like a scalded cat.'

'Thank you, Hannah. Take care. Don't sass them back or they may turn ugly. Please.' Shanna went down on one knee beside Tante Lea and took her in her arms. The woman trembled as if trying not to respond, then tears broke loose, coursing down over her cheeks, soaking Shanna's face. 'Tell me. Tell me everything.'

'You don't want to hear it, child. And I have to go. I am not fit to belong here any more, not after what that man did to me. Hanson. . .he. . .he and his men stopped us on our way back from Savannah that day. Pulled Benjamin and me from the cart. . . he tried to protect me, Lord, how that boy fought, but Hanson. . .' Her voice broke and she could not go on. Shanna smoothed back the lank hair from her face and kissed both thin cheeks. There were tears in her own eyes now, anger mingling with the happiness she was feeling at Tante Lea's return.

Hanson! She no longer felt sorry for the hideous way he had died.

'We have been through too much together to be parted now,' she whispered gently. 'Go on.'

'Hanson's men beat Benjamin. . .beat him until he didn't move any more. Then Hanson forced me, right in front of those grinning apes. He kept me to himself for a week and then he sold me to a slave trader. I was sold again three weeks later to a man who owned a plantation outside Macon. When the Yankees came past, they freed everyone, burnt the house and crops, the negroes turned on the master. . .' She did not elaborate and Shanna asked for no more details. After what had happened at the LaFontaine plantation she did not need to know any more. Tante Lea shook her head as Shanna smiled at her and squeezed her shoulders reassuringly. 'It is no good, child. How can I stay after. . .after being used so? Even Leon turned his back on me. . . Once he loved me. . .'

'Leon!' Rafe ejaculated from the bed. 'He knows all this?'

The woman nodded mutely. Rafe swung his legs over the side of the bed, pushing away his father's restraining hands.

'Wayne's back in the house, Tante. If Leon finds him. . .'

'He was in the drawing-room getting very drunk before the soldiers arrived,' Shanna said, moving forward to support him as he stood up, swayed and held tightly to her arm for a moment to steady himself. 'But. . . I haven't seen him since, not even when I was looking for Tante.'

'The coward is probably hiding himself somewhere

until it is safe to show his face again,' Alexander said fiercely. 'No backbone. Never did have.'

'We have to find him before Leon does. I bear him no love, but. . .'

Rafe reeled out of the room. Shanna followed in his wake, grabbing his arm as a soldier cannoned into him, almost making him lose his balance. He wheeled about immediately, his fists clenched, but the soldier had passed and she quickly helped him down the stairs, avoiding a potentially dangerous moment.

The soldiers seemed to be withdrawing from the house, having satisfied their orgy of destruction, but there was no sign of Wayne in the drawing-room nor the study. In the solar they found Leon standing beside the window, looking out across the lawn, watching blue-coated figures running, gathering their horses, mounting. In a chair sat Mimosa. As they entered she raised her head and they saw a vivid bruise on one cheek.

'No, not the soldiers,' Leon said in a flat tone as Shanna opened her mouth to ask that very question. 'Massa Wayne decided to find himself a safe place to hide until all this was over. He went into the monk's hole—found the things we had put there. Mimosa says he seemed to go out of his mind—started laughing about getting even. He was going to tell the soldiers about it—that you and Massa Alexander had arms hidden too. He wanted to see this place burned to the ground and the two of you dead. Mimosa tried to stop him and he knocked her out. I found him just coming out of the hole. . .'

He paused. No one else spoke. Instinctively both Shanna and Rafe knew Wayne was dead even before he continued. . .

'He had a knife, Massa Rafe. I tried to take it away from him, then he cut me. . .' He held out a bloody arm. 'I went crazy then. . .after what Lea had just told me. . .we fought. . .'

'Where is he?' Rafe asked. He felt no anger or sorrow at his brother's demise, only that so much unhappiness and pain had been brought about by the things he had done in his jealousy and ambition.

'Still in there. I thought it best. If the Yankees found him first. . .'

'We will leave him there until we can give him a decent burial. Every man deserves that, no matter how he lived his life.'

'And me, Massa Rafe?'

'You have a woman upstairs who needs you, my friend.' Rafe went to him, laid a hand upon his shoulder and the look that passed between them was more eloquent than a thousand words. 'Go to her.'

Shanna and Rafe stood arm in arm on the veranda steps, watching the last of the soldiers ride away. A few feet away lay some of the things that had been taken from the house. . .cut-glass decanters, a couple of paintings and a Persian rug.

'It isn't much out of what must have been taken. . .' The major reined in his horse in front of them. He had never offered his name, nor had he enquired theirs. It was as if he did not want to know anything about those unfortunates he encountered as he followed Sherman's orders, obeying, yet dispensing mercy as best he was able. 'We have confiscated your grain and most of the livestock, but. . .' He paused and stared into the two hostile faces staring up at him. 'I am not totally without compassion, despite the conduct of my men. I am aware of the hardship you will suffer with the winter months ahead. I have left half a dozen hogs and chickens and several sacks of flour. We have gathered more than enough for the needs of my men. With the main army almost outside Savannah by now, I doubt if you will be troubled again.'

'Are we expected to be grateful?' Rafe snapped, fists curling at his sides. 'You leave us with no weapons, our house in chaos, hardly enough food to survive. . .'

'You are alive,' the officer retorted stonily. 'Be grateful for that and for the lady there, who, I suspect, would have put a bullet between my eyes had you died, despite the consequences to herself. It is inappropriate to wish you a happy Christmas, but I wish you well. Believe it or not.'

In the kitchen late that evening sat seven exhausted people. No one could bother to eat the last of the stew Hannah had prepared, but they drank cupful after cupful of sweet black coffee. In a day or two there would be none left. The last of the fires had been extinguished, the chickens and hogs caught and confined inside a hastily made pen. Rafe had decided not to send for Balthazar and the other horses for a day or so until he was sure they would not be revisited. The rest of the horses in his stables had been taken, along with all their grain and winter vegetables. The bacon had been snatched from the smoke house before it had been burned, like every barn and shed on the plantation. Only the slave quarters had remained untouched and they now housed the negroes who had remained to try and clear away some of the devastation, as exhausted as the occupants of the kitchen.

Tante Lea had not gone with the soldiers. Rafe had known Leon would never have allowed it, which was why he had sent the man to her. She sat in a chair beside him, very quiet and downcast, but washed and wearing one of Shanna's warm dresses. Shanna herself had brushed her hair. She held very tightly to Leon's hand and occasionally he bent to whisper something in her ear and she managed to smile. Time would heal her wounds, Shanna thought as she watched them, as they had healed hers. And, like Shanna, she had love to help sustain her in the hard times ahead.

Alexander was almost asleep over his coffee-cup. Despite the handicap of his legs, he had still managed to work alongside them, until his strength gave out and Leon carried him back into the house.

Shanna sat on Rafe's knee, her head against his shoulder. Her face was smudged with dirt and smoke and his clothes reeked of it. As did hers, she realised. She needed a bath and fresh clothes and she needed Rafe to hold her and tell her everything was going to be all right. As if sensing her thoughts he said softly, his eyes tender as he looked into her tired face, 'I think we should all get some rest. Tomorrow is going to be a long, hard day and the ones after it no better. Not for a long while. We have fences to mend, a corral to build, fields to be planted. . .'

'And a minister to bring to the house,' Alexander said, suddenly awake.

'Maybe when you do, Massa Rafe, he will say the words for Lea and me too,' Leon said hopefully. 'We want to do things right, you understand.'

'I do not recall I have been proposed to yet, Alexander,' Shanna said, laughter rising in her eyes. Out of the chaos, the pain, the fear, there would come a future for them all. An uncertain future, but it was in their hands whether or not it blossomed. She knew it would.

The wicked light which sprang to Rafe's eyes matched hers. He rose to his feet, holding her still close against his chest, said as he moved purposefully towards the door, 'Then I shall take you somewhere very private and do so.' He chuckled. 'And we shall have a Christmas wedding.'

As the door closed behind them, they heard Alexander begin to laugh. It followed them up the winding staircase and along the corridor and into Shanna's room. . .